HANGMAN'S GAP

RACHEL AMPHLETT

LOCATION MAPS

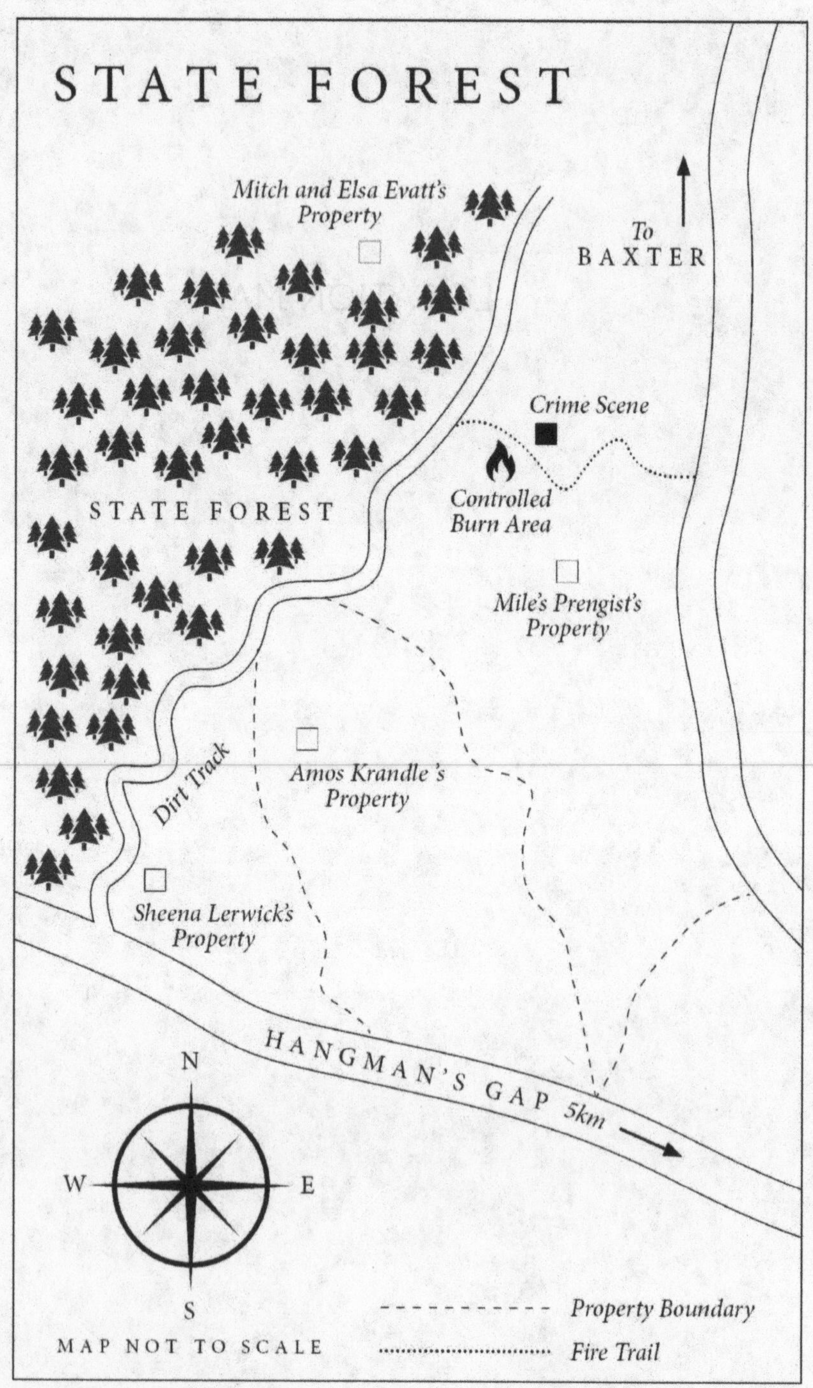
STATE FOREST
Mitch and Elsa Evatt's Property
To BAXTER
Crime Scene
Controlled Burn Area
STATE FOREST
Mile's Prengist's Property
Amos Krandle's Property
Dirt Track
Sheena Lerwick's Property
HANGMAN'S GAP 5km
N
W
E
S
MAP NOT TO SCALE
Property Boundary
Fire Trail

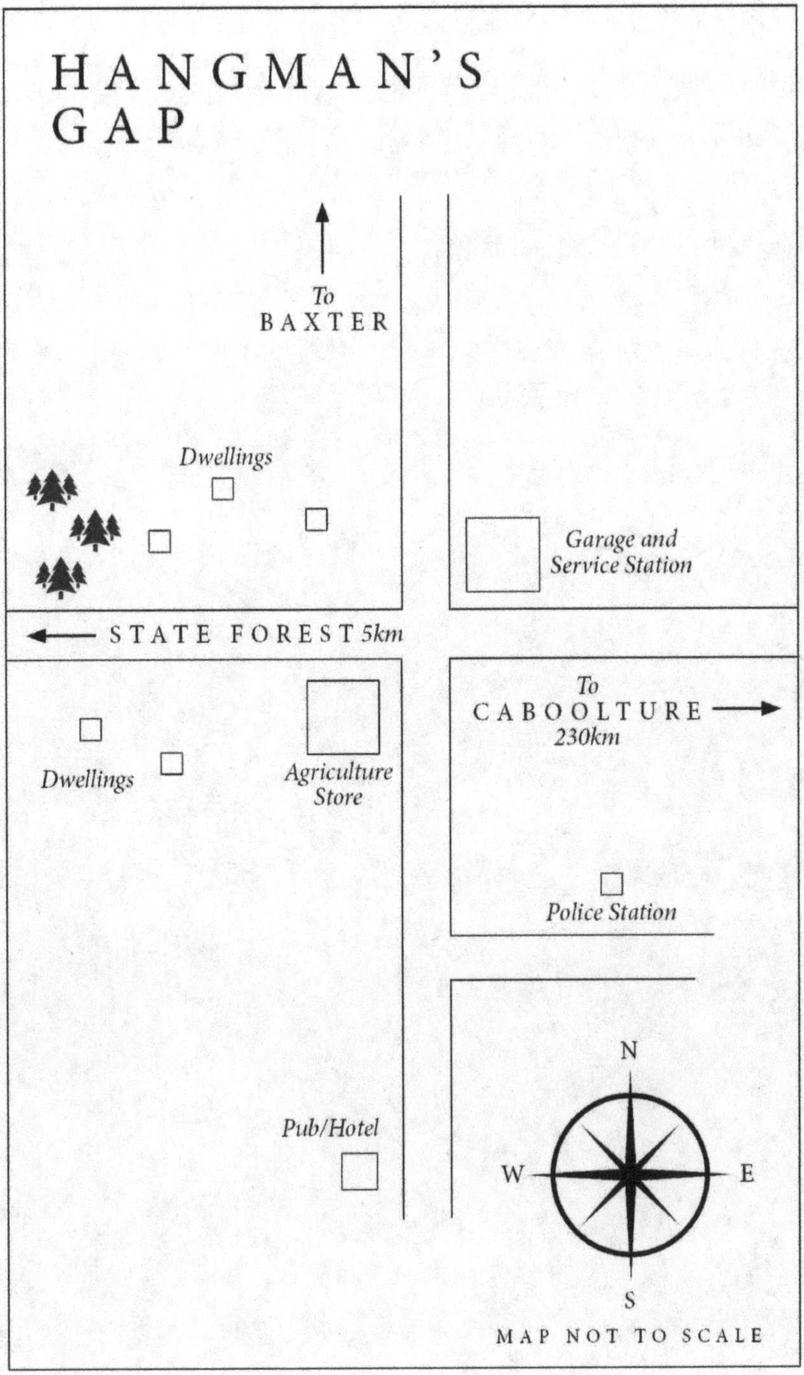

HANGMAN'S GAP

To
BAXTER

Dwellings

Garage and
Service Station

STATE FOREST 5km

To
CABOOLTURE
230km

Dwellings

Agriculture
Store

Police Station

Pub/Hotel

N
W
E
S

MAP NOT TO SCALE

ONE

Detective Sergeant Blake Harknell eyed the dusty white four-wheel drive that was slewed to a standstill beside a smouldering old eucalyptus stump, and rued the day he had left Melbourne.

The bittersweet tang of freshly ground coffee, the honk and shove of traffic outside his favourite café's window – even the sour stench of overflowing gutters and drains after a heavy downpour.

Anything but the smoky tang from the charred stumps that littered the ground at his feet, and the crawling sensation that close by, amongst the burned-out tendrils of ghost gum bark droppings, an Eastern brown snake was waiting to pounce.

Sidling between the rear end of a Queensland Police-issued vehicle and a mobile water tanker emblazoned with a Rural Fire Service logo, he stepped over a motley collection of breathing apparatus before raising his ID card in silence to an enquiring junior constable.

'Victoria Police?'

'I was told to report here.'

He received a cursory nod in response, and then he was past the first cordon of plastic crime scene tape that had been stretched between two door mirrors.

The undergrowth crackled under his shoes while he crunched over the remains of tree trunks felled by last year's lightning storms, now scorched and splintered to smithereens by the fire that had torn through here sixteen hours earlier.

The pungent stench of smoke clung to the air, scratching the back of his throat and stinging his eyes.

Not too far away, he could see ghostly figures wearing bulky orange high-visibility coveralls, the bright material dulled by dirt and grime, the volunteers' skin smudged by tiny particles of charcoal that had lifted skywards when the flames took hold.

They had finished dampening down now, extinguishing the embers and obliterating any chance the undergrowth had of sparking another blaze.

Hence the water tanker.

He hadn't experienced the Queensland heat before, but knew that the traditional torrential rains in these summer months were becoming rarer, and that the winters often meant the dams were dry.

He had seen the photographs from further out west of here

as well – the dehydrated skin hanging off dead cattle that had wandered for kilometres in search of fresh water, the deserted homesteads that families could no longer afford to keep, or had no wish to keep. And he had read the reports of suicide after suicide as farmers grew more and more desperate.

High above him, away from the remnant smoke that twisted its way around the gnarled tree trunks, a lone bellbird chimed, its constant pip reminiscent of a submarine's sonar array.

He could hear voices now, low murmurs that carried on a light breeze that spoke volumes, a deference to the utter destruction around him, no matter that it was man-made, and necessary.

Especially given the weather predictions for the coming weeks.

Movement at the base of one of the enormous gum trees caught his attention, and a young constable with sweat patches spreading under his uniform shirt raised an eyebrow in greeting, the rest of his face obscured by a paper mask that he had evidently donned to try to offset the poor air quality.

The man walked over to him, his manner brisk.

'Can I help you, sir?'

Blake cleared his throat. 'I got a phone call telling me to report to Detective Inspector Cameron Bragg. Is he around?'

'Yeah. He got here thirty minutes ago.' The constable looked him up and down. 'Do you want some coveralls?'

'Please. I usually carry some in my car, but…' He broke

off as two Rural Fire Service volunteers rambled towards him, their shoulders slumped.

Blake watched them walk past, their faces etched with exhaustion and a practised stoicism. 'When did they find the body?'

'A couple of hours ago, when they were dampening down after the controlled burn. It's another three hundred metres through there from the fire trail.'

'They look shattered.'

The man jerked his chin towards the retreating figures. 'Those two were meant to clock off yesterday afternoon, but the wind turned and they were scared the fire would get out of control, so it was all hands on deck. Bragg is through there by the way, beyond the cordoned-off area.'

'Okay.' Blake looked around. 'Where do I find those coveralls?'

In response, the constable led the way to a white polyester tent that had been erected a metre or so in front of a length of plastic crime scene tape tied between two ghost gums. He gestured to the opening then turned away, leaving Blake to push back the flap and discover a table laden with sealed packets of protective coveralls amongst other equipment the forensic specialists had unloaded from the van that Blake had parked behind moments earlier.

Blake bit back a yawn, the effects of the drive from Melbourne two days ago and the rush to check into his accommodation – a pub five kilometres away in Hangman's Gap – starting to take their toll.

Everything had happened so quickly.

He wasn't ready, never had been if he was truthful, and yet here he was, some 1,800 kilometres from home, in unfamiliar territory with a familiar dread lodged in the pit of his stomach.

Already, the questions were forming in his head.

There was a crinkling sound, and then the tent flap was shoved backwards by a woman in her mid-twenties. She was a couple of centimetres shorter than him with blonde hair tied back in a stumpy ponytail.

'You're DS Harknell, right? Are you ready? DI Bragg is looking for you.'

Blake tugged the protective booties over his shoes and then straightened. 'I am. Sorry, you are?'

'Senior Constable Angela Forbes. I'd shake your hand, but…' She held up gloved fingers, then dropped her elbow and let the tent flap fall back into place.

Blake followed, trudging beside her towards the crime scene tape. 'Do you report directly to Bragg?'

The smile disappeared. 'No.'

She lifted the tape, ducked underneath and then held it aloft while he did the same. Then she led the way along a demarcated path that zigzagged between the gum trees.

Here, the birds had fallen silent.

Even the persistent bellbird had disappeared.

The crime scene wasn't devoid of sound though, and as

they drew closer Blake could hear it – the steady drone of flies.

The air was full of them, great clouds clustering above the SOCOs and forensic technicians, the insects' fat, glossy bodies landing on his protective suit and colliding with the exposed parts of his face before he batted them away, grimacing.

They grew louder the closer he got, and then the wind turned and he could smell it.

Death.

A chill clutched at Blake's spine as his eyes found the numbered markers that dotted their approach.

What had the forensics team found?

Would it help them?

His gaze travelled to a group of four figures huddled together wearing identical protective suits while they peered at a tablet computer.

'Over here,' Forbes said, interrupting his thoughts, and then pointed at the earth. 'Watch yourself, the demarcation narrows as we get closer, so it's single file only.'

'Was the victim caught in the fire?'

'It wasn't the fire that killed him,' she said. 'That much even I can tell you.'

Blake swallowed, took a last inhalation of relatively fresh air, and hurried to catch up with her.

She stopped a reverent distance from where the forensic team worked, and from here Blake could only glimpse the tattered remains of a pair of shoes wrapped around charred feet that pointed skywards from behind a jagged knee-high granite boulder.

The ground was littered with large stones around here, adding to the difficulty of a terrain already made treacherous by the thick tangled tree roots that had miraculously escaped the flames.

'I was meant to be meeting Sergeant Mortlock this morning before I got a phone call from your HQ in Caboolture telling me to report out here to Bragg instead. Is Mortlock joining us?' Blake asked while they watched one of the figures straighten and turn away with a sealed evidence bag.

Forbes kept her gaze straight ahead, her jaw set for a moment, then: 'I doubt it very much.'

'But I thought he was the officer in charge around here.'

There was a shout then, and the taller of the protective suit-clad figures beckoned to them.

'Come on.' Forbes led the way over, then briefly introduced him. 'This is Jonathan Coker, our lead forensic expert.'

'Have you had a chance to speak to headquarters yet?' Coker said to her, nodding a brief greeting to Blake. 'It's just that…'

'There won't be anyone more senior than Bragg here for at least another hour.' She shrugged. 'Sorry.'

Coker sighed. 'All right, well we'll probably be ready to move him by then with any luck. Sigford's already left, and he said he'll be in touch about the post mortem.'

Blake watched while one of the forensic team used a fine brush to sweep at the dirt a few metres away. The woman's movements were meticulous, methodical, despite the rising humidity. He turned his attention back to Coker. 'What do you know so far?'

The forensic expert's brow creased, his eyes full of confusion as he adjusted the nitrile gloves against his fingers. 'When did you get up here?'

'Yesterday,' Blake said. 'I was just saying to Forbes, I haven't even had a chance to introduce myself to Sergeant Mortlock in person yet.'

The forensic expert sighed, placed a hand on his shoulder and turned him to walk around a large boulder.

A fresh swarm of flies lifted into the air as one of the technicians stepped aside, and Blake saw then.

Saw the burnt flesh torn away by the flames.

Saw the raw blistering wounds so deep that charred bones showed through, a skeletal hand clawing at the smoke-filled air.

Saw the twisted, melted metalwork of a belt buckle and—

Coker cleared his throat. 'DS Harknell, meet Senior Sergeant Ivan Mortlock.'

TWO

A pair of crows cackled above Blake's head as his gaze took in the obliterated features of a man who was once flesh and blood.

The fire had done its job – the skeletal form was now curled in on itself, forming an uncanny resemblance to a foetus in a womb, the baked earth around it a blurred background in a macabre mimicry of an ultrasound image.

A respectful silence accompanied him while he stepped carefully around Mortlock's charred remains, noting the blackened skull with its screaming open jaw, the pelvis and hips twisted towards the granite rock, the ribcage hollowed through and through by the unforgiving furnace that had ripped across the terrain.

Despite Blake's attempts to stifle his breathing, despite the protective mask he wore, his nostrils were still assaulted by the stench of charred flesh.

'How can you be sure it's him?'

Coker jerked his thumb over his shoulder. 'His car was found parked out near the back of Mike Prengist's property, about a kilometre through there. It's off a spur from an older fire trail that hasn't been used for a while. The keys were still in the ignition. No sign of a struggle, either.'

'What about a mobile phone?'

'What's left of it is there, on the left of his chest. He must have had it in his shirt pocket. There's very little signal out here, so he couldn't have used it anyway.'

Blake took in the lumpen mass of melted plastic, the outer casing of the phone unrecognisable. 'What are the chances of retrieving the SIM card from that?'

The forensic expert snorted. 'You've got to be kidding me.'

'What happened? Was he trapped before he could reach the firebreak, or…?'

'He wasn't out here for the hazard reduction burn,' said Coker. He crouched beside Mortlock's charred footwear. 'See? The soles are burned away but there's no metal left here. He wasn't wearing steel-capped boots. These look like ordinary work shoes to me, although keep that off the record until we've got him back to ours for a proper examination. Besides, this burn was publicised four weeks ago and the RFS lot did a drive-through here before they started to make sure there were no vehicles around.'

'You said you were meant to be meeting Mortlock. When did you last speak with him?' said Forbes, her green eyes peering at him over her mask.

'Yesterday, when I checked in to the pub.' Blake scratched at the plastic hoodie that rubbed against his cheek. 'He called me at about eleven o'clock, I reckon. Just to firm up some last-minute details before we met today.'

'Did he seem anxious about anything?'

He frowned. 'I didn't get that impression, no. Why? Do you think this was a suicide?'

'No, I don't.' She turned to Coker. 'Show him what Sigford found.'

The forensic technician shuffled sideways on his haunches until he reached Mortlock's skull, then gently turned it away so the hideous grimace faced the rock, before running his forefinger along the base of it. 'There's an indentation here, just behind where his ear would be. Michael Sigford, our pathologist, won't confirm anything until the PM but said off the record it's a blunt force trauma wound.'

'He fell and hit his head?'

Coker blinked. 'Not exactly, detective. Not the way he was found lying here, he didn't. His body would have taken a different trajectory.'

Blake felt a bead of sweat trickle through his hair,

accompanied by a swift shiver that spread across his shoulders. 'So, you're saying—'

'He was murdered,' said Forbes, her voice thick with emotion. 'Some bastard murdered him, and then after the RFS crew cleared the area his killer used the fire to try and hide the fact.'

'Jesus.' He took a step back and used the back of a gloved hand to wipe his forehead. 'You're sure?'

'As sure as we can be, until Mike Sigford's post mortem and any evidence we manage to find here confirms it, yes.' Coker straightened and nodded towards the fringes of the cordon. 'Hence why your lot have sent Detective Inspector Bragg from Caboolture HQ to watch over us. Met him yet?'

'He was talking to Brisbane HQ when I saw him, trying to get more resources sent up here,' said Forbes. 'I figured I'd introduce them after this.'

'Best get on with it then. Send him over here when you're done.' Coker batted away a fresh onslaught of flies from his face. 'I want him to be here when we move the body.'

'Will do.'

Forbes led the way back towards the outer cordon, her head bowed while she stepped carefully over twisted tree roots and coiled hoses that snaked across the demarcated path.

A strained silence accompanied them, broken only by a pair of RFS volunteers who nodded at them as they passed, one of them pausing briefly to murmur something to Forbes and then hurrying to catch up with his colleague.

'What was that about?' Blake said.

'Just passing on his condolences,' came the reply.

She kept walking.

Blake's tongue rasped against the roof of his mouth, the morning sun lifting the shadows amongst the smoky haze between the eucalypts and hoop pines beyond the outer cordon. It was another five degrees warmer since he'd arrived and the protective suit was clinging to him, suffocating his skin, shrouding him within its sticky sweaty grasp.

Ducking under the twisting crime scene tape, he staggered after Forbes into the white tent and tore away the mask, gulping in fresh air before peeling the hood from his head, running his hand over damp hair.

'Here.'

She stood beside a plastic crate laden with half-litre bottles of water, then tossed one to him.

He caught it one-handed, twisted the seal and swallowed half before catching his breath. 'Thanks.'

'No worries.' She peeled her protective suit away from a simple black T-shirt and jeans, then sipped delicately at her water, eyeing him while she did so. 'You do realise you might've been the last person to speak to Mortlock, don't you?'

'Wasn't he on duty yesterday?'

'He had a rostered day off. Wasn't due in until three this arvo – he pulled the late shift this week.'

'When did you last speak with him?'

A faint flush settled on her cheeks, and she turned away. 'Monday night. Just after nine.'

'So, how did he seem to you?'

'Normal, I suppose.' She stripped off the protective suit and shoved it into a biohazard bin beside the tent flap before turning back to him. 'Distracted, maybe, but not worried.'

'Has he had any threats recently?'

'Not that I'm aware of, no. But then, you never—' She broke off as voices grew louder outside the tent, then drained the last of her water. 'That's Bragg. I'd better introduce you before Coker gets hold of him.'

THREE

'Sir, can I have a word?'

Angela Forbes shifted the weight of her holstered pistol against her hip before tucking a loose strand of hair behind her ear, then heard the soft lisp of the tent flap fall back into place as Harknell hurried to join her.

Detective Inspector Cameron Bragg looked up from his phone, raising an eyebrow as she approached.

He still wore a tie despite the cloying humidity, although she noticed he had loosened the top button of his shirt, sweat patches showing under the arms.

No doubt he was missing the air-conditioned comfort of his office back at Caboolture headquarters.

'What is it? I've got Jon Coker wanting me to suit up so he can move the body, and Brisbane's just informed me that they're under-resourced and can't spare anyone to send up here, so make it quick.'

'I wanted to introduce you to Blake Harknell.' She had to lift her chin to meet his deep-set eyes, brown irises boring into her before his attention moved to Harknell.

'You're the new DS?'

'Yes, temporary secondment from Melbourne.'

She watched with interest as the two men sized each other up in the few seconds it took to shake hands, Harknell a couple of centimetres shorter than the inspector.

'I heard a rumour that Ivan was talking to you yesterday.' Bragg folded his arms across his chest. 'What was that about?'

'Just when I was due to get here, that sort of thing.'

'Did you talk about any active investigations?'

'No.' Harknell gave an apologetic shrug. 'Nothing like that. He wasn't very talkative – sounded like he was in a rush to be somewhere.'

'When was this?'

'About eleven. I'd just checked into the Royal in town.'

Bragg's nose wrinkled. 'That dump? Jesus. Whose idea was that?'

'Erm…' Harknell looked to Angela. 'Mortlock's.'

'Must've wanted to keep him close, sir,' she suggested.

'Even so…' Bragg shook his head. 'Why are you on secondment?'

'I had family near Morris Beach, an aunt who wasn't well. I was owed some leave so I asked for a short secondment.

Mortlock somehow got hold of my details and asked my boss to send me up here.' Harknell held up his hands in a what-can-you-do gesture. 'And here I am.'

'I know the area. Where does your aunt live?'

'She doesn't. She passed away six weeks ago. It was too late to cancel the secondment by then though.'

Bragg didn't bat an eyelid. 'Sorry for your loss. How long are you planning on staying up here for?'

'I don't know, I mean the secondment was for three months, so…'

'Good.' A shark-like smile crossed the inspector's face. 'We're low on resources, so consider yourself a part of my investigation now. I need a detective up here given that Brisbane's not going to help. Angela, he can partner with you—'

'Sir, with respect, we need to hit the ground running on this. I've got interviews backed up from this morning already, and…'

'It wasn't a request, constable.' Bragg glared at her, then jerked his head towards Harknell. 'He can help you with the interviews while you show him around. I don't need to remind you that we've just lost a valuable member of our team. A family man who dedicated over thirty years of his life to the police service. Do I?'

She felt the heat rising to her face under the scrutiny of the newcomer. 'No, sir.'

'Right then. Speak to the RFS crew leader while he's still

here, then go and interview Miles Prengist. After that you can set up the investigation centre back at the station, get Harknell up to speed with who's who there, then continue with the interviews. Get onto Mortlock's mobile phone provider when you get back to the station as well, and request the call and text records for the past six months.' Bragg glanced down at the phone in his hand as it began to ring. 'I'll speak to you later.'

Digging her nails into her palms, Angela watched him walk off towards the cordon with his phone to his ear, then gave herself a mental shake and then turned to Harknell.

'Looks like you're stuck with me,' he said, a rueful smile on his lips. 'Sorry.'

'Not your fault.' She squinted through the smoke drifting through the clearing and then jerked her chin towards a large man in his late fifties, short greying hair echoing the charcoal streaks flecking his face. 'That's Jeff Tanner, the RFS crew leader for this burn.'

'Okay.'

'Any problem if I lead the interview?'

'None at all.'

'Come on then.'

She led the way between the remnant stumps, the charred remains this side of the firebreak all that was left of the fledgling saplings that had taken hold over the summer and older trees that had rotted away or been sacrificed in the name of protecting the properties bordering the State-owned forest.

She held up a hand in greeting to Tanner. 'Jeff? Got a moment so I can take a statement from you?'

The older man tore thick work gloves from hands the size of bear paws and wiped his face against the collar of his hi-vis shirt. 'Five minutes, Ange, that's all. No offence, but thanks to Mortlock I've got twice as much paperwork to fill out when I get home, and head office wants to have a video conference call at twelve. Obviously they've forgotten how shit the signal is out here.'

Angela grimaced, taking out her notebook. 'Won't take long. But Bragg wants it done. So do I. We need some answers, especially before we tell Jill what's happened before she hears it through gossip.'

'Jesus.' Tanner turned his attention to Harknell. 'Haven't seen you around here before.'

'DS Blake Harknell. On secondment from Melbourne.'

'Melbourne, eh?' Tanner raised an eyebrow. 'Long way from home.'

'He was meant to be meeting Ivan this morning,' Angela explained.

'Shit, really?' The eyebrows lifted further. 'You knew him, then?'

'Jeff, the statement?' Angela popped her biro against the notebook and turned to a fresh page. 'What time did you get here?'

'Just before midday yesterday, once the crew had started prepping the area. I did a final drive around to check for any people or vehicles – Carl Upshott split the burn area with me so we could save a bit of time. After that, I spoke to the Parks and Wildlife rep to make sure the escape route matrix was clear, and then we started the burn at around two.'

Angela looked up. 'Why the delay?'

'The bloody wind turned on us at the last minute so we had to wait. Luckily, it was only a light breeze but…'

He didn't need to finish his sentence.

She had seen first-hand what happened when a hazard reduction burn got out of control a few years ago, and the memory sent goosebumps prickling across her forearms despite the humidity. 'Any sign of Ivan or his car while you were doing the final checks?'

'None at all. He must've turned up after we'd gone.'

'Were you here all night?'

'Yeah.' He bit back a yawn. 'And yes, I'm knackered.'

'Sorry, won't be much longer. Did you see anyone acting suspiciously?'

'No. I didn't see anyone who wasn't meant to be here. I've already told your boss – sorry, Bragg – that I'll give him a copy of the roster.'

Angela blinked, noting the slip and the hurried apology, but resisted the urge to comment.

The bloke truly looked knackered, after all.

'Okay,' she said, snapping shut the notebook. 'I'll probably need to speak to you again later in the week once we start processing all the information, but get yourself home, Jeff. You look like shit.'

He grinned, white teeth gleaming through the smuts that covered his face. 'Carl asked earlier if you'd be interested in joining him when he has a shower?'

'Tell him he can piss off.'

FOUR

Blake ducked under the thick tensile web of a golden orb spider stretching between two towering ghost gum trees and swept his gaze across the thickets of lantana that clung stubbornly to the wide trunks.

Despite the stark landscape caused by the controlled burn a few hundred metres away, the undergrowth flourished here, with tangling and twisted vines creeping across the path before winding their way around smaller saplings and bottlebrush shrubs, only broken when the grasses took over, dry and yellowing from the arid conditions.

'Will they be doing back-burning through here, too?' he called out to Forbes.

She didn't stop walking. 'Yes. All of this is a fire risk. Most of it's invasive species anyway but these grasses… If they catch light during a storm, it'd be a disaster. They're just doing it in stages to give the wildlife space to escape.'

He spotted the telltale smudges of an old lightning strike against the stubborn skeleton of a eucalyptus. 'When did the last fire rip through here?'

'About three years ago. I was only a junior constable then, but it took them six days to put out the last of the embers.' She trudged onwards, paused to lift the outer cordon tape and sign out, then waited while he did the same.

'Tell me about Jeff Tanner,' he said when they were on the move once more. 'What does he do when he's not managing planned burns like this one?'

'He owns the local servo and repair shop. You'd have driven past his place this morning – it's just down the road from the Royal.'

'Another volunteer, then?'

She frowned. 'They're all volunteers. The place isn't big enough to sustain full-time roles.'

'How many volunteers were working on this burn?'

'Fourteen. I'm planning to split the interviews between myself and Ryan Darke – you'll meet him when we get to the station.'

'Where does Carl Upshott work?'

'He's got his own business as a handyman. Does fencing repairs, bathroom renos, that sort of thing.' She wrinkled her nose. 'He gets most of his work out nearer Caboolture way though. There're loads of new housing developments sprouting up, lots of people moving up from your neck of the woods and Sydney.'

'You don't approve?'

Forbes shrugged. 'Makes everything twice as expensive for the rest of us. Even if you can find a job, the wages around here are pretty shit.'

He didn't have an answer to that, and instead pulled out his car keys as they approached the vehicles.

'Did you drive up from Melbourne?' she said, eyeing the licence plate on the dark grey wagon. 'You didn't fly?'

He blipped the fob and the indicator lights blinked. 'I figured it'd save money rather than hiring a car once I was up here.'

'How long did that take you?'

'Couple of days with a rest stop in between.' He opened the door and then took a step back as a fresh blast of warm air wafted over him. 'Thankfully, the air con works.'

She almost smiled at that, then pointed at the QPS four-wheel drive he'd parked behind. 'That's mine.'

Soon they were on the move, the steering wheel juddering under his grip as he tried to avoid the worst of the deep wheel ruts scoring the weather-beaten dirt track.

Here and there, termite mounds poked through the pale brown landscape, the towering dirt structures sticking up in the air like rudimentary milestones. They were interspersed with imposing granite boulders that had tumbled from the crevices and rocky outcrops that hung over the track, hugging the shallow valley.

All around him were the burned-out husks of trees, the soil between them blackened and ruined.

The two vehicles wound their way down the craggy hillside for another minute or so, and then the terrain levelled out.

The track twisted around a wide corner to reveal a dusty black panel van parked on the right-hand side in front of an off-white ute that appeared to have been abandoned. Scorch marks mixed with mud up the sides of the paintwork, and the windscreen was streaked with road grease and dead bugs.

'Shit.'

Blake stomped his foot to the floor as the brake lights on Forbes's vehicle flared, narrowly avoiding careening into the back of her four-wheel drive.

She crawled past the vehicles, and as he craned his neck to see around them he spotted a team of four forensic technicians scouring the terrain, heads bowed.

They glanced up, one raising a hand by way of greeting in the direction of the QPS four-wheel drive before returning to their work.

'Mortlock's ute,' Blake murmured.

It appeared to be in reasonable condition, with only the usual muck and dust associated with a vehicle used regularly but cleaned as and when its owner had time. There were no obvious signs of vandalism or other damage to the bodywork aside from that caused by the hazard reduction burn. Even the flames had only licked at the paintwork from a distance, nothing more, and so maybe the forensic team would find something to help the fledgling investigation.

But why had the senior sergeant parked here?

Had he walked to where his body had been found that morning, or had someone else been here with him?

Forbes picked up speed then, only stopping when she reached the end of the twisting dirt track and a T-junction.

An enormous scruffy blue road train thundered past, its two trailers pockmarked with ventilation holes. The soft white muzzles of Brahman cattle were just visible through the gaps as they sniffed at their last vestiges of freedom before they reached the slaughterhouse.

Forbes turned onto the potholed asphalt road, accelerating as soon as the four-wheel drive's tyres struck the tarmac.

They reached Miles Prengist's house via a convoluted route along a second dirt track that made Blake wonder why the landowner simply hadn't carved a direct access from the back of his property through to the State forest's dirt track.

By the time he parked alongside a large galvanised steel water tank, his coccyx was numb from the potholes and ruts, and he was sure the car suspension was in worse shape.

Climbing out, he groaned as his back protested, then wandered over to where Forbes stood next to her vehicle, eyeing the house.

It was a simple whitewashed clapboard affair, with a

shallow veranda clinging to the front of it and a gabled roof that hung over the top windows with a perpetual frown.

Straggly grass grew in clumps around the base of the wooden steps leading to the front door, and what might have been once an optimistic front lawn was now given over to abandoned rusting machinery, interspersed with weeds and stones.

'What can you tell me about Prengist?' he said.

'He's a fourth-generation cattle farmer. Mid-fifties, history of violence – doesn't like being told what to do, especially if it's about his property. His wife walked out on him four years ago when the last of the kids left for university. Her bruises cleared up after about three weeks.'

'Any history of gun ownership?'

'Yes, but Ivan confiscated his last registered rifle eighteen months ago.'

'Is he likely to kick off when we knock on the door?'

'It depends how much he's had to drink.'

'How big is his property?'

'Big enough. He has three hired hands to help out now that both his boys have left home.'

'Do they stay in touch with their dad?'

'Not as far as I know. One's working down in Sydney, the other buggered off to England as soon as he graduated. Neither have been back here, that's for sure. Someone would've told us otherwise.'

Blake scanned the three large timber-clad sheds that

towered over the thin line of macadamia trees to the left of the property, squinting against the late morning sunlight. 'How do you want to do this? Knock first, or have a look around?'

Forbes squared her shoulders. 'Let's see if he's in.'

'Perhaps I should go first?'

'He doesn't know you.' She was already walking towards the veranda. 'He might listen to me.'

He hurried to catch up, his skin prickling with anticipation as her boots found purchase on the steps leading to the front door.

As he drew closer, he saw that despite the state of the barren front yard, the veranda decking was swept clear of leaf litter and had been recently oiled.

Forbes beat her palm against a metal fly screen, then tried the handle.

It didn't give under her touch.

'Miles? It's Angela Forbes,' she called. 'You in?'

There was no answer.

'Want to try the sheds?' Blake ventured.

She said nothing, leading the way across to the first of three and peering in through the open sliding metal door. 'Miles? You around?'

No answer.

They had no luck with the other two either.

'Probably out hunting,' said Forbes, pushing her hair from her forehead with the back of her hand and looking at the house.

'With what? I thought you said Mortlock confiscated his guns?'

'He did.' Her mouth twisted. 'Or at least, he said he was going to.'

'So, there'll be something on file that might help us, right?'

'Maybe.' She sighed, dropping her hand. 'Okay, follow me back to the station and I'll introduce you to everyone properly.'

'Right-o.'

'Don't get too excited. There aren't many of us, which is why Bragg's pissed off with Brisbane. And evidently delighted that you're here.'

FIVE

Blake eased into his car, mindful of the searing heat emanating from the upholstery, and then started the engine and batted down the dashboard vents with his hand so they didn't blow warm gusts into his face while the air conditioning began to work.

He kept a reasonable distance from Forbes, dust and small stones spitting out from under the tyres of the four-wheel drive and into the high grass verges that lined the main road.

Risking a glance at the terrain that encroached on either side, Blake swallowed, throat dry despite the bottle of water he'd finished. He lifted his collar, then recoiled. His clothes stank, the reek of smoke clinging to his shirt and trousers, his hair…

A few kilometres later, the first of the small town's properties came into view, the only clues to their existence being metal mailboxes in various shades of decay at the end of driveways every couple of hundred metres.

Here and there, a tumbledown corrugated-roofed outbuilding of dubious construction or a dilapidated timber shed flashed past his window, and then they were slowing to fifty ks, passing the local Lions Club-sponsored sign welcoming him to Hangman's Gap.

He slowed a little as he passed it, squinting at a pair of rusting holes in the top right-hand corner of the faded lettering, sure he was looking at bullet holes, and then accelerated, wondering if it was a portent of what was waiting for him here.

The small town was as attractive as its name.

The main road – such as it was – cut a wide scar between dusty single-storey buildings that were a mixture of residential and commercial, although the only difference between the various squat wooden-slatted Queenslanders was the absence of signage in the windows or above the doors of the homes.

A few businessowners had made desultory attempts to spruce up the place by hanging a colourful banner or some sort of floral display from the worn awnings, although in most cases both the signage and flowers were wilting in the late morning heat.

He glanced down as his phone beeped, his top lip curling at the name displayed on the screen before he flicked the switch on the steering wheel and answered it. 'Boss.'

'What's going on? You were meant to report in an hour ago.'

'They found Ivan Mortlock's body this morning.' He saw Forbes turn left and indicated to follow her. 'I've been introduced to Cameron Bragg – he's the inspector running the investigation out of Caboolture HQ. He's teamed me up with a Senior Constable, Angela Forbes, given that I was supposed to be here on secondment.'

There was silence at the other end for a moment, then: 'Where are you now?'

'Following Forbes to the station in Hangman's Gap.' He saw her brake lights flash, and then she was slowing, her four-wheel drive passing through an open wire mesh gate in a matching fence that sagged in the middle. 'Looks like we're here.'

'I'll expect an update later.'

The call ended, and Blake ran a hand across tired eyes before climbing out.

Forbes pulled a duffel bag from the back seat of her four-wheel drive and swung it over her shoulder. 'FYI, there's a shower here but it doesn't always run hot water so if you want to go back to the hotel to get out of those clothes, you've got time before we're due to go and see Ivan's widow.'

He sniffed his shirt cuff, aware of the stink of smoke clinging to him. 'Thanks, I'll do that.'

She turned away and began walking towards the station

entrance, a pair of glass doors with stainless steel handrails. 'Well, I'll get you introduced, then we'll—'

Forbes stopped suddenly in her tracks, frozen to the spot.

'Woah.' Blake almost crashed into her, side-stepped to avoid a collision, then looked up at the deep blue corrugated steel roof to see what had caught her attention.

His stomach sank.

A portico provided a modicum of shade across the steps leading to the front doors.

High above that, beside a bird shit-covered satellite dish pointing south, the Australian flag was hanging at half-mast.

SIX

Blake gave Forbes a moment, then cleared his throat.

'Shall we?'

'Yeah. Sure.'

She gave a slight shake of her head, then strode towards the front doors of the station.

There were shutters across the windows either side of the doors, and he wondered whether they were pulled closed to keep the heat out or prevent prying eyes from looking in. A CCTV warning sign on the pale blue-painted slatted timber wall beside the door caught his eye, and he cocked his head to the right to see a security camera pointing at him, a red LED light glowing underneath the lens.

He followed her, noting the public opening hours stencilled in white paint on the glass and the greasy hand-shaped smears on the stainless steel vertical push-pull bars.

After closing the door behind him, he instinctively looked around for hand sanitiser, then gave up and settled for wiping his hands down his trousers, wrinkling his nose.

An aluminium ceiling fan wafted pitifully at the stale air clinging to the small reception area of the station.

It was only a couple of metres from the door to a rectangular hole cut into the opposite wall that evidently served as a reception desk, its opening shut off from the outside world by a sliding frosted Perspex window with a set of stickers peeling from the left-hand side of it that displayed a range of hotline numbers. The remainder of the reception space surrendered to wall-to-wall wooden panelling covered in various public notices and posters crinkling at the corners and yellowed with age. A sturdy-looking wooden door was off to his right that he guessed led through to the inner workings of the building.

Beyond the Perspex window, he could see the blurred outline of a stocky figure hunched over a desk, the murmur of a conversation bubbling through to where he stood.

He wondered if that was the man who had lowered the flag.

Forbes stabbed a six-digit code into a security panel beside the wooden door and beckoned him over at the sound of a soft *click*. 'The code is hashtag 040968, then an asterisk on the end.'

He opened his mouth to reply, but she rolled her eyes.

'Yeah, I know. We kept telling Ivan that his birthday

wasn't the best idea for a code, but he refused to change it.' Her face fell. 'I guess we'll have to think of another one.'

She wrenched open the door and stalked through it, dropping her duffel bag on the floor beside a scuffed grey metal filing cabinet. 'Terry, this is DS Blake Harknell, up from Melbourne.'

The broad man who Blake had spotted through the Perspex window looked over his computer screen, a scowl on his face while he replaced his desk phone in its cradle. Pitted skin covered his sun-damaged forehead and cheekbones, and a ruddiness stained his nose that hinted at a drinking habit sustained over several years. His thinning brown hair was flecked with white and cut close to his scalp. He blinked once, and then pushed his chair back and thrust out his hand when Blake drew near.

'Senior Constable Terry Doxon,' he said, his Queensland accent a laidback drawl that belied the shrewd look in his pale blue eyes.

'Good to meet you.'

'Terry's decided to take early retirement,' Forbes explained, perching on another desk across the narrow aisle from Doxon's and folding her arms. 'When's your last day?'

'Three weeks' time.' A faint flush rose up the man's thick neck. 'Talk about bloody timing, though.'

'No shit.' Forbes jerked her chin at the sound of a quiet curse and Blake turned to see a younger man in his mid-twenties struggling out of a side office with a stack of beige manila folders in his arms that were stuffed with curling papers. 'What've you got there, Ryan?'

'Some of the files that were on Mortlock's desk,' he said. 'Terry reckoned we ought to go through them in case there're any clues.'

'That all right, Angie?' The older constable asked, a leer to his voice.

Blake watched with interest as her attention snapped back to Doxon, her mouth open in retort before she cast a sideways glance his way.

'Bragg's taking over the investigation, Terry,' she said.

'I'm more than capable of managing it. He knows that.'

'Well, he's got Blake on board now, and like you said, you're retiring in three weeks so we need to make sure we've got continuity.' It was her turn to smirk now. 'And if he's got any questions, I'm here to help him.'

'Fine.' Doxon returned to his desk and slumped back into his seat, picking up his mobile phone and checking the screen.

'What shall I do with these files then?' Ryan ventured, half-turning back towards Mortlock's office.

'Put them back on the desk in there,' said Forbes. 'Terry's right, there could be something in those that'll help us but we need to make sure everything's properly recorded.'

'Don't you use QPRIME here?' Blake looked from her to Doxon.

'Of course we do,' he said scornfully. 'It's just that

Mortlock was a dinosaur – and he sometimes ran his own investigations into things.'

'He hated the political side of the job,' Forbes explained. 'All the stats and reports, the targets that were set, that sort of thing. So if he caught a whiff of something, sometimes he'd do a bit of digging around before entering it into the system. Just in case there was a way to fix things… amicably. It's a small town, remember. Everyone knows everyone, so…'

Blake eyed the folders sliding about in Ryan's hands. 'Are all those off the books then?'

'Dunno.' The young constable's eyes widened slightly. 'Maybe.'

Forbes caught Blake's incredulous glance. 'Put them back, Ryan. We'll take a look later once we've spoke with Jill.'

'Apart from what I found on the local community website – which hasn't been updated since 2019 – what is it like around here?' Blake said, pulling out his notebook. 'I mean, has anyone else died in suspicious circumstances recently, or—'

'Not in a while,' said Ryan, returning from Mortlock's office and easing behind a smaller desk squashed into a space in the far corner of the office. His lanky frame seemed awkward surrounded by a printer, a whiteboard on wheels and another battered filing cabinet. 'Not since—'

'There was an accident, out on the Baxter road three months ago,' said Forbes. 'A white ute with New South Wales plates skidded out of control and hit a tree. We still haven't managed to ID the victim.'

'Male or female?'

'Male. No sign of anyone else having been in the vehicle, but when the accident investigators opened the back door, they found a shovel in the footwell. There was blood on the blade.'

Blake stopped writing and stared at her. 'Animal, or…?'

'Human. We sent it off for testing. There were a few strands of hair, too.'

'Any sign of a body?'

'None, and even though we've checked what security camera footage there is along that road from private properties, that car hadn't been picked up until it pulled onto the main road west of Baxter,' said Doxon. 'We haven't had a new lead on that one for weeks now.'

Blake exhaled. 'Okay, so was Mortlock investigating that?'

'Yes, and not off the books,' said Forbes. 'He was leading our enquiries into it and reporting to Bragg, but I didn't get the impression that he was going off on a tangent, did you, Terry?'

Doxon shook his head in response.

'Okay, so we'll bear that in mind then.' Blake scrawled a note to himself, then paused. 'Is there anyone local who might've wanted to kill Mortlock? What's the population here in Hangman's Gap anyway?'

'It depends. We get a few tourists passing through – those who want to see more of the hinterland rather than the beaches. So at this time of year, with rental properties, guesthouses… about two to three thousand,' said Forbes. 'Give or take a—'

'Plus one.' Ryan returned from Mortlock's office, beaming. 'My older sister had a baby boy at Caboolture hospital last night.'

Blake looked up from his notes as the others voiced their congratulations. 'First one?'

'Second. Her daughter started at kindy last week.'

'What about you? Any kids?'

Forbes snorted. 'Don't be daft, he's only just out of diapers himself.'

'Young Molly at the Royal might have something to say about that.' Doxon winked theatrically.

Ryan blushed, turning away to his computer screen. 'We've only been going out for two months,' he mumbled.

Blake bit back a smile, the familiar to and fro of station banter lending a normality to the otherwise awkward undercurrent that cut beneath his questions.

'What about you, sarge?' said Doxon. 'Family?'

'Ex-wife, back in Melbourne,' he replied. 'No kids, but she got custody of the dog.'

'What d'you have?' said Ryan.

'Rescue greyhound. Going back to Mortlock – d'you reckon anyone passing through here had a problem with him?' Blake jerked his thumb towards the office at the end. 'Given that he had a habit of running his own investigations into things, you said.'

'Can't think of anyone,' said Forbes, shrugging. 'But we'll speak to his wife, Jill, and ask her.'

'I can't think of anyone either,' said Ryan. 'But he would've told us if he thought any of our lives were in danger though, right?'

Blake closed his notebook and glared at the ceiling fan that was doing nothing much apart from ruffling the paperwork on Doxon's desk. 'Okay, well thanks for the potted local history. I suppose I'd better make a couple of calls, see if I can find somewhere to stay in Caboolture before I report to headquarters in the morning.'

Forbes shook her head. 'Bragg doesn't want you at Caboolture, liaising with me over a phone. He wants you here. Every day. I thought that was clear when we spoke to him earlier.'

Blake frowned. 'But…'

'No buts. He said this was going to be the investigation centre for Mortlock's murder. The rate it's going around here with lack of resources, we'll be lucky if they send out anyone else either.'

Doxon shot him a malicious grin. 'Looks like you're stuck with us, mate. Guess you won't be needing that suit, either. Don't suppose you packed something more—'

'Practical? Yes, I did.' Blake checked his watch, then turned his attention back to Forbes. 'In fact, if you don't mind,

I'm going to head over to the pub for that shower and a change of clothes. Meet you back here in, say, thirty minutes?'

'Sounds good.'

Doxon's drawl carried to the door as Blake shoved it open. 'Don't get lost, will ya?'

SEVEN

Angela peered through the grey plastic blind covering the kitchen window and eyed Harknell's road-worn wagon.

It was a few years old, a popular model, and the tyres looked a little on the ragged side of a roadworthy certificate, but it had managed the uneven surface of the fire trail with gusto.

In front of it was Terry's personal vehicle, an SUV that wore its mud-spattered bodywork with aplomb. Despite Mortlock's requests, the Caboolture-based procurement department refused to provide additional funding for another four-wheel drive given Terry's imminent retirement, so he shared her QPS-issued four-wheel drive or Ryan's car when he was on shift, something she wouldn't miss once he retired.

Beside that was Mortlock's service vehicle, one that matched her own. It had already been dusted for prints by a team of forensic technicians that morning, and there were telltale streaks of powder across the door handles and bodywork. No doubt the upholstery was in a similar state.

Ryan's low-slung liveried sedan was beside that, a crooked radio antenna that seemed hellbent on hanging onto the roof for grim death, despite her telling the young copper he ought to get Jeff Tanner to fix it rather than wait for the procurement team at HQ to do something about it.

Her suggestion had been successfully ignored for the past three months, Ryan's optimism that HQ would do something before he had to speak to Tanner testing her patience to the point where – if it hadn't been for Mortlock's murder – she had planned to fix it herself that afternoon.

The sound of the kettle rumbling to a crescendo caught her attention and she let the blind snap back into place before flipping the switch as steam filled the air.

'Make us one, Angie,' Terry called.

'Plenty of water, help yourself,' she said, then clinked the spoon against the chipped mug, the sound ringing off the cheap plasterwork walls.

She could hear him grumbling under his breath for a moment before his phone rang.

Straining her ears to hear his side of the conversation, she relaxed a little when she realised it was simply the coroner's office confirming that the paperwork had been received for the post mortem.

Her hand shook as she fished out the sodden teabag, and

tannin-stained water slopped over the Formica worktop before she flipped it into a pedal bin beside the small refrigerator.

She closed her eyes for a moment, crossing her fingers until the call ended and she heard Terry push back his chair.

She glanced over her shoulder at the sound of his approach.

'The post mortem's scheduled for Friday morning at Coopers Plains,' he said. 'They've already heard from Bragg. He wants the new boy to go with him.'

Exhaling, she nodded. 'Okay.'

'Caught a break there, didn't you?' He winked, then disappeared.

She snarled at the empty air, then frowned as her mobile phone vibrated in her pocket. 'Not a great time, Mum.'

'Is it true? Is it Ivan?'

'I can't say, you know that,' she murmured, listening to Terry's voice in the other room. 'And I can't talk right now.'

Sandra Forbes had a formidable reputation as the co-chair of the local Country Women's Association, and Angela knew full well that reputation came with a predisposition to gossip where the town police station was concerned. Despite her efforts, despite her results, any rumours emanating from the community hall down the road on a Wednesday night were automatically assumed to have been passed from daughter to mother, and she was having none of it.

'Mum, I have to go. There's a lot to do here.'

'Call in later. The meeting isn't due to start until seven. Besides, your dad would love to see you.'

Guilt punched her in the chest, and she closed her eyes. 'I know, but I doubt I'll be leaving here before ten tonight, if that. He'll be asleep by then, right?'

Her mother sighed. 'Probably. You know what the painkillers do to him.'

'I'll call in as soon as I can. Love you.'

Angela ended the call before her mother could reply, then jumped as Terry appeared at the door.

'That your mum?'

'Yes.'

'How's your dad doing?'

'Same as always. Tired.'

'I'm going to nip out, see if I can make a head start on those landowner interviews.'

'I thought you were manning the phones.'

'Ryan can do that.'

'Terry, he needs the experience. I need him to get that experience, especially as you're leaving soon. Send him instead.' She saw the flash of anger in his eyes then, and put down her tea mug before taking a deep breath. 'Seriously? You want to have this argument now?'

'Just because Mortlock's dead, doesn't mean you're automatically officer-in-charge around here,' he said, his tone petulant. 'And Ryan's too wet behind the ears to know when someone's lying to his face.'

'Keep your voice down,' she hissed. 'It's only a matter of practice, and he's not exactly getting that thanks to you, is he? Come on, Terry. Please. I know you and I have had our differences but you're out of here in three weeks. Ryan's the only one around here who knows as many of the locals as us. What do you think's going to happen after you leave?'

'Probably nothing for a few months…'

'Exactly. And if we haven't found Mortlock's killer by then, or managed to get any headway on who the hell that bloke was in that car, we're fucked, right?'

'You are.'

'Oh, so you don't think people are going to ask you when you're down the pub why you didn't stick around to help, is that it? Old Terry Doxon goes ahead with early retirement even though his colleague and supposed friend is lying dead in a morgue – that's going to go down well, isn't it?'

'Everything all right in there?'

Angela clamped shut her jaw at the sound of Ryan's voice, his worry evident.

'We're fine,' Terry snapped, his eyes on her. 'Just sorting out some staffing issues.'

'Okay.'

'What's it going to be, Terry?' she said, holding his stare. 'After all, you never did explain why you left it six hours after finding that car crash before you called it in. Why was that?'

His jaw clenched in response, a hiss escaping through his teeth.

'Who was he?'

'I don't know,' he said eventually, his voice little more than a mutter.

'Are you sure about that?'

'Yes. And it didn't get called in straight away because I was using Ryan's vehicle and the radio died on me.'

'Could've used your phone.'

He snorted. 'Give me a break, Ange. You know what the signal's like out there. Piss poor at the best of times.'

A phone started to ring in the office, its tone persistent.

Picking up her mug once more, Angela's gaze travelled to the window as Harknell's imposing form cast a shadow across the blinds. 'Best get that, Terry. Might be important.'

'Screw you.'

EIGHT

There was a palpable sour atmosphere when Blake returned to the police station.

Even the supposed ocean-scented complimentary soap from the hotel's shower couldn't disguise the raised pungency of Terry Doxon's body odour as he slammed a desk phone back into its cradle and spun his chair so his back was to the room.

Except that wasn't it, not really.

There was something else about the small police station, something that sent a crackle of anticipation across Blake's shoulders as Forbes appeared from a door near the back of the building cradling a ceramic mug and looking for all the world if she would rather be somewhere else.

What had his presence interrupted?

He turned at the sound of a polite cough to see Ryan Darke fumbling with a set of car keys, his eyes keen.

'Right, Ange. Well, I'll be off to have a word with Marcus up at the dairy, then. That all right?'

'Sounds good. Just remember to take your time. Better to double check anything with him now rather than later. And don't forget to ask about security around the place while you're there. Any break-ins lately, the usual.'

'Will do.'

The young constable nodded at Blake, then scurried away, the front door banging shut in his wake before the roar of a V8 rumbled through the thin walls.

'I take it this Marcus has land that backs onto the controlled burn area?' said Blake.

'It does, at the far end.' Forbes shot him a tired smile. 'It's the furthest from the crime scene so it'll give Ryan some practice at least.'

Her gaze flittered to Doxon as the senior constable muttered something under his breath before she continued. 'And we should get going too if we're going to speak to Jill before the rumours start circulating.'

Five minutes later, air conditioning blasting an Arctic-like breeze across his shoulders, Blake held onto the door strap as Forbes swung her QPS four-wheel drive onto the main street and accelerated away from the police station.

'Did something happen while I was gone?' he ventured.

She glanced across at him, then back to the road and eased off the throttle. 'What do you mean?'

'It seemed a bit tense back there when I walked in.'

'Just some staffing issues. Nothing for you to worry about.'

'Right.' He loosened his grip on the strap and looked out the window as they passed the pub where he was staying. 'The bloke who owns the hotel reckons they'll be able to put me up for another two weeks, but then he's got a backpacker group from Germany turning up so I'll be homeless. Might have to find somewhere in Caboolture after all.'

'We'll see.' She tapped her fingers on the steering wheel for a moment. 'There are a few people around here that let out rooms from time to time.'

'To a copper on an active murder investigation? I can't see Bragg agreeing to that, can you?'

'Maybe not.'

They passed the town speed limit sign and she eased the accelerator to the floor, the last clapboard houses disappearing in the door mirror in seconds and the scenery returning to one of scrubby pasture and clumps of eucalyptus and ghost gums.

Long grass hugged the roadside verges, obscuring barbed wire fencing strung between wooden posts and encroaching onto the asphalt.

Blake swallowed, the dryness of the landscape palpable even from the comfort of the air-conditioned vehicle.

'There's a spare bottle of water in the glove compartment,' said Forbes.

'Thanks.'

He popped open the compartment, caught a flashlight before it tumbled into the footwell and then fished out the water bottle. 'Want some?'

'Got one here, thanks.' She rummaged in the door pocket beside her, then produced another bottle and clinked it against his. 'Cheers. Welcome, by the way. I don't think I got a chance to say that.'

'Cheers.' He took a long swig before smacking his lips. 'So what's Doxon's problem with you? Or is it just the thought of retirement?'

A bitter laugh escaped her. 'Probably a bit of both. Me, being a woman and a better copper than him when he was my age. And yeah, retirement. Not that he had a choice.'

'Oh? Being forced out, is he?'

'Something like that.'

'He doesn't seem that old. Is the service cost-cutting that much up this way?'

'It's more of a performance thing. And yeah, age too.'

'What sort of performance thing? Anything that's going to give us problems with this investigation?'

She sighed. 'I hope not.'

NINE

Ivan Mortlock's widow was waiting for them.

Wearing a scowl deepening a brow that looked as if it had seen many a frown over the years, she watched with arms crossed from the front veranda of a pale blue clapboard Queenslander while Forbes steered the four-wheel drive into a space beside an eight-year-old Holden wagon.

Blake averted his gaze, busying himself with his mobile phone as the engine died. 'We've been spotted.'

'I'd imagine Terry phoned ahead.'

'Seriously?'

She shrugged. 'Probably. Or anyone else we passed on the way here.'

'I only saw two cars.' Blake looked up from his phone. 'And the last one was five Ks back.'

'It's a small community. People talk.'

'How long had she and Ivan been together?'

Forbes released the door catch. 'Long enough.'

With that, she climbed out, leaving him to scramble after her, straightening his tie and wishing to hell he had sprayed more anti-perspirant under his cotton shirt.

The house had been constructed beyond a picket fence that resolutely separated it from the road despite evidence of termites in the wooden palings. The wide gate blocking the dirt driveway hung from hinges that had dropped over the years, and he waited while Forbes lifted it open with a practised hand.

He ran his hand over his neck, slicking away the perspiration that was already forming in the mid-afternoon heat, then ran his fingers down the sides of his trousers as he followed Forbes across spikes of yellowing grass that constituted a lawn in these parts.

'Jill,' she murmured as she drew closer to the porch, her head lowered.

'He's dead, isn't he?'

'Could we go inside?'

'Would it change anything?' Mortlock's wife shook her head, dropping her arms to her waistline and hugging herself. 'I always knew it'd bloody come to this. Two coppers on my doorstep, telling me he's never coming home again.'

Blake saw it then, the armour in the woman's glare slowly dissolving as her voice shook.

'Mrs Mortlock, For— Angela is right. We should go

indoors.' He climbed the three shallow steps up to the veranda, taking in Jill's rake-like form under a baggy T-shirt and leggings, then gestured to the screen door. 'Can I get you a drink of water?'

She jutted her chin out, pulling herself to her full height which was still a good four inches shorter than him. 'Reckon I could do with something stronger in the circumstances. Who are you?'

'Detective Sergeant Blake Harknell.'

'That's not a local accent. Where're you from?'

'Melbourne.'

'Seriously?' She peered around him to where Forbes remained at the foot of the steps. 'What the hell did Ivan get himself into?'

Fifteen minutes later, after the scant details that could be given about Ivan Mortlock's death and the sombre expressions of grief shared, Blake sat on a hard pine chair at a matching table in Jill Mortlock's kitchen, and wondered whether he would be considered rude if he asked for ice in the glass of cordial that had been poured for him.

Beads of condensation bobbled across the tumbler before dribbling steadily onto the wooden surface, forming a pool beside an old coffee stain.

'I spoke to your mother yesterday,' she said to Forbes,

easing herself into a seat opposite them. 'Reckon she's going to go for another year chairing the CWA. Got to say, I'm surprised given your dad's health. How is he by the way?'

'Same, thanks.'

Blake heard the dismissal in his colleague's voice, but kept his gaze firmly on Mortlock's widow as she took a sip from a crystal whisky tumbler before setting it down on the table with a dull thud.

She stared at it for a moment. 'We used to have six of these. They were a wedding present from his parents, the whole set of crystal glasses. Champagne flutes, the lot. All broken over the years. Ivan insisted on keeping this one. Said it was his favourite.' With that, her shoulders heaved and tears spilled over her cheeks. 'Oh, shit.'

The sound of her sobs filled the kitchen, her breathing coming in gasps as she leaned her elbows on the table and buried her head in her hands.

Forbes pushed away her chair, walked out the room and returned a moment later with a roll of toilet tissue, expertly unravelling it before holding out a wad. 'Here.'

'Thanks.' Jill snuffled, gasped for breath, and blew her nose loudly. 'Christ, sorry.'

'Mrs Mortlock, there's no need to apologise,' said Blake. 'Is there anyone we can call? Perhaps there's a friend nearby who can be with you?'

That elicited a bitter snort.

'You're joking.' She blew her nose again, pushed back her

chair and shoved the sodden tissue paper into an aluminium swing bin beside the back door. 'All anyone around here will want to do is find out what you've just told me so they can be first to say they know what's going on. Either that, or tell me he had it coming to him.'

'I'm sure that's not—'

'Oh yes it is.' Jill folded her arms and leaned against the sink. She bobbed her head towards Forbes. 'Ask her.'

'Jill, we don't know if this is work-related yet,' said his colleague. 'It's very early days.'

'It couldn't be anything else though, could it? I mean, work is all he did. Either that, or drink in the Royal – and even that was so he could keep an eye on things.' The woman shoved herself away from the sink and flopped back into her chair in one fluid movement. 'That was Ivan though, wasn't it? Couldn't keep his nose out of things.'

'Did he say anything to give you cause for concern these past few weeks?' said Blake, ignoring the glare that his colleague shot his way.

She might have been a senior constable and more familiar with the local area, but he ranked higher than her and there had been no prior discussion about who would lead any interviews.

Yet.

Jill straightened, dabbed at her eyes once more, then blinked. 'Ivan never spoke to me about his work. He was secretive like that.'

'Did you ask him about it?'

'What?'

'Did you ask him about his work, or was it an implicit understanding between you that he wouldn't talk about it?' Blake shared what he hoped was a shy smile. 'I know my ex-wife would rather not know about what I do for a living. Hated everything about the job actually.'

'Then you know what I mean.' Jill waved a hand towards the tired walls and paintwork. 'I'd been asking him for three years if we could decorate in here. I mean, look at it. It's embarrassing. He was always too busy though, either working or off on one of his tangents.'

Blake sensed Forbes stiffen beside him. 'What sort of tangents?' he said.

'Maybe ask your colleague there instead of me.' The woman gave a petulant shrug. 'After all, she and Ivan were spending a lot of time together these past few months. Weren't you, Angela?'

TEN

Cheeks still burning, Angela made her way back to the four-wheel drive, jostling the key fob between her hands as she stalked ahead of Harknell.

Jill had ushered them from the house after her scathing remark, telling them she would call the station if she thought of anything that might help the investigation, and listening with a dispassionate expression while Angela tried to explain what Mortlock's colleagues would be doing in their attempts to find his killer.

The screen door slapped against her heels before Harknell caught up with her, his hasty retreat accompanied by mumbled apologies and a promise to stay in touch with Ivan Mortlock's widow.

'Better you than her,' came the biting response.

Hissing between her teeth when the four-wheel drive's

leather upholstery burned through her uniform trousers, Angela twisted the key in the ignition and placed her hands on the fiery surface of the steering wheel, the burning sensation focusing her mind away from the myriad of rejoinders that now spun through her tumbling thoughts.

Harknell swore under his breath when he climbed in, then said nothing more as she accelerated away from the property in a cloud of stones and dust that she left in her wake.

The engine roared under her right foot, producing a satisfying growl from the diesel engine that vibrated through the wheels as the dirt track turned to asphalt.

'Where are we going? Back to the station?'

She blinked, Harknell's voice cutting through the police radio that chattered away in the background, and she reached out to toggle the volume.

'No. Let's see if Miles Prengist is home before we head back to the station. We still need to interview him as a priority.' She glanced across at him. 'Aren't you going to ask me what happened back there?'

He shrugged, and turned his attention back to the road. 'Figured you'd tell me in your own time.'

'Right.' She bit her lip, checked the mirrors, and took a deep breath. 'Everyone around here thinks me and Ivan were having an affair.'

'Were you?'

'Not exactly.'

He reached out and adjusted the air conditioning, said nothing, then settled back into his seat.

'We were close, okay?' Angela cleared her throat, a tightness to her voice that pinched at her heart. 'He was more like… a good friend. A really good friend.'

'Did you spend a lot of time together? Outside of work, I mean.'

'Yes. Probably too much, which is why the rumours started.'

'Any ideas about who might've killed him?'

'No. Not yet.'

'Did you know about the other cases he was working on?' Harknell shuffled in his seat until he faced her, although she kept her gaze firmly on the road ahead. 'The ones that weren't in the files in his office, that is.'

'Some of them, yes. But there were one or two he kept to himself.' She swallowed. 'He said it was better if I didn't know.'

'Did you try finding out?'

'Too damn right I did.' She risked a glance his way. 'Not that it did any good, did it?'

The drive to Miles Prengist's property took another twenty minutes, by which time the silence in the four-wheel drive had been broken once more only by Harknell's surprised exclamation when he spotted the landowner riding a battered quad bike alongside the highway.

A cloud of dust and a flea-bitten Kelpie followed close behind it, the dog easily keeping up with the machine as its rider spotted the QPS vehicle and accelerated towards a spur off the main road before braking to a standstill.

By the time Angela drew up alongside the bike, the rider was on his feet, his worn work boots planted firmly amongst the scrubby spikes of dry grass, and the dog lying beside him with its tongue lolling.

She heard its panting breaths as she climbed out and wandered over. 'Miles.'

'Angela.'

His voice was gruff, either from smoking or lack of use, she was never sure.

Prengist kept to himself, and expected others to do the same. Any interruption to his daily routine was seen as a threat to his existence.

And she knew turning up unannounced on his doorstep as it were would rile him.

She had only walked a few paces from the vehicle when his hand shot out.

'That's close enough,' he barked, then peered past her. 'And you can stay where you are.'

'Sure.'

She heard the calm in Harknell's voice, and said a silent

thanks that he hadn't pressed the matter. 'Just wanted a quick word, Miles, that's all.'

'This about the body out by the burn?'

'Yes. Who—'

He folded his arms across a substantial chest, biceps bulging from his faded T-shirt. 'Word gets around. Was it Ivan?'

'Yes.'

'Good.' He hawked noisily, then spat onto the dry brush at his feet. 'One less of youse to worry about.'

She let the barb slide without comment. 'Notice anything suspicious around here lately?'

'Nope.'

'Any strange vehicles on the road past here?'

'Not that I've seen, no.' He scuffed a toe across the dirt, a bored expression on his face. 'Just the usuals.'

'Amos?'

'Yeah, him. Plus Jeff Tanner. Just before the burn – doing the rounds I expect.'

She nodded. 'When was the last time you saw Ivan?'

'About three weeks ago.'

'Here?'

'Nah, over by Amos's place.'

'Amos?'

He shrugged. 'I was picking up a carburettor for the ute. Ivan was on the porch when I got there.'

'At Amos's place?'

'Yeah.'

She tried and failed to disguise the frown that formed. 'I didn't think those two were on speaking terms.'

'Didn't look like they were either.' He flashed a smile, his broken teeth mottled with brown gunk and decay. 'I could hear their voices when I pulled up.'

'What were they arguing about?'

'Not sure.'

'Miles…'

'What's it worth?'

'Oh, I don't know. Maybe not taking a closer look at that quad bike for roadworthiness.' She felt her heartbeat lurch but pressed on anyway. 'Or we take a look at the house now for firearms. What do you think?'

It was one hell of a risk, but it had the desired effect.

He held up his hands. 'There's nothing there. Ivan took a look a few months back. Check the record.'

'What were Amos and Mortlock arguing about?'

'I only heard the end of it. They shut up pretty fast when they saw me get out the ute.'

'Miles…'

'All I heard was Ivan say something like "deal with it, or I will". That's it.'

'Deal with what?'

He shrugged. 'Dunno. Didn't hear that bit.'

'Are you sure?' Narrowing her eyes at him, Angela risked another step forward. 'Think. This is important.'

The Kelpie growled.

She kept her gaze firmly on Prengist, ignoring the animal. 'Ivan's dead.'

'Yeah, you said.' He scratched at the scraggy beard clutching his jaw, then dropped his hand. 'There was something. I didn't hear anything else, I ain't lying about that. But Amos looked scared.'

'Scared?'

The man nodded. 'And I ain't ever seen Amos scared, have you?'

ELEVEN

Blake stared at the fan spinning lazily from a cable protruding from the patchwork plaster ceiling and let the voices and laughter from the bar downstairs wash over him.

There was a stubborn cicada stuck in the net curtain at the window emitting an occasional chirp, but he had long since given up trying to rescue it.

Instead, he listened as a V8 engine revved to life and a trio of shouts accompanied the roar while it hared away, followed by a muttered curse from the pavement below.

Whoever it was emitted a final drag on a cigarette before walking back inside, the waft of nicotine carrying on the gentle breeze through the open window before the sound of a boot being dragged across the spent butt filtered up to where he lay.

The muffled music became louder as the front door opened

then shut behind the smoker, and then a relative peace descended on the street outside.

Blake rubbed a hand across tired eyes, blinked to counteract the dryness from the fan's draught, and reached across to the bedside table for his phone.

The pub would close in another hour, but after a late debrief at the police station he had declined the gruff offer of a beer from Terry Doxon and instead retreated upstairs, ordering a simple pizza from the pub's menu and devouring it in his room while flicking between a limited selection of TV channels.

There were already two missed calls displayed on the phone screen.

The first conversation would be easy.

The second one would be complicated.

She picked up on the second ring, her voice clogged with grief. 'You're four hours too late.'

He sat up, heartbeat thrashing.

So much for easy.

'Sophia? What happened?'

'The ultrasound scans showed a growth in his stomach.' She sniffed, and then he heard the telltale splash of her wineglass being topped up. 'It was too big to operate on.'

'Soph…'

'Apparently it's common in greyhounds, sight hounds.' She slurped the wine noisily. 'And then they charged me three thousand dollars. Did you know a dog cremation costs four hundred? You get to choose the box the ashes are put in and everything. Iz a bargain, right?'

'How much have you had?' he said gently.

'Whadd'you care?'

'I care, because it won't help.'

'It's a good Shiraz.' She giggled. 'A very good Shiraz.'

'How much?'

'Only two glasses—'

He frowned.

'—from this bottle, anyway.' There was a sad hiccup, and then she groaned. 'Shit. Shit. Shit.'

'Put me on speaker phone. Tip the rest down the sink, now.'

'Okay.' The phone clattered to the kitchen counter. 'You there still, yeah?'

'Yes. And get a pint of water down you. I'll wait.'

''Kay.'

Blake sat up, planted his bare feet on the mottled red tones of the carpet and leaned forward, listening intently.

Sure enough, she knocked into something on her way to the sink, her muffled curse echoing through the kitchen.

'You okay?'

'Stupid thing.'

'No, you're not. Tip the wine away. Down the sink, not your throat.'

She laughed at that, and he almost smiled.

Then he heard the glug from the bottle, the splash as she

ran water down the sink to chase the Shiraz away, and then the noisy, desperate swallows as she drained the first of what would be several pints of water over the next few hours.

'What time do you have to be into work tomorrow?'

'I'm not going in. I phoned David earlier and he told me to work from home.' She belched, then groaned. 'Fuck.'

'Soph? Was it just the wine?' He gripped the phone tighter. 'Anything else?'

'Nothing else. Not this time.'

He exhaled, releasing a breath he hadn't been aware he'd been holding for so long. 'That's good.'

'Maybe.'

'When was the last time you checked in?'

''Bout a month or so ago.'

'Is there a meeting tomorrow? They have them at that place down the road from you on Thursdays, don't they?'

'Yeah.'

'Will you go? For me?'

'Okay.'

'Promise?'

'Pinky promise.' She sighed, and then he heard the water glass being topped up before she moved closer to the phone. 'I miss you.'

He closed his eyes. 'I know. Is Nigel around tonight?'

'Working in Adelaide for two days. Bastard.'

The new marriage was working out well, then.

'What about your mum? Can she come round?'

'Maybe.'

'Give her a call. Ask her to stay over.' He checked his watch. 'It won't take her long to get there this time of night.'

'Okay.'

'I've got to go, Soph. I'm meant to be working.'

She ended the call.

Blake stared at the carpet for a moment, then pressed the second number on the display. 'Boss.'

'You were meant to check in hours ago.'

'Been a bit busy up here.'

'What's the latest?'

'Early days.'

The cicada fluttered against the net curtain once more, then freed itself and began crawling across the chipped off-white paintwork covering the sill.

'They've started interviewing the landowners around the burn area,' he said, watching its progress. 'Have you come across someone called Miles Prengist?'

'Doesn't sound familiar. Why?'

'Not sure. Might be worth doing a check in the system. Apparently, he's had a few altercations up this way.'

'Interesting. Okay, will do. Did Mortlock know him?'

'Yes, given he's a local, but I don't know how well yet. He said he saw Mortlock three weeks ago, at another landowner's property. They were arguing.'

'What about?'

'He reckons he didn't overhear that much, but said that Mortlock told Amos to "deal with it", whatever "it" was.'

'Could be anything.'

'Exactly.' Blake rose to his feet and crossed to the window, cupped his hand around the cicada and felt its body writhing against his warm skin. 'Did you know Terry Doxon's retiring soon?'

'I'd heard a rumour, yes.'

'Any idea who his replacement is going to be?'

'Why, do you fancy staying up there?'

He shuddered, despite hearing the humour in the voice. Thought of Sophia. Slid open the window screen before dispatching the insect. 'Best not.'

'What are your plans for tomorrow?' There was an interruption at the other end, a voice in the background. 'Make it quick.'

'More interviews. And I want to find out who knows what about a car crash near here three months ago. The driver didn't survive but they found a blood-streaked shovel in the boot. Human, not animal.'

'Who was the driver?'

'Nobody knows. No ID, no one recognised what was left of his face, and the vehicle details had been filed away.'

There was an impatient grunt, then: 'Keep me up to date.'

'Will do.'

Blake tapped the phone screen to end the call, and raised

his eyebrows as it started ringing and a local number appeared on the screen. 'Blake Harknell.'

'Good evening, DS Harknell.'

'And to you, Senior Constable Forbes.' He frowned. 'Are you still at the station?'

'Just going through some paperwork while it's quiet. I'll be leaving in a minute.'

'What can I do for you?'

'You can be outside the hotel at eight o'clock tomorrow morning. I'll pick you up to save you driving. We're due at a property the other side of the valley to interview the landowner there, and it's over an hour away.'

'Thanks, that's good of you.'

'Don't thank me,' said Forbes. 'It was Terry's idea. Not all of the roads through the state forest are signposted. He figured this way you wouldn't get lost, and we won't have to waste time trying to find you.'

TWELVE

The next morning, Blake wrapped his fingers around the strap above the passenger door of the four-wheel drive, and resisted the urge to clench his jaw in case he lost a molar due to the deep potholes in the fire trail.

A pale blue sky had chased away the last of the dawn, and the haze on the horizon gave a subtle hint to the temperature expectations for the day. There was no breeze, no movement in the trees beyond the windscreen, and dust everywhere he looked.

Forbes was in her element, zigzagging her way between the ruts and washed-out gullies, and evidently at home amongst the ghost gums and ironbark trees that bordered the road.

He could smell the eucalyptus too, despite the closed

windows and pollen filters in the air conditioning. It was all-encompassing here, almost pungent.

The chassis wallowed from side to side while she steered a convoluted path between a fallen banksia and a rotten log, and then the road narrowed further.

'What do Mitch and Elsa Evatt farm all the way out here?' he said, eyeing the thick foliage either side of the roadside verges.

'They've got a smallholding, about seventy hectares, just the other side of the forest, but it's a more direct route going through the forest rather than using the main road,' Forbes said. 'They used to have more land when they had a dairy herd but sold off the cows five years ago when Elsa got sick. Now they just maintain the land and keep a small veggie garden.'

'Sick?'

'Kidney disease. She's been on the transplant list ever since.'

'That long?'

'That short. Most people around here are on that list for seven years, maybe longer.' Forbes shot him a sideways glance. 'Plus there's some sort of complication with her blood type, Mitch says. So she's on home dialysis until they can get her a new kidney. She has other health issues too.'

Up ahead, a wallaby launched itself from behind an ironbark tree, and she braked to a crawling pace until it took off across the track. Blake tried to spot where it had disappeared to as they passed, but it had dissolved into the trees, forever hidden from view.

The foliage began to thin after another couple of kilometres and the streaks of sunlight that had bathed the road now pooled into swathes of heat that filled the four-wheel drive.

Scrubby grasses broke up the stony sides of the road as it widened, and the dirt track transformed into pitted asphalt once more, reducing the noise in the four-wheel drive to a steady rumble.

Then Forbes swung across the road and between two wooden gate posts obscured by creeping vines, the tyres travelling over an iron cattle grid before spitting up stones and gravel from a driveway that wound around tired-looking mango trees.

A little way in the distance, Blake could see a corrugated iron shed, its four doors open to the elements, and the back of an old Holden ute poking out from the darkened interior in the left-hand opening. There was a steady trail of farming equipment and machinery leading from the shed towards them, and then Forbes rounded the corner and he could see the house.

The Evatts' property was a long squat home clad in a pale green timber that had seen better days. There was a dirt-streaked satellite dish poking out from the galvanised steel roof, jostling for space beside a solar hot water collector that had fared little better. A veranda traced its way around the front and away to the sides, providing shade but little relief from the rising temperature.

As Blake climbed out of the vehicle and walked towards the house beside Forbes, he batted away a fly and squinted at the screen door leading out onto the veranda, then took a step back as a rough-looking mongrel lifted its chin from its paws and eyed him beadily from the doormat.

'It's okay, Roscoe doesn't bite,' Forbes said. 'He's hardly got any teeth left these days.'

'Good to know.'

Three wooden steps led up to the veranda, each one creaking under his foot.

The dog raised its nose to Forbes's outstretched hand, then heaved itself up from the doormat and shuffled away to the far corner of the veranda, evidently satisfied the visitors posed no threat.

'Mitch, are you in?' she called. 'It's Angela.'

A hacking cough reached them, and Blake spotted movement beyond the screen door before a man in his early fifties wrenched it open and beamed at Forbes.

'Ange, this is a nice surprise.' His gaze shifted to Blake, then back. 'What brings you out here?'

'You haven't heard the news?'

'What news?' Then he frowned. 'What's happened? D'you want to come in?'

'That'd probably be best. This is my colleague, DS Blake Harknell.'

'Mitch Evatt.' The man's handshake was strong. 'Come through to the living room – Elsa's in there.'

Blake followed him and Forbes into a short hallway that dog-legged past an antique mahogany dresser with an array of framed photographs on top of it.

Glancing at the larger images as he passed, he spotted a familial resemblance between Evatt and the younger man, and guessed it was his son.

'Els, it's Ange,' the man said as he led the way through a plasterwork archway. 'And…'

'Blake. Blake Harknell,' he provided, nodding to the frail woman sitting at the far end beside a patio window.

She beamed at Ange, enveloping her in a heartfelt hug as the senior constable bent over and murmured a few comforting words, then peered around her at Blake. 'New partner?'

'A visitor. From interstate,' said Forbes.

'There's iced tea,' Mitch said. 'D'you want some?'

'That'd be great, thanks.'

'Mr Harknell?'

'Please. Thanks.'

'What are you doing here, Ange?' said Elsa, fidgeting with a thin blanket that covered her legs. A shaking hand held a plastic nebulising mask that she hugged to her chest. A green tube protruded from the end of it before snaking across her lap and over the side of the armchair to where a black oxygen tank was encased within an aluminium frame. She pointed the mask at Blake. 'And why is he with you? Where's Terry?'

'Terry's retiring in three weeks,' Forbes replied, her gaze following Mitch's departure from the room. 'DS Harknell happened to be visiting up here so Caboolture HQ paired him with me.'

'That Bragg?'

'Yeah, him.'

Elsa tutted. 'Thought you said Ivan told you he was moving on to Roma Street or somewhere. Out of your hair, anyway.'

'Not yet.' Forbes caught Blake watching her, and blushed. Before Elsa could question her further, she straightened and patted the woman's hand. 'How are you doing, anyway?'

Elsa coughed then, a wracking rumble emanating from her chest before she gasped. Placing the mask over her mouth, she closed her eyes and took gulps of oxygen before slowing lowering it once more. 'I was doing okay until they started the back burning.'

'It's set off her asthma real bad,' Mitch added, his reappearance accompanied by the tinkle of glass.

He held a tray in his hand laden with a large pitcher of iced tea and four differently coloured beakers. Condensation ran down the jug, and Blake swallowed at the sight of the amber liquid.

'Reckon you ought to get some of this down your throats before telling us what's going on,' their host said with a theatrical wink. 'You both look like you could do with it.'

After waiting while Mitch busied himself handing out the

drinks, Forbes perched on the arm of the sofa beside Elsa's chair and contemplated her glass for a moment before speaking.

'There's no easy way to tell you this,' she began, 'but Ivan was found dead yesterday morning.'

Elsa gasped, setting off another coughing fit, and spluttered into her mask. Her husband put down his drink and hurried over to her, expertly manoeuvring her into a more comfortable position until the spasms subsided, then peered over his shoulder at Forbes.

'How?'

'He was murdered,' she said, her words accompanied by a slight shrug that oozed regret. 'Out by the old Pedersen property. We're interviewing everyone with land around the back-burn area.'

'Including Miles Prengist?'

'Yes, including Prengist.' Forbes took a sip of her drink while Mitch returned to his armchair. 'Did you see or hear anything unusual these past few days? Particularly… Tuesday wasn't it, when you spoke to him?'

She aimed this question at Blake, an eyebrow cocked.

'Yeah. Tuesday arvo,' he said.

'Can't say I did,' said Mitch. 'Jeff Tanner called in just after lunch to say they were going to make a start on the burn that afternoon – as soon as he'd gone I closed all the doors and windows so the smoke wouldn't set off Elsa's asthma.' He looked a little sheepish. 'To be fair, it gave us a chance to binge watch that new reality TV show everyone's been talking about. I don't get much time to do that these days.'

'Have you seen anyone around the property since the burning finished yesterday?'

'You're the first visitors we've had since Jeff was here. I took the dog out with me yesterday to check the fences in case any 'roos broke through getting away from the fires, but didn't notice anything unusual.'

'Okay.' Forbes set down her glass and rose to her feet. 'Do me a favour? Let me know if you do hear anything.'

'And you come and see us more often,' said Elsa, reaching out and grasping her hand. 'We know how much Ivan meant to you.'

Blake saw Forbes stiffen a split second before she bent over and kissed the other woman's cheek. 'I will, and thanks.'

Her husband followed them out to the vehicle, the dog ambling down the veranda steps before padding alongside.

'How is she holding up?' said Forbes. 'Truthfully, Mitch.'

He gave a stoical shrug and shoved his hands in his jeans pockets, boot scuffing at the dirt. 'As well as can be expected. We've got a meeting with her consultant on Tuesday in Brissy. Maybe they'll have some news for her, maybe they won't. The courier's due with another month's supply of dialysis drugs on Monday anyway. He couldn't get here this week because of the burn.'

'And what about you?'

The man shot a sideways look at Blake, then gave another shrug by way of response.

'Phone me if you need anything, Mitch. Anything at all.'

After saying their goodbyes, they climbed into the four-wheel drive, Blake easing himself onto the seat with trepidation as heat escaped. Winding down his window, he leaned his elbow on the sill and watched in the door mirror as Mitch Evatt raised his hand in farewell, his figure disappearing in a growing cloud of dust as Forbes accelerated away.

On each side of the vehicle, pale scrubby grasses filled empty grazing land. Any trace of the dairy herd that once roamed the Evatts' land was lost to time, and all that remained was the occasional rusting water tank or dilapidated timber shed.

'Air con's kicked in,' Forbes said, pulling him from his thoughts.

'Right.' Buzzing up his window, he jerked his chin towards the undulating track in front of them, leading back through the forest. 'Are there any more controlled burns planned for this area?'

'One more, on Monday. If it goes ahead, after what's happened.'

'What happens if the courier can't get to them next week with Elsa's dialysis drugs?'

He looked across at her in time to see her swallow.

'He'll be here,' she said eventually. 'He'll be here.'

THIRTEEN

Ryan Darke was waiting for them when Forbes pulled up outside the police station.

The young constable was holding open the front door, shifting from foot to foot, a frown creasing his brow.

'What's up?' Forbes said, shielding her eyes with her hand.

'Bragg phoned ten minutes ago. He wants a briefing in five.'

'Shit.'

'Is he here?' said Blake, scanning the cars in the car park. 'Or…'

'Video conference call, sarge. He's got another meeting to go to straight afterwards with the Crime and Intelligence Command.' Ryan's eyes narrowed. 'I think they're expecting answers.'

Forbes snorted. 'And yet, they refuse to send out anyone else to help.'

She brushed past him, stalking through the reception area without a backward glance.

'How did Bragg sound when he phoned?' asked Blake.

'Busy.' Ryan shrugged. 'I suppose.'

'How'd you get on with interviewing… who was it, yesterday?'

'Marcus. He owns the dairy up past Prengist's place.'

'Everything okay there?'

'I was going to tell everyone at the same time at the briefing, to save repeating it.' Ryan looked pointedly at his wristwatch, a smart device that no doubt told him how many steps he had taken that day, and whether his resting heart rate was that of an eighteen-year-old or a fifty-year-old.

Blake didn't suspect the latter.

'Fine – let's go.'

When he entered the office, Forbes had her mobile to her ear, her voice no more than a murmur, and her mumbled farewell was accompanied by a faint flush that coloured her jawline.

'Which computer are we using?' she asked. 'And where's Terry?'

'He's at the ag store, talking to Amos.' Ryan headed towards Mortlock's office. 'And I figured we could do the briefing in here – we can get three chairs in front of the screen better.'

'Didn't he interview Amos yesterday?' Forbes wheeled a weather-beaten chair on four casters in front of her as she followed him and Blake.

'He tried, but Amos wasn't around. Day off, apparently.'

'Did he say why?'

'No, but I figure the fish must've been biting out at the dam, knowing him.'

Blake hovered beside one of the chairs Ryan had already placed beside Mortlock's desk while the constable turned the screen to face them and set up the call. Once that was done, he took the one on the far side, content to let Forbes lead the opening introductions.

Detective Inspector Cameron Bragg was already waiting for them when the call connected.

His back was to a beige plasterwork wall with a framed mass-produced landscape painting taking up most of the available space. The corner of a teak-coloured filing cabinet could be seen over his right shoulder.

With his mouth set into a fine line, he glanced up at the camera before returning his gaze to an agenda he held in his hand.

'Is Doxon not available?'

'He's currently doing an interview, sir,' said Forbes. 'I'd be happy to provide him with an update when he returns.'

'Do that. Right, where are you up to with interviews?'

'We're concentrating on landowners bordering the burn area as a priority, with a view to expanding that to egress routes through the area next,' she said. 'Ryan's also put in a request for CCTV images from businesses in the area, and property owners are being asked via our social media page to get in touch if they have any security footage showing unusual vehicles or other activity over the past week. That way, we have more opportunities to spot anyone acting suspiciously, especially if Ivan's killer was recce'ing the area prior to his murder.'

'Anything come out of those landowner interviews?'

'Not yet, sir.'

'Okay, what have forensics given you so far?'

'Nothing yet. I was planning to give Jonathan Coker a call this arvo.'

'This morning would've been better.'

Forbes opened her mouth to reply, but Blake interrupted.

'That was my bad,' he said. 'I'm not familiar with the area so she's having to chauffeur me around at the present time so we can get the landowner interviews completed. If you could arrange to send maybe two or three constables to—'

'That's not going to happen,' said Bragg. He held up a hand to prevent another interruption from anyone. 'And that's the final answer in the matter. Unfortunately we're dealing with an expanded caseload here in Caboolture, and Kilcoy and Woodford are under too much pressure as it is without expecting them to provide additional manpower to Hangman's Gap. When's Doxon's retirement date?'

'Two and a half weeks away now,' said Forbes. 'And we

haven't yet heard about a replacement for him, sir. Any idea when—'

'You'll find out when I find out, Angela.' He paused and lowered his gaze for a moment, the sound of a pen scratching across a notebook filtering through the speakers. 'I'll make a note to chase up HR in Brisbane though. Do you think he'd consider staying on if that was an option?'

Blake heard a surprised grunt emanate from Ryan.

'I don't know,' Forbes said, her voice tight. 'I'm not sure whether that's a good idea though, sir.'

Bragg's head snapped up, his eyes boring into the lens. 'Meaning?'

'I've seen it before with people retiring,' she said. 'I'm not saying it's happening at the moment, because it isn't, but if Terry's winding down with a view to walking out the door in a little under three weeks, it could be difficult motivating him if he stays.'

'Your concerns are noted, constable. However, it may be the only option if you want the manpower,' Bragg said pointedly. 'Harknell – any thoughts about progress to date?'

'Just something that might be worth considering,' said Blake. 'The property owner closest to where Mortlock's body was found – a Miles Prengist – apparently wasn't too happy with him when his gun licence got revoked last year.'

'Have you interviewed him?' Bragg leaned closer to the screen. 'And why was his licence revoked?'

'We spoke to him yesterday,' said Forbes. 'He said he didn't see anyone acting suspiciously. He lost his licence because he walked into the pub last February pissed as a fart and stuck a rifle under Jeff Tanner's nose saying that he'd ripped him off.'

'Who's Jeff Tanner? Remind me.'

'The RFS team leader you met yesterday. Owns the local servo.'

'Who made the arrest?'

'Myself and Ivan.'

'Any threats made by Prengist at the time?'

Forbes shrugged. 'Just the usual ones we get from time to time. I didn't take it seriously though, and neither did Ivan. Once he'd sobered up, Prengist tried arguing that he needed the licence for pest control around the farm, but we couldn't risk it.'

'Reckon he's still got weapons at the property?'

'Potentially, yes. But he's kept to himself since that incident, and only comes into town for supplies. I don't think he's been in the pub since that incident.'

'What about Jeff Tanner? Any trouble?'

'None at all, sir. Certainly not with Ivan.'

'Right,' said Bragg. 'Well, in that case I shouldn't have to remind you that we need results, and fast. Losing a member of the community like this is bad enough, let alone one of our own.'

He ended the call without further comment, leaving the three of them to stare at a blank screen.

Ryan cleared his throat. 'So, does anyone want to hear about my interview with Marcus?'

FOURTEEN

Angela stared at the whiteboard that she had wheeled to one end of the office, her jaw set.

The far corner of the space had been cleared of old files and overflowing paperwork and now served as a temporary incident room, safely out of sight from any prying eyes at the reception hatch when it was open.

She had placed a cork board next to it to act as a screen though, just in case.

Beside her, Harknell stood with his notebook open while they listened to Ryan.

'So, Marcus reckons he didn't see anything yesterday morning,' said the constable. 'But he said he thought he *might* have heard gunshots Tuesday lunchtime.'

'Did he have any idea of the direction they came from?' she asked.

'He said they were in the distance, so he wasn't sure. He only heard them because he was having a smoke break. But he says probably south-east of his place.'

'How many?' said Harknell.

'Three, in quick succession. And he reckons small calibre, not a rifle.'

Angela scrolled through her phone contacts and found Jonathan Coker's number.

The forensic pathologist answered just before it went to voicemail.

'My preliminary report won't be with you until at least tomorrow afternoon,' he said by way of greeting. 'And I've already told Bragg that too.'

'Never mind the report, but thanks anyway. Any sign of shell casings at the crime scene?'

'Not to date. I've still got a team working there on a wider perimeter search though. They should be finished tomorrow – it would've been sooner, but the RFS crews are still dampening down.'

'Okay. Let me know if they find anything, will you?'

'The pathologist on scene never mentioned anything about Ivan being shot. I thought it was the head wound that killed him.'

She could hear the surprise in Coker's voice. 'We won't know for sure until the post mortem's done tomorrow, but we're keeping an open mind.'

'Well, likewise – let me know if anything changes. I'll

need to widen the scope of our side of the investigation.'

'Thanks.' Ending the call, she eyed the map that had been pinned to the centre of the whiteboard. Ryan had marked the perimeter of each landowner's property with a red marker pen. 'Prengist's land is south of Marcus's dairy.'

They turned at the sound of movement in the reception area before the familiar beeps of the security panel carried across the room and Doxon appeared, his features turning to one of confusion.

'Was there a briefing?'

'Ten minutes ago, with Bragg,' she said as he hurried over. 'And Ryan was just filling us in about his trip over to Marcus's dairy yesterday.'

'Oh?' Doxon stood before the whiteboard, arms crossed, hiding the sweat marks on his short-sleeved shirt. 'Like what?'

'He said he heard three gunshots,' said Ryan. 'He can't be certain from what direction, but we think it might've been over Prengist's way.'

'Or it could've been from the forest,' Harknell added, pointing at the map. 'Hard to tell. Both properties border it in that direction, and this escarpment might form an acoustic baffle. Whose property is this beside Prengist's?'

'Amos Krandle's,' said Angela. 'Speaking of which, how did you get on talking to him this morning, Terry?'

'He wasn't at the ag store – he was out doing a delivery,' said the older constable. 'But I got talking to Sheena Lerwick. She says she didn't see anyone out near her place on Tuesday arvo and that's on the southern entry to the fire trail.'

'Who's she?' said Harknell.

'Part-time cashier.'

'What does she do with the rest of her time?'

'Gossips,' said Angela. 'So if she *did* spot someone, you can be sure we'd have heard about it by now.'

'Amos… wasn't he the bloke Prengist said he saw arguing with Mortlock?' Harknell flicked through his notebook. 'Yeah, it was. When's he back from doing that delivery?'

'He won't be – he's doing that, then going straight home. Won't be back there until after seven tonight, according to Sheena.' She saw Harknell raise an eyebrow. 'We'll talk to him tomorrow, don't worry. But Amos argues with everyone at some point or another so don't read too much into what Prengist said.'

'Okay.' He turned back to the whiteboard. 'Are there any hiking trails through the forest near Marcus's dairy?'

'One or two, but they're overgrown – hence the burn this week,' said Doxon. He reached out and tapped the map with his forefinger. 'There's a track here that's used by local kids with motorbikes, that sort of thing. Mostly at weekends though.'

'Anyone under sixteen have a run-in with Mortlock lately?'

Angela shook her head. 'No, and the only warning given out in the past month was to Carl Upshott's eldest, Connor.

That was for kicking off in the pub after one too many drinks with his workmates one Friday night. And I attended that one, not Ivan.'

'Would've hated to have been that lad when his dad found out,' Doxon snorted.

Harknell ignored Ryan's splutter of amusement and continued staring at the map. 'If these trails are used by the locals on a regular basis, that gives us a wide suspect pool to work through, especially given the lack of officers available to help.'

'*If* it was someone local who murdered Ivan.' Angela glared at the scant notes on the board, then him. 'And we're going to have to be bloody careful when we interview them.'

'Why? One of them might know something. Or be responsible for Mortlock's murder.'

'Because some of us have to live here once this is over. You don't.'

FIFTEEN

Mid-morning the next day, Blake leaned against the door of his dust-covered wagon and squinted against the sunlight glaring off the sand-coloured walls of the hospital.

He finished checking his emails, replied to two texts, then tucked his phone in his pocket and crossed his arms over his chest, settling in to wait.

A mixture of mature royal palm and eucalyptus trees framed the landscaped exterior of the hospital complex, the upper boughs rocking lazily from side to side in a breeze that did little to counteract the rising humidity.

A steady stream of outpatients, visitors and hospital staff had entered the building since his arrival, some being dropped off under the shaded concrete portico above the wide reception doors, others walking – either from parked cars or one of the nearby bus stops.

He ran his tongue over dry lips, wondered whether to take a swig from the bottle of tepid water tucked into the coffee holder in the car, then changed his mind.

The last thing he wanted to do was excuse himself from the imminent post mortem to take a piss.

He had left Hangman's Gap early, telling Forbes he needed to meet with his aunt's solicitor in Brisbane prior to the post mortem in the southern suburbs.

The solicitor didn't exist, but the excuse meant he could avoid anyone suggesting that he and Cameron Bragg travel together.

Instead, the inspector had told him to meet him in the car park outside the hospital, which was why he now watched each passing vehicle with a wary eye.

After another five minutes, a smart dark-blue sedan swung into the entrance, the driver's chiselled features cast in shadow from the lowered sun visor. As it passed him, the driver peered through the passenger window and raised a hand in greeting.

'Here we go then,' Blake muttered.

He reached up and straightened his tie, brushed off the back of his trousers from leaning against the car, then strolled over to where Bragg had parked under a drooping jacaranda.

'Morning, guv,' he said by way of greeting.

Bragg nodded in return, shrugged a dark grey suit jacket over his shoulders and led the way towards the hospital. 'Been waiting long?'

'Got here ten minutes ago. Made good time.' Blake

increased his pace to keep up with the inspector's long strides. 'Who's doing the PM?'

'Mike Sigford. He's one of the best, and attended the crime scene on Wednesday morning, so Mortlock's in good hands.'

A shiver crossed Blake's shoulders. 'Worked with him before then?'

'Too many times, sadly,' Bragg said, stepping out of the way of a hospital orderly who was pushing an empty wheelchair through the front doors towards a waiting taxi. 'What do you think of Forbes?'

'Pardon?'

'Angela Forbes. Is she capable of managing the station out at Hangman's Gap do you think?'

'Well, I've only been working with her for a couple of days, but she seems to have everything under control, yes.'

'Good.'

The detective inspector strode ahead, and Blake found himself blinking to counteract the sudden change in light as they entered an expansive reception area.

His shoes squeaked across a spotlessly clean tiled floor, the surface still wet in places as he skirted around a yellow plastic sign warning of the same. A curving suite of ash desks took up the far wall, with the top halves encased behind safety glass – whether to protect the staff from unruly patients or airborne viruses, Blake wasn't sure.

'The morgue's upstairs,' Bragg said over his shoulder, already striding towards a lift door to one side of the desks.

They rode upwards in silence, Blake shuffling to the back beside an aluminium handrail as the lift stopped on the first floor and a large man and woman joined them.

As a waft of stale body odour washed over him when the doors swished closed, he wondered why Bragg didn't just take the stairs, and held his breath until they rose another level.

When the doors opened, he pushed past the couple and stumbled out into the corridor, ignoring the bemused look that Bragg shot his way, and followed the inspector towards a wooden door at the far end that remained resolutely closed.

There was no glass panel to peer through like the others they had passed, and no free access granted either given the security keypad set into it.

Bragg rapped his knuckles against the door, and moments later a sprightly man in his late forties appeared.

'Cameron, thanks for being on time.'

'No worries. This is DS Blake Harknell, on secondment from Victoria. Blake, meet Michael Sigford.'

'Call me Mike.' The man's grip was firm, which was no surprise given his enormous shoulders.

'Rugby player?' said Blake.

'Used to be. Most I can manage these days is the occasional game of touch footy, if time allows. Please, come in and we'll get you suited up so we can make a start.'

'Did you get the email Angela Forbes sent yesterday?'

Blake said, following Bragg and Sigford into an air-conditioned reception area several times smaller than the one on the ground floor.

'I did. So you think Ivan was shot, do you?' Sigford approached a desk behind the reception counter and swept up a manila folder, flipping it open as he spoke. 'On what basis?'

'One of the landowners we've interviewed said he heard three gunshots in quick succession around Tuesday lunchtime,' said Blake, noting Bragg's raised eyebrows. 'The information only came to light after our briefing yesterday, guv, which is why she copied you in on the email.'

'Haven't had a chance to read it yet,' said Bragg, recovering his composure. He cleared his throat. 'Management meetings, et cetera.'

'Not to worry.' Sigford's tone remained calm. 'We'll keep a lookout for anything like that, although I have to say, given the damage sustained by the body because of the fire, I may have to resort to X-rays if the physical examination proves fruitless. What about other forensic evidence?'

'Coker's team have been delayed by the dampening down,' said Blake. 'But they're hoping to finalise their search today. He'll let Forbes know if he finds anything to substantiate the witness statement.'

'All right. Well, in that case let's get on with it.' Sigford pointed to a door off to the left. 'Cameron, if you could show him where to get changed, I'll see you both in the examination room. Emma's assisting today, so we'll make a start while you're doing that.'

It took ten minutes of rummaging through a stack of sealed protective suits to find one long enough to cover Bragg's large frame, but once they were both ensconced in overalls, gloves and masks, the inspector led the way back through the reception area and along a short corridor with a pair of stainless steel doors at the end.

As soon as Blake followed him through them, he felt cool air brush against the back of his neck through a gap in the suit, and shivered at the sight of the body laid out on an examination table in the middle of the room.

He had attended many post mortems over the years, but the shock never wore off.

In truth, he was grateful for that. It reminded him he was human, despite all the horrors he had witnessed in his role.

Especially burn victims.

Those were the worst.

Sigford's assistant, Emma, looked up from her examination of Mortlock's jaw as Blake moved closer.

She afforded him no more than a passing glance before returning to her work, her long fingers cradling the blackened remains of the man's skull with a tenderness that belied the gruelling work at hand.

'Cameron, Blake, if you'd like to join me,' Sigford said, beckoning to them from where he stood level with Mortlock's knees. 'I'll show you some of the problems we're going to have today.'

'That's obvious – he's still curled up like a baby,' said Bragg, cocking his masked face to one side as he ran his gaze along the dead sergeant's remains. 'So how the hell are you going to do this?'

'Carefully.' Sigford sighed, his breath creating a slight billow in his mask. 'So I hope you don't have to be anywhere in a hurry.'

'I'm good until four. Blake, what about you?'

'I haven't been made aware of any pressing need to get back to the station.'

'Good man.' Bragg turned back to the pathologist. 'It seems we're all yours.'

'Okay. I'm proposing to run the PM as I would any other, and if we don't find any bullet casings during this examination then I'll do what I said and run some X-rays while you're here. That way, if we do find something to help you, you can action it straight away. Sound good?'

Blake nodded, hearing an agreeable grunt emanate from Bragg.

'All right, then let's begin.' Sigford nodded to Emma, who was already brandishing a scalpel. 'Stand back, please gents.'

Blake didn't need telling twice.

Over the next two hours he watched – most of the time – while the pathologist and his assistant carefully dissected the remains of Ivan Mortlock, their movements meticulous.

Sigford provided a running commentary as they worked, with his words recorded by a microphone dangling from a cable above the examination table.

Starting with a practised cut from the collarbone to the abdomen, he removed what was left of the internal organs, carefully passing each to Emma.

Blake watched while she recorded and took tissue samples that would be sent to the onsite laboratory for testing, but then turned away while Sigford started up an evil-looking saw and made his way towards Mortlock's head.

As the motor died away, he looked up to see Bragg's jaw tighten beneath the hem of his mask, the detective inspector's gaze never leaving the examination table. Fists clenched, he stood with his feet apart, waiting while the pathologist's work continued.

Finally, Sigford signalled he was finished and switched off the microphone. 'Well, gentlemen, I can confirm what I suspected at the crime scene, which is to say Ivan suffered a head trauma.'

'Was it enough to kill him?' said Bragg.

'Hard to say. I would posit that it was hard enough to knock him out. Whether or not it killed him is difficult to establish given the damage the fire has caused to his body.'

'Christ, d'you mean he could've been alive when the controlled burn ripped through there?'

'Perhaps.' Sigford looked over his shoulder at the prone form on the examination table. 'Although in what state of consciousness, I couldn't tell you. But if he tripped and fell before clipping his head on the rock where he was found, I would hope he didn't suffer.'

'What about gunshot wounds?' Blake blurted, then swallowed. 'Sorry.'

'Not at all.' The pathologist beckoned them over to a stainless steel sink where he preceded to strip off his protective gloves and place them in a biohazard bin before washing his hands. 'That remains inconclusive. There are fracture wounds to his limbs but I'm reluctant to posit a theory about those. They might've been caused by the extreme temperatures his body was exposed to during the burn, after all. Then I have to account for the fact that nothing untoward was found in his chest or abdominal cavities. The internal organs are in a state due to the fire damage, but there were no foreign objects in those either.'

'What are your next steps then?' said Bragg.

'X-rays.' Sigford tore a strip of blue paper towel from a roll beside the sink and then checked the clock above the door. 'So if you want the results of those today, rather than waiting for my report on Monday, you'd best go and find somewhere to have a coffee.'

SIXTEEN

Blake shuffled his weight in the orange plastic seat to try and alleviate the numbness spreading through his backside, then winced when pins and needles shot through his left leg.

An empty takeaway cup stood on the Formica table beside his right hand, its inner plastic lining stained with coffee.

A pervading stench of fat-laden hot food wafted across from the hospital's café, and he wrinkled his nose as an gaunt man in a dressing gown shuffled past, his body odour leaving a vapour trail in his wake.

The ham sandwich Blake had bought with the first round of coffees lay opened and ignored, pushed away to the far end of the table where it would eventually be removed by one of the cleaners who stalked the premises.

Bragg had demolished his food with gusto upon taking the

seat opposite, brushing crumbs aside before slurping half his coffee in one go, despite the scorching temperature.

That had been almost an hour ago, time enough for the woman behind the till at the far end of the café to glare at their lack of custom several times before the inspector had checked his watch.

'How long does it take to do X-rays of a dead man?' He had pushed his chair back after that, pointed to Blake's empty cup and mimed a refill.

Blake had muttered his thanks before watching the other man weave his way between the tables towards the till.

At least the woman over there perked up at his approach, her movements mimicking efficiency while a reluctant smile was plastered to her lips.

Blake lowered his gaze to his hands, his thoughts turning to the myriad of investigative threads that were starting to form.

Even if Sigford found no evidence of gunshot wounds, there was still the fact that the head wound suggested that Mortlock was either hit from behind or had stumbled and knocked himself out.

Which didn't explain what Mortlock was doing wandering around a signposted controlled burn area hours before it had been lit.

Or – given the sort of footwear that remained – why he probably wasn't dressed for a walk in the bush in the middle of the day.

Blake flexed his fingers, then looked up to see Bragg heading back his way, two more cups of weak coffee in his hands.

'Guv, we need to ask Jill Mortlock if any of her husband's clothes are missing. Thanks.' He took the cup from the inspector and winced at the heat seeping through the cheap surface. 'He wasn't wearing the sort of boots I'd be lacing to my feet if I was traipsing through that area. Not with all that long grass.'

'I've been thinking the same,' said Bragg. His brow knitted together. 'Never mind the snakes, the ground's so bloody uneven. One of Coker's team nearly twisted an ankle when they first got there as it was.'

'And I'm presuming that given Mortlock was a local, he'd have carried a spare pair of boots in his vehicle anyway.'

'Still…' Bragg took a sip of coffee and then pointed the cup at him. 'Keep on top of it, Blake. I'm counting on you. I had a feeling Ivan was running off-the-books investigations, but I could never prove it. I'd like to know what the bloody hell he got himself into to wind up on Mike's table upstairs.'

'Don't worry – I'll have a word with Forbes when I'm back at the station to make sure I haven't missed anything else. I expect—'

He broke off as the inspector's mobile phone vibrated, and saw a flitter of excitement cross the man's face.

'Speak of the devil,' Bragg said before answering. 'Mike – got anything for us? Really? Okay, we're on our way.' He simultaneously pushed back his chair and ended the call. 'The X-ray results are in. Let's go.'

Five minutes later, having wrestled their way into a lift amongst a gaggle of exhausted student doctors, Blake followed Bragg along the corridor towards the morgue.

Sigford opened the door before they reached it, ushering them inside. 'I must say, DS Harknell, that your witness information has dampened the impact of what I'm about to tell you, but they were right about hearing gunshots. Come and take a look.'

Blake's heart ratcheted up a notch, his throat dry as he followed the two men through into the examination room.

Emma had been busy in the time since the post mortem, clearing away the bloodied detritus and washing down the instruments and tiled floor. She was now perched on a stool beside a metal desk at the far end of the room in front of a laptop computer, only glancing over her shoulder before returning to her work.

Mortlock's ravaged remains had been covered by a light blue sheet, and Sigford expertly twitched it away to reveal the man's legs.

'I can only posit that your witness managed to hear the shots due to the way the land lies, because he was right in telling you that it sounded like a small calibre weapon.' He slipped on a pair of protective gloves and used his little finger to point out a tiny cavity in Mortlock's right calf. 'Here, see? I had to cut away most of the burnt tissue from around the fibula to retrieve it.'

'You've got the bullet?' Bragg said, his tone incredulous.

'Emma's just doing the paperwork so you can get it into evidence.' Sigford straightened. 'And given the position of the wound, I'd be confident in suggesting Ivan wasn't facing his killer.'

'You mean he was shot while trying to run away?'

The pathologist gave a tired smile. 'You know me better than that, Cameron. That's for your team to find out. I do have a second bullet for you though. We dug that one out of his left shoulder, and given how well it was embedded, I'd suggest that was discharged at a closer range.'

'So one to the leg to slow him down, the second to stop him?'

'And then he hit his head as he fell. It's entirely plausible.'

'The witness said he heard three shots.'

'Well, only two found their mark. The X-rays haven't picked up anything else.' The pathologist dropped the sheet back into place and slipped off the gloves, balling them into the biohazard bin. 'We're behind schedule today, but I'll do my best to get my report emailed to you over the weekend. I know how important this one is for you.'

'Thanks, Mike. We'll see ourselves out.'

They were passing through the exit doors when Bragg next spoke. 'Got any plans for this evening?'

'Er, not really, guv.' Blake risked a sideways glance at the other man. 'Figured I might order room service and try and get an early night. Although I think they've got a live band in from nine o'clock so that might be a bit optimistic.'

They crossed the road to the car park, his grey wagon now bookended by a scruffy off-white hatchback and a black SUV.

'I reckon you should make a point of staying in the hotel bar,' said Bragg, stopping in his tracks and eyeing the hatchback with nonchalant interest. 'It'll be busy, and Mortlock's murder will be all anyone's talking about.'

'Guv, with respect I'm trying to keep a low profile. Y'know, in case people start asking too many questions. It's a case that's going to affect the whole community, especially if his killer is a local. I feel like I'm under a microscope there as it is.'

'All the same, it's a Friday night, the beers will be flowing, and it'll loosen people's tongues.' Bragg shot him a predatory smile. 'Who knows what you might hear?'

'Okay. Good point.' He fished his car key from his pocket and aimed it at the car, hearing a satisfying *thunk* as it unlocked. 'Shall I give you a call Monday to check in, unless I have something urgent to report?'

'Do that.' Bragg turned to go, then stopped. 'And Blake?'

'Guv?'

'Keep an eye on Forbes for me, will you?'

'Is there a problem?'

Bragg looked away then, casting his gaze across the

swathe of vehicles as an ambulance roared from the exit, lights blazing before its siren whooped to life.

'Just a rumour, that's all,' he said eventually.

'What sort of rumour? Does it have any bearing on Mortlock's death?'

'Maybe. Perhaps. Best keep an open mind at the moment.'

'What's the rumour?'

Bragg studied him for a moment, then exhaled. 'That allegedly, she was having an affair with Mortlock.'

'Yes, I heard something to that effect. There was one hell of an age gap though, wasn't there?'

'It's still something that should be borne in mind. After all, maybe she's been after the top job in Hangman's Gap for a while, especially given Terry Doxon's imminent retirement.'

'Just what are you implying, guv?'

'Well, it makes you wonder how far she'd go to get that promotion, doesn't it? Especially as she and Ivan were seen arguing on Saturday night in that shithole of a pub you're staying in.'

'Were they?' Blake frowned. 'The others haven't mentioned it.'

Bragg pulled his phone from his pocket and peered at the screen. 'I've got a meeting at Roma Street in forty minutes. Like I said, keep an open mind. You know what small towns can be like.'

'Yeah,' muttered Blake as he watched the other man hurry back to his car. 'Yeah, I do.'

SEVENTEEN

A weariness spread across Blake's shoulders when he parked beside Ryan Darke's liveried patrol car three hours later.

The traffic around Brisbane had been abysmal, and given the reluctance of his superiors to reimburse his expenses in a timely manner on previous cases, he was reluctant to fork out for the toll road option.

Instead, he had turned down the police radio, tuned into a local station, and tapped his fingers on the steering wheel to a playlist that relied heavily on eighties and nineties rock anthems while he crawled northwards behind a steady stream of trucks, hire cars and rented camper vans.

The spur road off the M1 that wound towards Hangman's Gap had quietened the closer he got to the small town, and the radio signal fizzled out somewhere west of Kilcoy, leaving him to choose between political commentaries or country and western music that had seen better days.

He chose silence instead for the last thirty kilometres.

Climbing out, he saw that the sun had already started its descent over the galvanised steel roof. The flag drooped at half-mast and his thoughts returned to the twisted remains that now lay in one of a number of metal refrigerated drawers within the Coopers Plains morgue.

He shivered, despite the heat, and then remembered Bragg's words.

Forbes had some explaining to do.

She was sitting with her mobile phone to her ear when he walked into the small office. Neither Doxon nor Ryan were around, so he made a beeline for a spare desk, dropped his backpack onto it and crossed to the whiteboard.

His gaze roamed the assembled pins until he found the one for Miles Prengist's property on the fringes of the state forest.

'How'd it go?'

He turned at her voice. 'I didn't hear you finish your call.'

'You were miles away.' Forbes managed a small smile. 'I've already asked you twice if you wanted a cuppa. How was it?'

'Probably best you didn't go.' He watched as her smile faded, sadness clouding her eyes. 'And yes, I'll have that cuppa thanks.'

'Coming right up.'

After she had walked away, Blake faced the whiteboard

once more and compared the single track at the rear of Prengist's property with the fire trail used to access the crime scene two days before.

The lines were similar in width, and yet the fire trail one was deliberately straighter, cutting a diagonal between the north-western tip of the cattle farmer's land with that belonging to Amos Krandle, and through to the main highway after passing Sheena Lerwick's place.

Blake's gaze swept back to Krandle's land.

It was smaller than the rest, narrowing at the northern tip where it met with the towering granite slope of Hangman's Hill.

He traced the name with his forefinger, then glanced over his shoulder as Forbes returned with two chipped ceramic mugs.

'Sorry – no one's had a chance to wash up so we're down to the back of the cupboard,' she said by way of explanation.

'Doesn't matter. It'll do the job.' He took a slurp. 'If Mortlock drove his own car out to the forest, where's his work vehicle?'

'It's out there next to mine, the other four-wheel drive. Although he hadn't driven it since Saturday – like I said, he was off duty when he… when he died.'

'Holiday?'

She shrugged. 'He didn't say. Just told us he was taking Sunday to Tuesday off to catch up on some stuff at home.'

'What sort of stuff?'

'I don't know. He didn't tell me.'

'But I thought you two were pretty close?'

'Meaning?'

He cocked an eyebrow. 'You said yourself people around here thought you two were having an affair because you spent so much time together. So don't you find it strange he didn't tell you what his plans were?'

'No.' She looked away while she picked up her tea mug once more. 'He didn't tell me everything.'

'What were you arguing about with him on Saturday night in the pub?'

Her mouth dropped open as she spun to face him, cheeks flushing. 'Who told you that?'

He said nothing, and waited.

'Whatever,' she said. 'It doesn't matter. We were discussing work. We'd been working late here, and Ivan suggested we get something to eat, so we went to the pub. It wasn't the first time we'd done that, you know.'

'So what was the argument about?'

Forbes sighed. 'I suggested we take another look at that car accident I told you about that happened three months ago, out on the Baxter road. He flat-out refused.'

'Why?'

'He said he was waiting to hear from a witness he reckoned he'd tracked down, and that when he had something concrete to share he'd tell me so we could come up with an investigation strategy. He told me to concentrate on my existing case load, and not to worry about it.'

'What's your case load? I mean, prior to Mortlock's death.'

'Three break-ins, one stolen vehicle, and a domestic violence case that's about to head to court.' She shrugged. 'Trust me, I had plenty of time on my hands to investigate that accident.'

'But Mortlock wouldn't hear of it?'

'And that's why we argued.'

Blake glanced past her towards Mortlock's office. 'Where's the file on the accident? In there?'

'I can't find it. I've looked everywhere, including his safe—'

'How d'you get into his safe?'

'I told you – he used the same code for everything. But it wasn't in there.'

'What was in there?'

'Some other case files, two passports – one for him, one for Jill – and two thousand bucks in tens and twenties.'

'Seriously?'

'Seriously.'

'When were the passports issued?'

'Three weeks ago. And before you ask, no. They've never travelled overseas before. Not as far as I know, anyway.'

'Makes you wonder why Mortlock had them then, doesn't it?'

'Yes, it does.' She put down the mug. 'In other news, I managed to pin down Amos Krandle long enough to interview him about his whereabouts on Tuesday. He says he was at the southern end of his property mending fences. I asked whether he saw or heard anything unusual, but he says not.'

'Do you believe him?'

'For now.'

'Did you ask what he and Mortlock were seen arguing about?'

'Not outright. I didn't want him to know that Prengist had overheard them. I did ask whether he'd had any issues with Mortlock recently though.'

'What did he say?'

'He said they'd had words about him not having a wrecker licence for selling used cars and parts. Reckoned that's all it was, and that he'd sent off the application paperwork earlier this week.'

Blake scratched his jaw, eyed the notes criss-crossing the whiteboard, then sighed. 'That dairy farmer who Ryan spoke to was right. According to the pathologist this morning, Mortlock was shot twice – probably while trying to outrun his killer.'

'Why the hell would anyone want to shoot him?' Forbes said, her voice barely above a whisper. 'He was just a small-town copper. I mean okay, he liked to try and sort out some stuff off the books, but that's the point. All he ever wanted to do was keep the peace. All this… The way he was left out there… That's—'

'Not the Ivan you knew?' Blake said, and drained his tea. 'Makes you wonder what else you didn't know about him, doesn't it?'

EIGHTEEN

Blake ran a comb through his freshly showered hair, then hung the towel on the aluminium rail set into the wall and padded barefoot out of the bathroom.

He selected a fresh short-sleeved cotton shirt from the flimsy pine wardrobe and placed it on the bed, pulled on a pair of boxers and picked up his phone.

There were no new messages.

The pub downstairs was busy, with a steady Friday afternoon trade turning into a raucous evening as several locals made inroads into weekly pay cheques and a covers band began to tune up.

A bass drum thundered upwards through the floorboards, its steady beat resonating under his feet while an accompanying snare tapped in time, both mingling with the rising volume of voices determined to be heard over the growing throng.

The ceiling fan wicked away remnant moisture from his skin while he pulled on a pair of jeans and tucked his wallet and phone into the pockets, then after slipping on the shirt and a pair of casual shoes he squared his shoulders and faced the door.

Suddenly, a cold beer seemed like a bloody good idea.

His room was one of six, located at the far end of a narrow corridor that had been painted a duck-egg blue and festooned with bucolic photographs depicting Hangman's Gap through the decades. A flight of narrow stairs that must have only just passed a fire regulatory test led down to an uneven passageway that acted as a main thoroughfare for the main pub, with the toilets off to the right.

Turning left, he passed the swing doors leading to the kitchen, then pushed through a second door that spat him out into the public bar.

The volume of voices hit him in the chest, closely followed by a surly man who elbowed his way past.

A young woman in her early twenties called after at him as he went. 'And you can keep your bloody hands to yourself, you bastard.'

'Hey.' Blake glared at him.

'Sorry.' The man held up his hands in apology. 'Didn't see you there.'

'English?'

'Yeah.'

'Mind how you go.'

The man turned and pushed his way through the doors without a backward glance.

The assault on Blake's ears reached a crescendo as he pushed his way towards the row of beer taps.

There was a seated area beyond the bar that the publican David Bressett and his wife Simone used to serve his breakfast. He peered along the length of the bar into the dining space and saw that there were two couples having dinner, and that the breakfast condiments had been swapped out for candles to encourage a semblance of romantic ambience.

No matter that the ambience was somewhat spoiled by the two televisions set above the bar, one playing a live rugby league match from a stadium in Brisbane, and the other showing regular Keno games.

'Usual?'

David's voice carried over the throng, and Blake turned to see the landlord ambling towards him.

'Please, yeah. Who's the English bloke?'

'A tourist.'

'Who's the woman over there? She seemed pissed off with him about something. Everything all right?'

'Yeah, no worries.' David gave him a weary smile. 'We might've been giving him a bit of stick about the way the poms have been playing in the Third Test. No way they're going to win the Ashes at that rate. He lost interest in the twenty-twenty tour match we were watching and decided it'd be a good idea to chat up Molly Tanner.'

'Ah, that explains the fuck-off vibes.' Blake grinned. 'Is that Jeff Tanner's daughter?'

'Yeah. Helps out here a few nights a week.'

'Ryan's girlfriend, right?'

'She is, yes.'

'Who's the band?'

'A four-piece over from Patchton. Not bad. Had them here about six months ago, and they went down well. If you want to eat, I'll put you in the dining room. Won't be any tables free out here.'

'No worries, thanks.' Blake swiped his card for the beer. 'Might have another of these first.'

'Night off?'

'Yeah, unless I get called in.'

'Make the most of it then.' David's attention turned to the next customer, his movements efficient as the woman reeled off a list of drinks in between giggling with the man next to her.

Blake moved away from the bar, found a supporting pillar away from the band's instruments and leaned against it, his gaze travelling lazily over the pub's clientele.

He recognised one or two faces from the previous night, and gave each of the men a cursory nod before looking away. A woman sitting with a group of three friends at a table over at the far side made eye contact, lowering her eyelashes before leaning over to whisper in the ear of one of her girlfriends.

Their laughter carried across to where he stood, and he casually turned his attention to his mobile phone, not wishing to engage in any conversation that could complicate his stay – or the investigation.

And yet…

Bragg was right.

Someone in here might know how Ivan Mortlock ended up dead with two gunshot wounds.

And who he was running away from at the time.

Blake cursed the detective inspector under his breath, then turned at a familiar voice.

'Thought you weren't going to put in an appearance.' Terry Doxon appeared at his elbow, the man's eyes beady. 'What took you so long?'

'Couple of phone calls to make.' Blake sipped at his beer. 'You here for the band?'

'Not really my thing.' Doxon nodded towards a group of four men who were standing over near the far wall, their conversation animated. 'Just sorting out a fishing trip with a bunch of mates.'

'Local?'

'We'll take the boat out to the lake on the other side of the forest in a week or so.' He scowled. 'Just got to wait for the back burning to finish now that's been delayed.'

'What sort of fish d'you catch out there?'

'Perch mostly. Maybe one or two bass if we're lucky.'

'Good eating?'

'Yeah, not bad.'

'How did you get on interviewing the tourists that are staying here?'

'Angie spoke to them. Two Germans and an English bloke. Passports all checked out, none of them have outstayed their visas, and not one of them knew Mortlock.'

'Bugger.'

Blake drained the last of his beer and pointed at Doxon's half-empty schooner. 'Want another?'

'Ah, you're all right – the boys will shout me.'

'Come on. I'm having one anyway and it'll save you waiting while they fight their way to the bar. Looks like they're going to be a while.'

Doxon peered over his shoulder to where his friends were talking, then ran his tongue over his lips. 'Yeah, go on then.'

Pushing his way through the crowd, elbows out and an easy smile to anyone who took umbrage before letting him pass, Blake approached the young woman who was helping David behind the bar.

Her dark hair was pulled back into a low ponytail, and immaculate nails caught the light reflecting off the beer taps while she poured glass after glass. Heavy make-up accentuated her eyes, and Blake tried to place where he had seen the resemblance behind the mask.

Unable to latch onto it, he shook away the thought and held up the two empty glasses.

'What'll it be?' she called above the noise of the band starting up.

'What does Terry Doxon drink?'

'Anything,' said a man next to him, cackling. 'Especially if he's not paying.'

Before Blake could respond, the woman had snatched the glasses from his hands and was already pouring.

'Thanks. Sorry – I don't know your name.'

'Laura. Are you the copper who's staying here?'

'Yeah.'

At that moment, the guitarist launched into a well-known AC/DC riff and the crowd cheered.

Blake gave up the conversation with a rueful smile.

Moments later, refreshed glasses in his hands and ears already ringing, he pushed his way through the regulars.

Doxon was no longer in the far corner, and after craning his neck to see whether the man had returned to his friends, Blake eventually found him in a large alcove towards the front of the pub that allowed a modicum of respite from the music volume.

He was hovering beside a slot machine, the bright lights from the game illuminating his features, and turned with a start when Blake approached.

'Here – Tooheys all right?'

'Yeah. Cheers.'

'Cheers.' Blake watched with interest as the older policeman slurped greedily at the lager, downing almost half the glass in one go. 'How well did you know Mortlock, then?'

Doxon coughed, patted his chest, and eyed him warily. 'Why?'

'Just wondered, that's all. I mean, you're the longest serving copper around here, right?'

'What's Forbes been saying?'

'Nothing. It was just a question. I mean, I get the impression you got on all right with him, given you're taking the time to hang the flag at half-mast every morning.'

'Yeah, well.' The other man lowered his glass and stared at the floor. 'He was good to me over the years. Helped me out a few times here and there.'

'On cases?'

Doxon's wistfulness was replaced with a sneer. 'None of your business.'

'Fair enough.'

Then someone bumped into him, jostling his shoulder from behind and he side-stepped to avoid spilling his beer.

One of Doxon's friends slurred a drunken apology, then raised his voice over a raucous guitar solo.

'Oi, Terry. Olly says his nephew wants to join us next week, and I reckon on the boat not being big enough.'

Doxon rolled his eyes. 'For fuck's sake. I've already told him he can't come. The kid's a pain in the backside.' He raised his glass to Blake. 'Thanks for the drink.'

'No worries.'

He watched the two men stagger back to their friends, then spent the next twenty minutes listening as the band played a well-received mixture of classic rock anthems.

When they announced they would take a short break after the next number, he ambled back towards the bar as the song finished and the singer aimed a good-natured barb at the crowd.

David was busy serving at the far end, while Laura was deep in conversation with a pair of men in their fifties, so he made a beeline for her, hopeful of a quick refill.

One of the men saw him coming and walked away with a scowl, his large hand clutching a tumbler of rum and coke.

'How long d'you think Terry's going to keep lowering that bloody flag?' grumbled the other man as he nursed a refreshed beer glass, his long beard mottled with grey and white.

'Until after the funeral, I reckon,' said Laura. 'Only proper, right?'

The regular shook his head, then turned away muttering about needing a piss, his scuffed work boots slapping across the bare floorboards.

Blake jerked his chin towards the man's back when he reached the door. 'Who's that?'

'Amos Krandle,' she said, pouring his beer into a fresh glass while she spoke. 'He works part-time for the agri merchants. Y'know, the big warehouse as you're heading out of town towards Brissy. He lives—'

'Yeah, I know where he lives.' Blake paid, then raised his drink. 'Thanks.'

He wandered over to the door leading out to the toilets and turned his back to it, his gaze scanning the crowded pub.

None of the other witnesses were in tonight, and he wondered if the likes of Miles Prengist ventured into town on a regular basis, or kept to themselves.

He gave it another minute, then positioned himself closer to the door and waited.

It didn't take long.

Krandle pushed it open, knocking Blake's elbow and sending the top half of his beer slopping over his hand and onto the floor.

'Shit,' he said, loud enough to turn heads.

'Christ – sorry, mate,' Krandle said, hands raised. Then he took a step back, eyes keen. 'You're the new copper, right?'

'Yeah.'

The man stuck out his hand. 'Amos Krandle. Heard you might be in here tonight.'

'Did you?'

'Well, Sheena at the store mentioned you were staying here.' He winked. 'And you'd be a right sad fuck if you stayed in a pub and didn't drink, right?'

Blake laughed, despite himself. 'Right.'

'Get you another beer?'

He held up his glass. 'I've had three. I wasn't…'

'In that case, let's have rum and coke. Won't do you any

harm. Besides, the band's about to start up again so you're going to get fuck-all sleep anyway.'

With that, Krandle turned away and walked back towards the bar.

'Got you,' Blake muttered.

NINETEEN

It soon transpired that Amos Krandle was as keen to learn more about the new policeman in town as Blake was to meet the elusive landowner.

After returning from the bar with two fresh drinks, the older man pointed out a table near the doors through to the kitchen and headed towards it without a backward glance.

The band started their second set with a classic Powderfinger track, and Blake fought his way through a burgeoning crowd that was more interested in yelling along with the chorus than making way for him to pass.

He reached the table unscathed and tipped his glass towards Krandle. 'Cheers.'

The man returned the gesture in silence, then waited until the song ended before speaking. 'How come a copper from Victoria's helping Angie to find out who killed her boss then?'

'I just happened to be in the area, that's all.'

'That right?' Krandle eyed him over the rim of his glass. 'So, are you a permanent fixture now, or what?'

'Temporary.'

'Unless you lot don't find who did it.'

'Any ideas?'

'Nope. You?'

'You know I can't comment on an investigation,' said Blake. 'What about you? Have you always lived in the area?'

'No, Rocky originally. I bought the chicken farm off the previous owners a few years ago.' He swigged from his glass. 'I suppose you're going to want to ask me about Mortlock's murder.'

'Why would I do that? Forbes took your statement earlier, didn't she?'

'Yeah.' Krandle shrugged. 'Just figured you would, that's all.'

'Only if you wanted to tell me something you forgot to tell her.' Blake watched him. 'Did you?'

'What?'

'Forget to tell her something.'

'Nah. It's all good.'

'Sure?'

Krandle shifted his weight, checked over his shoulder, then leaned closer. 'How come none of you have spoken to Sheena? She's me neighbour after all.'

'Sheena Lerwick? The ag store manager?'

'The very same.'

'Terry caught up with her.'

'When?'

'Thursday afternoon.'

'Not according to Sheena.' Krandle frowned. 'You sure?'

'I thought he had.' Blake gave what he hoped was a nonchalant shrug, then sent a silent prayer of thanks towards the band who launched into the next song in their set list, preventing further enquiry for a few minutes.

When the final bars of the eighties hit finished, he turned to the man once more. 'Does Sheena reckon she saw something then?'

'Don't know. I think she was more pissed off that she didn't get a chance to get the gossip about what's going on.' Krandle shot him a sly look. 'Makes you wonder where Terry was if he wasn't speaking to her like he told you, doesn't it?'

Blake checked his watch to break the man's penetrating stare. Cursing the decision to accept another drink, he tried to focus on what he was hearing.

If Doxon wasn't at the agriculture store interviewing Sheena on Thursday afternoon, then where the hell had he been for over an hour?

And what had he been doing?

He looked up and raised his voice over the next song. 'How'd you get on with Mortlock?'

Krandle chewed his lip for a moment. 'Most of the time,

okay. We had our disagreements about things from time to time.'

'Such as?'

'None of your fucking business.' The man smiled to take the edge off his words, yet the hardness in his eyes remained. 'You should be careful, poking around here y'know.'

Blake narrowed his eyes. 'Is that a threat?'

'No, you daft bugger. A friendly word of advice, that's all. It's a small town, you're new, nobody knows you. And yet here you are, asking all these bloody questions like you belong here.'

'So don't rock the boat. Is that what you're telling me?'

'Now you're catching on,' Krandle said with a wink.

'I'll bear it in mind. What about Mortlock?'

Krandle's smile faded. He eyed the condensation running down his glass and ran his thumb over it, then sighed.

'He was a boat rocker, that's for sure.'

TWENTY

Angela tapped her fingers on the steering wheel along to a Top 40 track and hummed under her breath while she watched half a dozen stragglers stumble out from the pub.

The clock on the display above the radio station's callsign read a quarter to midnight, the soft glow from the dashboard catching on the metal strap of the watch she had inherited from her grandmother.

'Come on,' she murmured. 'Where are you?'

The band were ferrying equipment out the door and across a darkened patch of grass towards their vehicles, a procession of compact flight cases and instruments that dwindled to a pair of backpacks before they were finished.

The four men returned to the pub veranda and paused to smoke cigarettes beneath the light from a single lamp hanging from a supporting beam, their posture relaxed now that the money had been earned and the adrenaline was starting to dissipate.

She wound down the window a little more, tweaked the radio volume until it was a mere murmur and let the sound of cicadas wash over her, the voices from the band carrying on a light breeze to where she sat.

Waiting.

Above the pub, two of the guest room lights remained switched on.

Neither was Harknell's room.

His was around the back of the building.

David had told her yesterday when she'd asked, after slipping her question into a conversation about the guest register and who had stayed over the past few weeks before the German couple and the man from the UK had arrived. All were checking out in the morning, and David reckoned on the German couple being divorced by the end of their planned two-month trip.

The pub's main door swung open, casting a dull light across the veranda.

A lone figure emerged, her silhouette slight compared to those of the band members who stepped aside to let her pass and called out farewells as she descended the short flight of wooden steps to the pavement.

'At last,' Angela murmured, then leaned across and opened the door. 'What took you so long?'

'Simone wanted to sort out a couple of extra shifts for next week.' Laura climbed in, slipped her seatbelt across her chest and then leaned her head back before closing her eyes. 'Shit, I'm knackered.'

'You and me both.' Angela reversed out the parking space and pulled away. 'The sooner you pass your test, the better.'

'Third time lucky, right?'

'Right. Especially if you don't tell the examiner that he's a stupid—'

'Don't. I've already had that conversation with Mum and Dad more times than I care to remember.' Laura reached out to turn up the radio. 'You stink of smoke.'

'I only had the one while I was waiting. What were the band like?'

'Okay, actually. Better than the lot David got in two weeks ago. They were shit.'

'Was Harknell there?' said Angela.

'He was,' said her sister, looking at her sideways. 'He was talking to Terry, and then Amos. Why?'

'Just curious. I mean, he turns up here and suddenly Bragg has him more or less running this investigation. We don't know anything about him.'

'Maybe you should have come in. Bought him a beer, and asked him perhaps?'

'Yeah, right.'

Laura shifted in her seat, pulled her mobile phone from her pocket and jabbed at the screen for a moment. 'Ugh. Connor's messaged to ask if I'll go to the beach with them on Sunday.'

'I thought you two had split up?'

'Me too. Jesus.' Laura typed out a reply, then lowered her phone. 'Your police friend is a bit of all right, isn't he?'

Angela risked a quick look at her sister, then turned her attention back to the road. 'He's too old for you.'

'I wasn't thinking of me.'

Angela exhaled. 'Now's really not the time, sis.'

'Sorry.' The music got turned down again. 'Any news?'

'Not yet. It's too early anyway. We're still interviewing people, trying to understand what happened.'

'And why.'

'Yeah. And that's all you're getting out of me. You know I can't discuss work stuff.'

'I know.' Laura tucked her phone away. 'But why have they got someone from Victoria to help? I mean, he doesn't know the area or anything, does he?'

'Apparently he and Ivan were due to meet this week.'

'What about?'

'I don't know.' She saw her sister's face turn to her, and held up a warning hand. 'And if I did, I couldn't tell you.'

'Okay.' There was a pout to her words, but the questions stopped.

Angela turned into a side road four kilometres from the pub and slowed as a wallaby emerged from the darkness before disappearing into the long grass on the other side.

A series of mailboxes flashed by the window, and then she was pulling in to a narrow unpaved driveway that zigzagged between decades-old mango trees before depositing them outside a low-set brick home.

The property was in darkness, save for a security light that came on as she eased to a standstill, its narrow beam illuminating the front door.

'You coming in for a cuppa?' said Laura.

'No. Early start. Let Mum and Dad know I'll pop round on Sunday if I get the chance?'

'Will do. Thanks for the lift.'

'No worries. Love you.'

'Love you too.'

Angela managed a tired smile as her sister slammed the car door shut, then waited until she had disappeared into the house before slipping the engine into gear and crawling back to the road.

Reaching the centre of Hangman's Gap ten minutes later, she spotted the bare flagstaff above the police station's roof, and then cursed as a familiar stinging sensation pricked the corners of her eyes.

'Dammit, Ivan. What the fuck were you playing at?' she muttered. 'And why the hell didn't you tell me everything?'

Wiping away the tears, she turned right after a small pharmacy and slowed to a crawl to keep the engine noise down as she drove along a street lined with thirty-year-old properties.

Cars were parked on short driveways beside trailers, compact campers and small dinghies – all the weekend detritus that her neighbours would ferry their kids into the next day amongst bickering and sulking. Here and there, older neighbours had given up maintaining a lawn and chosen to landscape their gardens instead with desert grasses, large rocks and coloured stones, with the occasional bottlebrush adding a splash of colour in an otherwise barren display.

Her shoulders relaxed as her gaze roamed the houses, a calmness settling over her while she took in the familiar surroundings.

And then she swung into her own driveway and stomped on the brakes, her heart lurching.

Angela swallowed, her mouth dry as she read the words that were sprayed in red paint across the garage door.

You're next bitch.

TWENTY-ONE

Bright sunlight poked through the dusty blinds in Mortlock's office the next morning, dust motes churning in the air while Blake cupped his hand around a mug of strong coffee.

He stared at the dead man's looping handwriting that covered the reports' pages while a niggling pain scratched at his temples and a rasping dryness clutched at his throat.

A large glass of water with his pub breakfast had failed to cure either of them.

His heel tapped the floorboards while he worked through the man's notes, breaking the silence that enshrouded the small police station.

The phones were quiet at the moment, with all calls being diverted through to Caboolture until the shift began at eight o'clock.

There was no sign of Ryan or Forbes, and he wondered if Doxon would make an early appearance or whether the previous night's drinking session would see him turn up later in the day.

Blake winced and shifted in his seat, wrapping his hand around the steaming mug.

The fabric-covered chair had seen better days, one of its loose springs stabbing his left buttock with an intensity bordering on abuse while he read the contents of the manila folder.

Rubbing the back of his neck, wondering whether he would find any painkillers tucked away in a drawer somewhere in the compact kitchen, he refocused on the words in front of him.

There were several folders strewn across Mortlock's desk despite Ryan's attempts to tidy, but it was this one that had piqued Blake's interest the most.

It was the one that referred to the car accident three months ago, and the subsequent discovery of a dead man in possession of a shovel that was smeared with traces of human blood.

Mortlock and his team had followed procedure, as far as he could tell from the senior sergeant's records. His handwritten notes were supplemented by regular formal updates that had been entered into the system and printed out to join the rest of the paperwork in the file. These were accompanied by reports from Jonathan Coker's forensics team and Michael Sigford's post mortem.

The autopsy had concluded that the man had died from a severe whiplash injury, supported by Coker's findings that a large animal – probably a grey kangaroo with a predisposition for suicide – had collided with the vehicle. Coker's report included a series of photographs from the scene, half a dozen of which showed various angles around the crash site.

There were no skid marks on the asphalt, so whatever had forced the car off the road hadn't given the driver time to react.

There were no noticeable scars or tattoos on the victim's body either, making identification impossible to date. He was white, possibly in his mid-forties, and – according to Sigford's post mortem report – with arteries that would have led to a heart attack before reaching his next decade if his car hadn't careened into a vicious-looking red gum stump after hitting the kangaroo.

But where he was going, what he had been doing, and why there was human blood on that shovel, remained a mystery.

'You're in early.'

He jumped, slopping coffee over his hand. 'Shit.'

'Sorry.' Forbes crossed over to the window sill and plucked a handful of paper tissues from a box before holding them out. 'The boss kept these for emergencies. He always did get uncomfortable around grieving relatives.'

'Thanks.' Wiping his hand, Blake managed a surreptitious glance at her face, and wondered why she looked so pale. 'Thought I'd take a look at that car accident from a few months back before we crack on with the briefing.'

'Oh, right.' She took a step back. 'Well, let me know if you spot anything we missed. It's a frustrating one, that's for sure.'

'No fresh leads?'

'No leads full stop. He's not local – no one recognised his face.'

'Yeah, I saw his car had NT plates on it. Where is it now?'

'At the towing company's yard in Tarnock. About half an hour from here.'

'I wouldn't mind taking a look.'

'Why? Jon's already finished the forensics on it.'

He balled the tissues into the bin under Mortlock's desk. 'Just curiosity.'

'Okay.'

'Where's the body? The one from the accident.'

'Still in the morgue at Coopers Plains.'

'Shit.' Blake pushed the paperwork back into the folder and slapped it shut. 'I could've taken a look at him while I was there yesterday if I'd known.'

Forbes folded her arms. 'Do you think he's connected to Mortlock's murder?'

'I don't know. Worth keeping an open mind though. Bit weird anyway, isn't it?'

'Yeah, it is.' She glanced over her shoulder at movement in the outer office. 'Through here, Ryan.'

The younger constable appeared, his eyes wide. 'Molly told me what happened. You all right?'

'I'm fine,' she said. 'It was just some paint, that's all.'

'Yeah, but—'

'What's going on?' said Blake. 'What did I miss?'

'It's nothing, it's—'

'Someone spray-painted a threat on her garage door last night, while she was picking up Laura from work,' Ryan blurted, then blushed as Forbes aimed a glare at him.

Blake stared at her until she met his gaze. 'Laura… She's your sister?'

'Yes.'

'What did the threat say?'

'That I was next.'

'Recognise the writing?'

'No.'

'Filed a report?'

'I only just walked through the door.'

'Did you take pictures? I presume that's why you look so tired this morning, that you washed it off last night.'

'I did, and I did.'

Blake checked his watch. 'I can't imagine Doxon's going to be in much before nine. Go and file a report, and we'll have the briefing when he gets here.'

'It might be nothing.'

He could hear the doubt creeping into her voice, and raised an eyebrow. 'Is that what you think?'

Forbes sighed. 'No.'

'Go and file the report.' He pushed back the chair. 'And if either of you have got some painkillers, now would be the time to tell me.

TWENTY-TWO

Terry Doxon slouched into the police station at ten to nine wearing a scowl and a crumpled uniform shirt.

Although the man was freshly shaved, Blake could smell the alcohol emanating from his skin beneath a sandalwood-infused soap aroma as he passed. He spun his chair around to face Doxon as he slumped behind his desk and groaned. 'Here,' he said, and chucked the packet of painkillers across. 'Forbes found those in the kitchen.'

'Thanks,' came the mumbled response.

Blake turned away at the sound of the foil wrapper crinkling and ran his gaze over the agenda that was still warm from the printer. 'Get a coffee down you. We're doing the briefing in five, and then we'll divvy out the tasks for the day. Are you legal to drive?'

'Probably not.'

'So you get phone duty, and you can act as exhibits officer today. Are you still planning on a day off tomorrow?'

'Yeah, I'm going fishing, remember?'

'Morning, Terry.' Ryan wandered past, his jauntiness eliciting a curse from the older officer. 'Good night, was it?'

Doxon pushed back his chair and hurried from the office, the toilet door slamming shut a moment later.

'Jesus.' Blake shook his head, and then crossed over to the whiteboard as Forbes put down her desk phone.

'Okay, that's confirmed,' she said, joining him and Ryan. 'The towing company says you can visit the yard on Monday morning to have a look at the car. It's obviously within a fenced-off area so you'll need to sign in.'

'Thanks. Want to go?'

She shrugged. 'Could do, I suppose. Wouldn't hurt to have a second look.'

Blake checked his watch and noted the time at the top of the agenda in his hand. 'Might as well make a start if Terry's out of action today and tomorrow. How long is it until he retires?'

'T minus two and a half weeks,' said Ryan without rancour. He grinned. 'Wonder if we'll notice when he's gone?'

'Cheeky. Okay, first things first,' Blake said turning to Forbes. 'The spray paint on your garage door. Report filed?'

'Yes,' she said. 'And no, I don't think I'm in danger. I just think someone's using Ivan's death to have a go at me.'

'Any ideas who yet?'

She sighed. 'Look, I'm a copper, and a woman, and Jill and a whole bunch of people around here thought I was having an affair with her husband. Take your pick – I'm fair game, as far as most of this town is concerned.'

'Still…'

'If anything changes, I'll let you know. But for now…' She jerked her chin towards the whiteboard. 'Can we concentrate on Ivan's murder?'

'Point taken.' Blake looked over his shoulder as Doxon appeared with a glass of water in his hand and a wan expression. 'Care to join us?'

The senior constable walked over, a sneer on his lips. 'Heard you had the decorators in last night, Angie.'

'Screw you, Terry.'

'Enough,' Blake snapped. He lowered the agenda and glared at Doxon. 'Christ Almighty, you're lucky you're not getting a disciplinary turning up here pissed, so at least have the decency to pull your head in when one of your colleagues has been threatened.'

'I was only joking.'

'It wasn't funny.' Blake squared his shoulders, found his notes, and tried again. 'Right, Sigford's post mortem report will be emailed over on Monday but after running some X-rays he found two bullets. Based on the position of the first one, he reckons Mortlock turned away from his killer, and was trying to escape when he fell and hit his head after the second shot got him.'

A stunned silence met his words.

Eventually, Ryan spoke, his tone hushed. 'Did Sigford think Ivan would've survived if he hadn't hit his head?'

'No, but if he had and I was the shooter, I'd have fired a third time if I was that determined to kill him,' said Blake. He gave Forbes an apologetic shrug as she paled. 'That's a scenario we have to consider. Someone was determined Mortlock wasn't coming out of that forest alive, weren't they?'

'Who would do that?' she demanded. 'I mean, to hunt him down like a… like an animal…'

'Bastard,' said Doxon.

'There's more – Sigford reckons the slugs are .22 calibre, so we need to start making a list of who has registered weapons that size around here first of all, and cross-reference that with the witness statements.'

Ryan's eyes widened. 'But that's probably half the population around here.'

'And they're all on the system, right? So run off a report, and work your way through it.' Blake waited while the young constable scribbled in his notebook. 'Once you've eliminated anyone who wasn't in the area over the weekend through to Tuesday night, let myself or Forbes have the list and we'll go from there.'

'And if Mortlock's killer is someone from out of town, what then?' said Forbes.

'We've got to start somewhere. Any better ideas?' Blake

cocked an eyebrow at his colleagues. 'No? Then we go with that course of action.'

'What about unregistered weapons?' said Doxon.

'That's something we also need to bear in mind, yes. Is Miles Prengist the only one around here under suspicion for those?'

'Yeah, and Prengist told us that Mortlock didn't find anything,' she said. 'The system supports that – I checked.'

'Easy enough to hide weapons,' said Doxon. 'Under the floorboards, for instance. I mean, let's face it, Ivan's idea of policing was complacent at the best of times, right? Anything to keep the peace around here, and all that.'

'Do you think he was telling the truth about finding no unregistered weapons at Prengist's then?' said Blake.

Doxon mouth twisted. 'I ain't saying anything, I'm just suggesting it's a possibility Miles was hiding them.'

'Why would Ivan lie?' Forbes said, her eyes blazing. 'Just what are you implying?'

'Nothing,' said Blake, raising his hands. 'I'm trying to keep an open mind here. Someone shot him twice, and so far we've got no motive, and no suspects have we?'

'Yeah, but there's playing devil's advocate, and then there's insulting a dead man,' Doxon said. 'She's got a point.'

Blake sighed. 'Okay, what would you suggest we do then? Based on your years of experience?'

The older sergeant was saved from answering by Forbes's mobile phone bursting into song.

She blushed, then glanced down at the number. 'It's Jonathan Coker.'

'Put him on speaker,' said Blake.

'Jon? I'm here with DS Harknell, Terry and Ryan,' she said by way of introduction. 'Are you packing up?'

'We are, but I've got an update for you,' said the forensic investigator. 'We found a bullet in the remains of one of the trees about fifty metres from where Ivan's body was found.'

Blake crossed to the whiteboard and stared at a diagram of the crime scene that had been tacked to the left of the growing list of notes. 'Which direction was the bullet travelling?'

'I'll email you the exact coordinates, but if you imagine standing by the rock where Ivan was found, then roughly his six o'clock position.'

Blake's gaze travelled to the map. 'That's towards Miles Prengist's property line. What size calibre?'

The sound of an evidence bag crackling carried over Coker's phone. 'It's punched out of shape, but I reckon a this is a 9mm round and likely from a pistol. We just don't know which brand fired it… yet.'

'That's the same as our service pistols,' said Forbes. 'Maybe Ivan managed to get a shot off at his killer.'

'Maybe,' said Blake, turning to face her. 'So, where's his gun?'

TWENTY-THREE

Angela stared at Harknell, her throat dry.

'Was there anything left after the fire to suggest he was wearing his uniform at the time?' she managed.

'Sigford took tissue samples so he'll run tests on those for any remnant fibres. He didn't mention that there were any obvious traces of clothing left,' said Blake. 'But he was off duty on Tuesday, wasn't he?'

'Yes, all day. So normally, he'd keep his service pistol in his gun cabinet at home for safe-keeping.'

'Unless he was doing something out there and felt he needed a weapon.

She glared at him. 'Ivan was a good officer. He might not have done everything by the book to make things work around here, but he got things done.'

'He got himself killed.'

'Might not have been Ivan who fired,' said Doxon. He turned to Angela's outstretched phone. 'Any idea how long that bullet had been in the tree for, Jonathan?'

'We've left the bullet in situ and cut the tree around it so I'll run some tests back at the lab,' said the forensic investigator. 'But I'm not sure I'll be able to give you a definitive answer, given the fire damage.'

'Thanks, Jon – chat later.' Angela ended the call, then looked up from her phone screen to see Harknell staring at her. 'What?'

'Have any of you checked to see if Mortlock's gun is still at his home?' he said.

She opened her mouth to respond, then clamped it shut, heat rising to her cheeks.

Ryan said nothing, and simply shuffled from foot to foot, his gaze lowered to the floor.

'Angela – did you ask Jill before we left on Wednesday?'

'No. I… I didn't get the chance.'

He cocked an eyebrow. 'How long have you been a copper?'

'I've been too busy interviewing,' Doxon muttered.

Harknell rounded on him. 'Speaking of which, where's your typed-up report from your meeting with Sheena Lerwick?'

'I…'

'Never spoke to her. Why not? And why did you tell us that you had?'

'I was going to, but she was busy when I got to the store,' Doxon wheedled. 'I figured if she had seen anything, she'd have told me, right?'

The two men glowered at each other.

'I'll head over to Jill's now to see if Ivan's gun is there,' Angela said, sweeping her keys off her desk. 'I'm sorry. It slipped my mind when we spoke to her with everything else going on.'

As she pushed through the front door seconds later, she raised a hand to shield her eyes from the blazing sunlight, her mind racing while she berated herself.

Why hadn't she thought to ask Jill if Mortlock left his house on Tuesday with his gun?

Would his wife have noticed?

Or did he secrete it under his clothing?

Crossing to her four-wheel drive, she heard the front door slam behind her and then footsteps crunching over the dirt towards her.

She stopped, and waited until he had caught up. 'I can handle Jill on my own.'

'All the same, I'd like to see Mortlock's gun cabinet for myself,' said Harknell. He raised an eyebrow. 'You don't mind, do you?'

'Get in.' She blipped the remote locking and climbed

behind the wheel, batting down the sun visor to check for spiders before closing the door.

They drove in silence to Jill Mortlock's house.

There was washing on the line stretching across the barren turf, and Angela bit her lip as she recognised Ivan's shirts and a pair of uniform trousers. A worn pair of cargo shorts was hanging at the far end, the hems frayed. Beside that, a T-shirt with a faded cartoon across the front hung upside down, the sleeves cut off at the shoulders.

Unlatching the front gate, she led Harknell up the three steps to the veranda and rapped her knuckles against the screen door.

'Jill? It's Angela Forbes. You in?'

Mortlock's widow appeared a moment later, staring at them through unfocused eyes. Her hair was tangled on one side, and her blouse was creased over a pair of cotton shorts that reached her knees.

'Found the bastard who killed him, have you?' she said, her voice groggy with sleep.

'Not yet, no. Could we come in?'

'Why?'

Harknell stepped forward. 'We need to inspect your husband's gun cabinet.'

'Why?'

'Can we take a look? Then we'll explain.'

Jill sighed, and flung open the screen door, narrowly missing Angela's toes. 'Come on then. It's in the utility room.'

Angela followed her through the kitchen and into an ante room leading to the back of the property.

There was stained grouting between the pale-coloured floor tiles, an older model washing machine tucked under a countertop that ran the length of the left-hand side of the space, and a plastic laundry basket with various shirts and underwear on top of that.

'I figured I may as well donate his stuff to one of the charity shops in Caboolture,' said Jill, waving a hand at it. She jutted out her chin. 'I suppose you think it's too soon, given he isn't even in the ground yet.'

'People deal with grief in different ways,' said Angela. 'And a charity shop is a good idea.'

'Patronising bitch,' sneered Jill, then waved her hand at a steel cabinet on the other side of the room. 'Have at it. And before you ask – no, I don't know the code, so good luck with that.'

She stomped off, and a few seconds later Angela heard the television from the living room, some sort of daytime cookery show.

Brushing past Harknell, she knelt in front of the gun cabinet and dialled in Ivan's usual code.

The lock clicked, and she glanced over her shoulder.

Harknell nodded, his gaze never leaving the cabinet.

She swung it open, then rocked back on her heels.

Ivan's service pistol was on the second shelf, the clip on

the shelf below that, together with a small box of 9mm ammunition.

'Shit,' she said.

'You realise what this means, don't you?' said Harknell.

'Yes.' She slammed shut the door and rose to her feet. 'There was someone else at the scene of Mortlock's murder.'

'Or, he had another gun.'

TWENTY-FOUR

Blake tapped his fist against the door sill, a faint gasp of a breeze emanating from the air conditioning vent on the dashboard brushing his skin.

Forbes drove fast, her hands tight on the steering wheel, lost in thought.

He cast a surreptitious glance her way every now and again, but she seemed intent on the road ahead and oblivious to his presence.

Another kilometre, and then he cleared his throat. 'Is there anything on file to suggest Mortlock submitted a possession request to headquarters so he could keep another weapon?'

'No, there isn't. He got me to manage all the admin stuff for the station, so I would've known about it if he had.'

'How many residents d'you think have 9mm weapons?'

'I don't know off the top of my head,' she said. 'We'll

have to ask Ryan to identify them on that list he's working through.'

'While he's doing that, let's speak to Sheena Lerwick, given that another of this bloody town's coppers lied about her giving a witness statement. Christ.' He gave the sill a final punch. 'Anyone would think you lot don't want to find out who killed Mortlock.'

'That's not true.' Forbes braked, hard, slewing the four-wheel drive into the stony verge.

Blake eased the seatbelt away from his chest, heart racing. He glanced across at her, saw her fingers wrapped around the steering wheel, her jaw set while she stared through the windscreen at nothing. 'What was he doing out there?'

'I don't know,' she murmured. 'And don't think I haven't been asking myself that since he was found. I reckoned on him telling me everything – that's the sort of person he was. Not all these secrets, the cash, the passports…'

'The extra-curricular caseload,' Blake added. 'Let's not forget that.'

She sighed. 'And that. Look, I realise I made a mistake not checking the whereabouts of his service weapon but believe me, I want his killer caught. No matter what Ivan was up to, he didn't deserve to die like that. Nobody deserves to die like that.'

'Is there anything else that's been overlooked?'

Forbes met his gaze. 'Only that we didn't ask his widow about the cash and passports.'

'Not yet. Not until we have more information. Just in case she's involved somehow.' He saw the shock register. 'Well, it doesn't look like there was any love lost there, does it?'

'Even so…'

'Keep it to yourself for now.'

She blinked. 'Sheena's place is ten minutes away.'

'Ready whenever you are.'

After a slight shake of her head, she checked her mirrors and pulled away.

Signposts for the state forest flicked past Blake's window, the tree canopy thickening the closer they got to the turning. Eucalypt jostled for space alongside ironbark and ghost gum, bark peeling from the trunks and littering the asphalt on either side of the road.

Forbes slowed for the last half a kilometre, eventually turning left between a galvanised steel mailbox and an enormous red gum stump.

'This is it,' she said. 'Sheena's husband died about six years ago, so she's been running the place on her own.'

Blake peered through the window at the fruit trees lining the makeshift driveway. 'What's she growing?'

'Macadamias, some fruit – most of it goes to one of the wholesalers out near Kilcoy, and some of it she sells to businesses in Maleny and Montville.' She braked to a standstill outside a cream-coloured Queenslander with green gabling and a matching tiled roof. 'Her family's farmed this land for three generations, but I don't know if either of her kids will take it over when she goes. She doesn't rely on it for an income thankfully – she and her husband had a few investment properties along the coast so I think it's more a family pride thing that keeps her here.'

'Where are her kids?'

'Sonia's in Coolangatta, and Jared's down your way in Geelong. They're both working in the finance industry I think. Last I heard, anyway.' She led the way over to the house, and lowered her voice. 'All right, Sheena's got a reputation as a gossip but I reckon it's just because she's lonely. It's probably why she works part-time in the ag store.'

Despite himself, Blake snorted. 'Point taken.'

Before Forbes could ring the doorbell, movement caught his eye and he turned to see a woman in her late sixties walking over from the direction of a neat galvanised steel panelled barn.

She peeled off a pair of work gloves as she drew closer, her eyes shaded by a cream-coloured floppy hat. A well-worn pale denim shirt hung over baggy shorts and she wore an inquisitive expression as she took in Forbes's uniform.

'Formal visit, Angela?' she said, then eyed Blake. 'You must be the copper from Melbourne everyone's talking about.'

'DS Blake Harknell, this is Sheena Lerwick,' said Forbes. She stepped aside as the woman brushed past her and stomped up the veranda steps. 'We just wanted to speak to you about—'

'Ivan.' Sheena narrowed her eyes while she toed off her

work boots. 'Thought you might. I'm surprised none of you have been to see me yet. After all, it's been, what, four days?'

'There was a misunderstanding. We were told one of our colleagues had taken your statement on Thursday.'

'Yeah, I'd heard Terry was in the store. I presume that's who we're talking about?'

'I can't comment, sor—'

'I know, but I also know I'm right.' Sheena flapped her gloves at Forbes. 'The sooner he buggers off, the better. Always was a lazy bastard. D'you two want to come in? I'm presuming you can't have a beer on duty so there're soft drinks for you.'

With that, she led the way into the house. 'Sit yourselves down in the living room while I get the drinks. The kitchen looks like a bomb's hit it.'

Blake followed Forbes into a comfortable room off to the left that captured an abundance of light from a north-facing window without adding unwanted heat to the living space.

The walls were taken up on the right-hand side with floor-to-ceiling bookshelves that warped in the middle from the weight of paperbacks lining the shelves. A wood-burning stove took up the far corner, with two sofas angled towards it for the colder months and a rectangular pine coffee table placed between them. Framed photographs lined a dresser, and Blake wandered over, taking in the images of a man and a woman strikingly similar to their mother.

He glanced over his shoulder as Sheena entered the room carrying three tin cans – two soft drinks and a beer.

'Might as well sit down,' she said, nodding towards the sofas. 'I need to put my feet up anyway. Been working my backside off this morning.'

'I thought you were getting some more part-time help,' said Forbes, before cracking open her drink and taking a sip. She pointed the can at the piles of documents strewn across the coffee table. 'At least with the manual side of things, even if you still have to do the paperwork.'

'I thought I was too, but you try getting someone to come out here and work these days.' Sheena sat amongst a pile of cushions at one end of a sofa. 'It's not like it used to be. And now I sound like my mother. Jesus.'

She chuckled, and gulped the beer while Blake positioned himself at the far end of the other sofa and Forbes extracted her notebook before sitting next to her.

'Okay, so first things first,' Forbes said. 'Where were you on Tuesday, Sheena, say from eleven in the morning?'

'Easy. I was at the ag store all day through to four – Andrew was out having a meeting with his accountant in Caboolture so he needed me to do some extra hours to look after the place while he was gone.' Sheena squinted at the ceiling. 'Must have left there about half past, got back here just after five and then I had to check the irrigation on the seedlings so that took me through to gone six. I crashed out after that – made dinner and watched a film.'

'Spot anything unusual around here lately?'

'Not really.' The woman's eyes sparkled as she glanced at Blake. 'And trust me, I don't miss much.'

He smiled. 'So I've heard.'

She laughed at that, an explosive sound that filled the room. 'I'll bet you have.'

Forbes's mouth twitched, but she kept her gaze on her open notebook. 'Any issues with Miles Prengist lately?'

'No, none at all. Keeps to himself most of the time. If he drives past here and I see him, he might nod in greeting, but that's it.'

'What about Amos?'

'Nope.' Sheena took a long gulp of beer. 'Not since Ivan had a word with him.'

'That's good to hear.'

'What was the problem?' said Blake.

'He got a bit too trigger-happy taking pot shots at vermin – his story – on my property boundary back in March,' Sheena said. 'And I was bloody worried he'd get me with a stray shot. I've got heirloom trees out that way that I can only check on foot – I didn't want to cop a bullet by accident. Amos told me where to stick it when I tried speaking to him, so I asked Ivan to have a word instead.'

'Do you get a lot of issues with vermin?'

'I live in the country, of course I do.' She lowered the can of beer, her expression thoughtful. 'No idea why Amos gave a shit about rats that far away from the house. Knowing him though, he was probably just riled up about something and needed to let off steam.'

'Does he do that regularly?'

She shrugged. 'Not so much now. A few years ago, yes.'

'When did you last see Ivan?' said Forbes.

'Monday. I was on my way to Caboolture and his car passed mine. Raised his hand.'

'His service vehicle?'

'Yeah.'

Blake saw the frown cross Forbes's brow a split second before she relaxed her face once more, her voice remaining business-like.

'Is there anything else you can think of that might help our investigation?' she said. 'Did you spot any vehicles out this way on Tuesday?'

'Only RFS ones and the neighbours' – Amos and Miles. That was first thing, before I left for work, so before nine o'clock. I never saw Mitch Evatt's vehicle but then Elsa had to stay indoors because of the back-burn affecting her asthma, didn't she?' She put the empty can on the coffee table and wrinkled her nose. 'Reckon they had the best idea. It's taken until today to get the bloody smoke stench out of my bedroom. Stupid me forgot to close the window before I went to work.'

TWENTY-FIVE

Blake swore under his breath as his hand brushed against the scorching metal door handle of the four-wheel drive before he wrenched it open.

Sinking into the passenger seat while Forbes started the engine, he bit back a sigh of relief when the air conditioning kicked in and the breeze from the dashboard vents turned from tepid to bearable.

'I reckon we should go and have a word with Amos next,' he said.

'Why? Amos said he was mending fences at the southern end of his property on Tuesday. And Ivan's body was found closer to Miles Prengist's land anyway.'

'Because Sheena's just told us that Amos is trigger-happy and Mortlock had to have words with him earlier this year. Did Mortlock ever mention anything about that to you?'

'No...'

'And Prengist told us he saw Mortlock and Amos arguing three weeks ago. Amos reckons that was about the lack of a wrecker's licence. Anything about that on file?'

'No, but that's just because—'

'It was one of Mortlock's informal conversations, is that what you're going to say?'

'Must have been.'

'All right, well I want to find out more, especially as Prengist thought Amos looked scared. Those were his words, weren't they?'

'Yeah.'

'Does Amos have any weapons apart from the rifle he was using back then?'

'I don't know – I'd need to look at the system.'

'Was Mortlock the only one who managed the gun checks around here then?'

'Yes.'

'Give me your phone.'

'Why?'

'Because I need to ask Ryan to find out from the system what Amos has got and when there was last a weapons inspection at his place before we walk in there, and I don't have his number in my phone.'

She pulled her phone from the back of her uniform trousers, unlocked the screen with her thumb and hit the speed dial before placing it on the seat beside her.

As soon as it started to ring, she eased the four-wheel drive into gear and headed for the fire trail, the wheels bucking over the potholed dirt track that led out from Sheena's property.

When the young constable answered, Blake raised his voice over the noise from the unpaved road. 'Ryan, can you check the system to see when Amos Krandle last had a weapons check?'

'Will do.' The sound of fingers on a keyboard reached Forbes, and then: 'Four months ago. All looks okay. One rifle, that's all.'

'Calibre?'

'Says here it's a .22.'

'Any other issues?'

'Nothing reported.'

'Okay, thanks.' Blake ended the call, and exhaled. 'It doesn't mean he hasn't got other weapons. Ever had reason to be worried about him?'

'No. But then I've never accused Amos of killing someone before either.'

'We're not accusing him of anything. We're just going to check where he was on Tuesday. And do a weapons check while we're there – we can say it's routine in the circumstances.'

'Okay.'

'I'll lead it. Keep an eye on him though. Just in case.'

A sultriness clung to the air by the time Forbes turned off the forest trail and drove between a pair of timber fence posts that leaned precariously close to the vehicle as they passed.

Blake looked through his window to see a rusting metal sign nailed to the post on his side, the single word "Krandle" painted in black at some point in the preceding years but now faded with time.

Grit and stones spat up into the wheel arches, pinging off the axles and creating a cloud of dust in their wake despite Forbes easing off the accelerator.

The dirt track ran alongside a wide dam on the right, its shallow depth just visible through a ring of dried grasses that withered within a metre of the water's edge. To the left, Blake saw the fringes of the state forest in the distance, the undulating pasture barren of any livestock.

After another hundred metres or so, two enormous corrugated iron sheds reared from the landscape, the pale-coloured sheeting reflecting the sun's light to such an extent that he squinted despite his sunglasses. Along the sides were four large open doors, but the contents remained hidden from view as they passed, the interior obscured by shadows.

'What are those?'

'Broiler sheds.' Forbes cursed loudly at a zigzagging pothole resembling a First World War trench that split the track in two, and slowed to a crawl while the suspension creaked and grumbled. 'There are two more on the other side of those silos.'

'Does he have any help managing this place?' Blake said, once he was sure his teeth wouldn't rattle from his mouth the minute he tried speaking.

'Sometimes, not always,' she replied. 'It depends.'

'On what?'

'How little people are willing to work for.' She shrugged. 'He can't afford much, so he does most of it himself. Like a lot of people around here. And he hasn't got family, so…'

'Hard life.'

'That it is. Lonely, too. I think that's why he sometimes helps out at the ag store too. Probably got better things to do out here, except it's not exactly inviting for visitors.'

'What's his history? I mean, did his family farm this land?'

'No. Amos is relatively new compared with most around here. He bought this place about fifteen years ago. The previous owners upped and left for Proserpine – switched chickens for sugar cane, though God knows why. Prior to this, Amos was managing a cattle place west of Rockhampton.'

They fell silent as the track curved to the left around a tangled scrub of vines and overgrown ghost gums, and then Blake straightened in his seat as a timber-clad single-storey building came into view.

A polyurethane gutter surrounded a galvanised steel roof that was once grey and was now mottled with a green lichen that clung to the metal ridges and valleys. It camouflaged the house at a distance, but the closer they drew he realised that the gutters were clean, and there was no foliage surrounding the building save for a stunted bottlebrush tree beside an old rusting water tank.

What remained of a garden was dirt and rock, with sharp stones that crackled under his boots when he got out.

He wrinkled his nose at the stench of ammonia carrying on the light breeze from the nearest shed, while the sound of squawking accompanied the chirrup of cicadas in the long yellowing grass beside the vehicle.

There was no shade out in the open, and he raised a hand to shield his eyes before peering across the bare earth towards the shuttered windows of the house.

'Is he in?'

'His car's there.' Forbes pointed to a pair of dilapidated timber sheds, each the size of a double garage. The nose of a grubby blue ute poked out from the open doors of one, its headlights covered in dead bugs and dust. She adjusted her utility belt, her hand falling to her pistol before sliding away. 'Might as well knock on the door.'

'Wait. Get behind me.' He glared at her when she paused. 'And make sure you're at least a couple of metres behind me, just in case. Got your sat phone?'

She tapped her belt in reply.

'Okay.' He set off towards the front door, sweat prickling his collar, his palms greasy.

Three windows were on this side of the house, all with wire-mesh fly screens across them, all obscuring his view of anyone watching his progress. There was a chair outside the front door, its wooden frame mottled with age and a pair of dusty boots kicked off beside it. Those had been abandoned together with a large worn hammer and a small open hessian bag that, on closer inspection, revealed a motley collection of different-sized nails.

Blake checked his watch.

Half one.

'Must've taken a break,' he murmured. He banged his fist against the screen door twice. 'Amos? You in there? It's DS Blake Harknell. We spoke in the pub last night.'

The sorrowful cry of a Brahminy kite carried on the wind, and he glanced up as the bird soared overhead, riding the thermals.

There was no sound from within the house.

'Amos?' He put his hand on the worn metal door handle, and grunted as it gave way under his touch. 'I'm coming in, mate.'

'D'you want to check the sheds first?' said Forbes.

'In a minute.' He held up his hand as she stepped forward. 'Stay there. Just in case he comes back and wonders what the hell we're doing in his house.'

Entering a narrow hallway that was painted in a depressing beige, he let the screen door snap back into place on his heels. 'Amos?'

Still nothing.

Venturing further into the house, he peered through an archway to his right and found the living room.

A mustiness clung to the air despite the open door. Various invoices and copies of the area's local newspaper were strewn across a battered wooden coffee table that squatted between two sagging armchairs, the seams of which were torn and frayed.

Off to the left was the kitchen, pale blue paint doing nothing to lift the gloominess of the space, and a distinct stench of stale coffee and fried food clinging to the worn Formica work surfaces. A square pine table and two matching chairs were thrust against the back wall beside a refrigerator, its motor humming under duress.

Two bedrooms, one used as a storage space for boxes and an abandoned weights bench, took up the back of the house, bookending a bathroom that was in desperate need of a deep clean and a re-grouting exercise, with mould clinging to the shower tray and plastic curtain.

'Blake!'

He spun at Forbes's shout, racing to the front door and wrenching it open.

She was standing outside the nearest timber shed, shading her eyes as he appeared, staring into the darkened interior beyond the battered ute.

'What's wrong?' he said, drawing closer.

Lowering her hand, she turned to him, a tightness to her jaw.

'It's Amos. I think he's dead.'

TWENTY-SIX

Angela watched as Harknell crouched on his haunches and resisted the urge to ask any of the questions that were troubling her.

Those could wait.

Right now, half an hour after she had thumbed her radio to life and informed the control room staff and then Cameron Bragg that there was another suspected homicide victim in Hangman's Gap, she was too intent on photographing the new crime scene.

Amos Krandle's battered form lay beside an ageing steel workbench at the back of the timber shed, his eye sockets and nose smeared with congealed blood.

One of his arms twisted away from his body at an impossible angle, and in the dust motes that spun amongst the fingers of light threading through the wooden wall panels, she could see the drag marks in the dirt floor interspersed with blood and piss that had led away from the ute's driver door to here.

At some point, Amos had tried to crawl away from his killer.

She could see where his hand had clawed at the ground, where he had tried to dig in his heels to compensate for the broken arm in order to slide along the earth, and where a pair of footprints had once been as he was followed.

Once been, because someone had taken the time to kick them away before leaving the old man to the flies that were swarming.

All that was left now were dusty rainbows and no clues.

Yet it wasn't the beating that had killed Amos.

A black snaking jump lead wound around his neck, the cable undercutting his Adam's apple in a vicious arc.

His purple and swollen tongue protruded from between his teeth, his dead eyes full of horror.

Angela lowered her phone and looked away.

'I've flagged the tyre marks outside as well,' she said. 'Did you touch anything inside the house?'

'No. Just the handle on the screen door each side.' Harknell peered over his shoulder at her, then rose to his feet. 'You okay?'

'Yes.' She swallowed. 'Poor bugger.'

He looked past her at the sound of vehicles approaching. 'Sounds like the cavalry's here.'

She recognised Bragg's vehicle, which was closely followed by Michael Sigford, who emerged from his car with a protective suit in a sealed bag tucked under his arm.

After greeting her with a resigned nod, the pathologist walked over to the timber shed, disappearing from view once he had donned the disposable overalls.

Stomping across to meet the inspector, Angela battened down the hope that Harknell would be asked to attend the second post mortem in as many weeks and instead straightened her shoulders.

'Officer Forbes,' Bragg began. He paused and waited while a panel van roared up the track towards them before it eased between his car and Sigford's. 'Ah, Coker's here. Good timing.'

The forensic investigator swung open the passenger door before his colleagues started to unpack their equipment and made his way over. 'Sorry, Ange. Traffic was a bitch up the M1.'

'Well, it's not like our victim's going anywhere in a hurry,' said Bragg before turning back to her. 'What can you tell us?'

'I've identified the victim as Amos Krandle, the owner of this place,' Angela said. 'He was beaten and then strangled with a jump lead – one of his, because the matching one is still on the workbench in the shed where we found him.' She pointed to the flags sticking out of the dirt. 'Those tyre tracks aren't mine. Amos has… had… two vehicles. The ute in the shed where we found him, and the runaround over in that one, the fifteen-year-old hatchback. He used to use that one to go on longer trips.'

'That so?' Bragg eyed the two vehicles, then the flags. 'So if we're lucky we might get a vehicle match for tracks that aren't those?'

'Hang on a minute,' said Coker, his voice rising. 'That's a long shot. Let's not get ahead of ourselves.'

'Of course not.' The inspector shot a tight smile at the man, then stepped aside as Sigford returned. 'What can you tell me?'

The pathologist grimaced. 'I'd reckon on him being dead no longer than five or six hours based on lividity. He certainly wasn't out here overnight.'

'Cause of death?'

'Asphyxiation by strangulation – but don't write that down, not until I've done the PM so we can make it official.' Sigford pulled off his gloves and bundled them into a biohazard bin that had been placed beside Jonathan Coker's van. 'And I've just told Harknell that's likely to be Tuesday.'

Bragg cocked an eyebrow. 'Busy night in the city last night, was it?'

'And Thursday. I'll see what I can do once I'm in the office on Monday to bring that forward though.'

'Good. Where's Harknell?' The detective inspector looked past Angela. 'Is he still poking around in the shed?'

'He was waiting for Jonathan,' she said. 'We were going to show him the surfaces we touched so he can mark them out.'

'Lead the way, then,' said Bragg. 'I might as well suit up and take a look while I'm here, eh?'

Ten minutes later, now encased head to toe within a protective suit that swallowed her slight frame, Angela scuffed back towards the shed where Harknell waited.

He was wearing similar white coveralls to her own now, a sheen to his forehead while he twirled a face mask between his fingers and stood aside to let Bragg and Coker pass by.

'We'd better visit Prengist as soon as we're done here,' he murmured as she joined him. 'Is there another way out of his place, or does he have to pass by here?'

'This road's the only decent one. There'll be cattle tracks off his property on the other side, but he'll only be able to access those using that quad bike of his.' She watched as Bragg and Coker listened with bowed heads while Sigford knelt beside Amos's body, his commentary washing over her, then back to Harknell. 'Do you think Miles killed him then?'

'Do you?'

She frowned. 'It was Mortlock and Amos he saw arguing, or so he said. Why? Do you think this is connected to Ivan's murder?'

'Hell of a coincidence otherwise, isn't it? And we've only got Prengist's word about what he thinks he saw and heard. No one else that has been interviewed has mentioned anything about those two arguing anywhere, have they?'

'No, but…'

'Blake, a word?' Bragg emerged from the shed, cocked his

head towards his car and led the way, the two men conversing in low voices as the sound of the coroner's trolley rattling across the gravel towards her filled the air.

'What do you think those two are talking about?' said Coker, snapping his protective gloves against his wrists absentmindedly while he stared after them.

'Fuck knows,' she muttered.

TWENTY-SEVEN

'When I asked you to stay, I expected a quick result – not another dead man.'

Blake let the inspector's barb wash over him and gave a rueful smile. 'Not what I expected when I accepted this assignment to be honest.'

Despite himself, Bragg snorted under his breath. He gave an almost imperceptible nod towards Forbes. 'What do you make of Mortlock's lot?'

'Between you and me, she's the only capable one there. Ryan's too young and inexperienced, and Doxon's a—'

'Drunk, bitter man with a chip on his shoulder.'

'How come he's only retiring now?'

'Because Mortlock kept him sweet I expect.'

'How?'

'Easy caseload, turned a blind eye to the drinking…' Bragg shook his head in wonder. 'God knows what else. Still, only two weeks to go and then he's no longer my problem.'

'Even so, we could do with some more manpower here. Especially now.'

'There won't be anyone joining you here. The best I can do is allocate a dozen officers to help remotely from Caboolture.'

'But…'

'Budget cuts from above, sorry.' Bragg's top lip curled. 'Even with the murder of one of their own, they won't change their minds. You should see the recruitment budget that's being released later this year though. We'll have more new officers than we'll know what to do with.'

'Bit late by then.' Blake saw the look of annoyance that crossed the other man's face. 'With respect.'

'You're not wrong. And rest assured, I'm doing all I can. What's your take on this? Reckon it's linked to Mortlock?'

'That's my gut feel. But why… I don't know. We have a witness who says he saw Mortlock and Amos arguing a few weeks back – that's why we were here. I wanted to ask Amos about it. He seemed affable enough in the pub last night when I saw him.'

'You spoke to him?'

'Yeah.'

'How'd he get home?'

'No idea – that's on my list of things to find out today once we're finished up here.' Blake eyed the steady stream of evidence containers being put into the back of Coker's van. 'Which'll be sunset the way things are going. Then we'll interview his neighbour, Miles Prengist. That's the bloke who reckoned he saw Amos and Mortlock arguing when he came round here to get a carburettor off the old guy.'

Bragg looked at his watch. 'I'd best get back to Caboolture and organise that remote support. You've got my number – as soon as there's anything to report, you'll let me know?'

'Will do.'

'And, Blake?' The man cast a sideways glance to where Forbes was deep in conversation with Jonathan Coker. 'Keep an eye on her and the others. Mortlock was involved in something, otherwise he wouldn't have got himself killed. God knows how far the rot spread. Watch yourself.'

Blake nodded in response, his throat dry as he watched Bragg walk away.

The inspector made a beeline for Forbes, the woman folding her arms across her chest when he approached, her stance one of defiance while she listened to him before giving a curt nod.

Coker kept his distance, the forensic technician busying himself with two of his colleagues who disappeared into the gloom of the shed to begin the painstaking work of piecing together Amos Krandle's final moments.

After Bragg finished talking to Forbes and his car pulled

away, Blake wandered over. 'Apparently we're not getting any more help except for some remote staffing back at Caboolture.'

'So I hear.' She rolled her shoulders, then sighed. 'Right, shall we make a start on the house?'

TWENTY-EIGHT

'Where do you want to start? Here, or the bedrooms?' Forbes stood in the middle of the living room and scratched at the protective hoodie covering her hair while she surveyed the paperwork strewn across the coffee table.

'I'll make a start here,' said Blake. 'You do the kitchen. We'll work our way back through the house.'

'Okay.' She turned to leave, then paused. 'What did Bragg say to you out there?'

'Just that we're on our own until he can convince headquarters otherwise, apart from some admin help from his lot at Caboolture.'

'Right.'

'Doesn't it seem strange to you?'

'What?'

'We've got one dead copper, another dead man out there

who may or may not be linked to Mortlock's death, and no one seems to give a shit,' said Blake. 'This place should be crawling with people. And yet Bragg seems intent on keeping us at arm's length.'

'He's always been like that. Ambitious, I mean. After all, it doesn't look good does it?' said Forbes. 'One of his senior ranking officers going off on a tangent investigating things off the books and being murdered.'

'What's his problem with you?' said Blake.

'What do you mean?'

He arched an eyebrow in reply, and said nothing.

Her shoulders sagged. 'He thinks I'm not capable. That I shouldn't be doing this job.'

'Why?'

'Because a long time ago, we had… a relationship. While we were both in training college. It didn't work out.'

'Ah.'

'Are we done with the questions? Because I've got a kitchen to search.'

'Sure.'

Forbes spun on her heel and stalked away. A few seconds later he heard her wrenching drawers open, the sound of rattling cutlery carrying through to the living room.

Turning his attention to piles of paperwork, Blake knelt by the coffee table and started to sift through it.

He shook the newspapers before folding them into one pile, his hopes diminishing with each issue that something might have been caught up between the pages that would help the investigation. That done, he started on the invoices.

It was evident that Amos spent a lot of his time doing his paperwork while either drinking coffee or something stronger. Most of the documents bore the telltale signs of stains from mugs or were wrinkled from condensation in circular patterns that resembled the same stubby coolers used by the pub.

Blake wondered how many of the establishment's schooner glasses were squirrelled away in Amos's kitchen cupboards.

Most of the invoices related to feed, veterinary bills and equipment the man used to run his property. There were one or two handwritten notes amongst these along with receipts for reconditioned car parts, and Blake realised that despite not having a wrecker's licence yet, Amos might have been doing a steady trade in cash sales.

And then there were the final demands. Bright red capitalised words splattered across the tops of overdue payments, veiled and not so subtle threats of asset seizure, and notices of loan repayments that included staggering amounts of interest owing.

Setting the last of the invoices aside, Blake stretched his legs and turned his attention to the two armchairs, pulling away the cushions and running his fingers down the seams, then unzipped them and checked inside.

Nothing.

Biting back a sigh, unsure of what he was really looking

for, Blake tossed the cushions back into place and spent the next half an hour inspecting the rest of the room.

'Left anything for us?' Jonathan Coker appeared at the door, an aluminium case in his hand. 'Found anything?'

'Nothing yet.' Blake gestured to the piles of paperwork he had set aside. 'I'll log that lot, but it's just the carpets and electrical sockets left. No sign of a struggle in here, but I'll leave that to you to confirm.'

'No worries.' Coker stepped aside as Forbes joined him.

'No luck in the kitchen either,' she said. 'Bedrooms next?'

'Sounds like a plan.' Blake traipsed after her. 'Which one do you want to do?'

'I'll take the spare room. God knows what he got up to in his.'

'I don't want to think about it.' He stood on the threshold while Forbes went into the spare room and started moving boxes and weights out of the way.

Amos's bed was unmade, the blue sheets crumpled and faded with age. Two pillows were bunched up against the cheap pine headboard and an old crocheted blanket lay in a heap on the floor in the corner, no doubt abandoned until the cooler months set in.

A metal ceiling fan hung above the bed, its edges frayed with rust, and a single bedside table made from the same cheap pine as the bed was home to a digital alarm clock and a reading lamp.

There were no photographs, only a stock reproduction

print hanging above the bed that depicted a surf beach somewhere.

'Hey, has Amos got any family, or next of kin we need to notify?' he said.

The sound of rummaging in the other room stopped. 'No wife or kids, as far as I'm aware. Not around here anyway. I think he might have an aunt or someone up near Rocky. I haven't found a mobile phone or an address book yet. Have you?'

'Not yet. Might be something in here. I'll let you know.'

He started with the bedside table, opening the single drawer and grimacing at the bunched-up tissues inside. Biting back the urge to gag, his gloved fingers pushed those aside and found a yellowing erotic magazine. Next to that were a handful of mixed coins, five and ten cents dulled with age. Then there was an old packet of analgesic tablets half used, the curled and peeled foil crinkling under his touch, together with a tube of unidentifiable cream, the generic labelling leaving no clues as to its use.

Blake tossed it back inside and slammed the drawer, then knelt and peered under the bed.

Nothing, except for two mismatched socks and a grubby T-shirt that had been abandoned some time ago, given the layer of dust covering it.

Running his hand under the mattress, he lifted it to find only the bare boards of the pine bed, and let it drop with a thud.

A metallic rattling carried through the fly screen, and he crossed to the window to see Sigford and an assistant using a trolley.

On it, a black body-shaped bag rocked and swayed as it was manoeuvred towards a waiting unmarked panel van for the journey to the morgue.

'Blake – you need to see this.'

His heart thrust against his ribs at the sudden interruption, and he spun around to see Forbes in the doorway, consternation etched across what he could see of her face.

She held a plastic card between gloved fingers, its surface catching the light from the window.

'What is it?'

'A driver's licence,' she said. 'With a Cairns address on the back.'

'Cairns?' Blake heard the van doors slam shut and an engine starting. 'What was Amos doing with a Cairns address?'

'It's not his. It's the bloke who died in that car accident three months ago.'

He snatched the card from her, turning it in his hand. 'Are you sure?'

'Yes,' she said, her eyes sparkling. 'I attended the post mortem with Ivan. It's him all right.'

TWENTY-NINE

Angela picked up the remote switch and dialled the ancient air conditioning unit up a notch, the gentle breeze feathering the piles of paperwork on her desk and tickling her fringe.

Beyond the closed blinds she could hear the soft chirp of cicadas, the security light under the eaves casting a halo around the window that was offset by the glow from her desk lamp.

The phones were quiet now, re-routed to Caboolture for the evening.

Ryan was nowhere to be seen and, given that his shift had ended two hours before she and Harknell had returned from Amos's property, was probably with his girlfriend Molly at the Royal.

As for Doxon…

She huffed her hair from her eyes and refocused on the computer screen, scanning the open tabs that popped up one by one.

Across the desk from her, Harknell had his head bowed while he re-read the contents of Mortlock's file on the car crash, occasionally pausing to write something on his notepad.

'What exactly are you looking for? Coker's lot took that car apart.'

'I don't know.' He slapped the folder shut and shoved it away. 'But there's nothing in there about a DNA test – did Mortlock order one?'

'Yes, that's how we found out the blood on the shovel was human, not from an animal.'

'I didn't mean the shovel. I meant the dead bloke. Tim Charterman.'

She frowned. 'I did ask him if he was going to. I just assumed it was delayed.'

'By three months?'

'It was his case, not mine.'

'Didn't you ask him about it?'

'Yes.' She swallowed, a fleeting memory of evenings spent alone here, talking about cases, life, future plans, anything. 'He told me not to worry about it. So I didn't. I just assumed he'd tell us when he had a breakthrough.'

Harknell tapped his forefinger on the folder. 'He never ordered a DNA test. There's nothing in here, and there's nothing on the system. And I'll bet when I phone the lab on Monday that they never received an order either.'

'I can do the paperwork tonight before I leave and email the request.'

His face softened. 'Do it Monday. It's late enough as it is, and you won't get a response until then anyway. But we need to find out if there's a link between this Tim Charterman and the blood on the shovel. What've you found out about him?'

'He had two previous arrests for drug possession, and was meant to do a stint for assault.'

'Meant to?'

'The person he assaulted withdrew their statement. Refused to change their mind, then moved. To Perth.'

'Huh.' Harknell scratched his chin and stared at the ceiling for a moment. 'Anything else?'

'I found his social media account. Most of it's locked down as private, but there are some photos, look.'

He moved around the desks to join her, standing at her shoulder while she enlarged the images and flicked through them.

Charterman was a thick-set man with a scar above his right eye, a nose that looked as if it had been broken more than twice, and had a habit of sneering at whoever was taking a photograph of him.

'A charmer then,' said Harknell as she flicked back to their online system. 'He's got the same look in these arrest shots.'

'I've identified all the other people in those photos,' she said, gesturing to her notebook. 'Looks like some were taken at a community footy club. The others are private parties and stuff like that. I'll get Ryan to track down numbers and phone them while we're looking at the car on Monday.'

'Tomorrow.'

'What?'

'We need to look at the car tomorrow, not Monday.'

'But—'

'And make sure Ryan's here tomorrow to make those calls. Without letting on to any of those people that we know what's happened to Charterman. Not until we understand what's been going on, and why Amos had his driver's licence. He can just tell them the car was found dumped. Who was it registered to anyway? That wasn't in Mortlock's report either.'

'The plates were stolen off a ute in Gympie. The owner reported it, but the locals didn't find the originals dumped anywhere so Mortlock assumed they'd been tossed somewhere on the way here.'

'Okay. Message Ryan.' He slipped his mobile phone into his pocket. 'I'll walk back to the pub. Pick me up at eight tomorrow?'

'I—'

He left without waiting for her to finish the sentence, the door through to the reception area snapping shut on its hydraulic hinge with a soft click.

For a moment, only the sound of the cicadas filled the small office.

Then Angela eyed her mobile phone as it started to ring.

It was her mother.

'Shit.'

THIRTY

The next morning, dressed in jeans and an old black T-shirt, Blake rubbed at sleep-deprived eyes and fought back a yawn before flipping down the sun visor with a growl.

Beside him, Forbes drove the four-wheel drive at a steady speed, her hands light on the steering wheel.

She had picked him up without a word at eight o'clock, with a surly glance at the cooked breakfasts being ferried from the kitchen to the dining room by David and Simone.

'If it makes you feel better, I didn't have one,' said Blake. 'And we can get a coffee when we get to Tarnock.'

'You'd best buy Alf one as well. He's not best pleased about having to open up on a Sunday.'

'Tough shit. We need to look at that car.'

'I still don't get why. I mean, Jonathan's team almost took

it apart. They checked air vents, the washer reservoir, the ventilation hoses…'

'But they were looking for evidence in relation to a dead body, right?'

'Right. But they tested for drugs too.'

'Did they find anything?'

'No.'

'Was there anything to suggest the vehicle was used to transport drugs?'

'No.'

'Which, given Tim Charterman's history of drug usage, seems strange doesn't it? So that's why we're looking again.'

'What for?' She risked a look at him before her gaze returned to the road. 'What did they miss? What did Ivan miss?'

'I'm not sure, but we'll find out.' He angled the sun visor a little lower. 'Did you get hold of Ryan last night?'

'Yes. He said he'd be in at nine.'

'Okay. We'll have a briefing back at the station once we're done at the car yard to see what he's managed to come up with. How'd he get on with Mortlock?'

'Ivan liked him.' A faint smile crossed her lips. 'I think he sort of saw him as the son he never had. He spent a lot of time getting him settled in when he moved up here from Logan after training college.'

'And Ryan? Did he like Mortlock?'

She sighed. 'To be honest, he was starting to get frustrated about how little he was doing to progress his career. I think he sees Hangman's Gap as a stepping stone to something bigger. He hasn't said much since you've been here, but he was always whinging about how he wasn't going to get on Bragg's radar by working on petty thefts and domestic abuse cases.'

'Ambitious then?'

'Yeah, a bit.'

'And you?'

'What about me?' The vehicle sidled to the left a little as she shot a glance at him before correcting the wheel.

'Are you ambitious?'

'What do you mean?'

'Exactly what I said. Do you want to stay in Hangman's Gap all your life, or move to Brissy, or apply for a promotion in Caboolture…?'

'I haven't really thought about it.'

'How long have you been a copper?'

'Six years.'

'And you've never thought about it?'

'No.' She sighed, shrugged. 'My parents are here. My sister too. I grew up here.'

'So you know everyone, the area, people's history and habits.'

'Exactly.'

'Scared of change then?'

'What?'

'Well, I mean it's only three or four hours to Brisbane on a bad day. It's not like you'd be a million miles away from your folks if you got a promotion there, or even in Caboolture, would it?'

'I like it here.'

'Even now that Mortlock is dead?'

He didn't get a response.

Alf Merriott's car yard was on the fringes of Tarnock in an industrial complex that had seen better days by the time the new millennium had come around.

Now, it was just one property amongst a half dozen that could be best described as ramshackle. They were a mixture of weather-beaten corrugated iron sheds set behind barbed wire or mesh fencing with varying examples of warning signs attached.

Outside one, a mean-looking Staffordshire terrier glared at Blake, its owner lifting old mattresses onto a flatbed truck with a dented passenger door, studiously ignoring the Queensland Police-liveried vehicle as it passed.

Beside that building, a closed-up unit with its warehouse door firmly shut and a bright yellow alarm box under the eaves promised cheap white goods, according to the signage above the door – just not on Sundays.

Merriott's business was positioned at the far end, almost as if the neighbouring properties had shunned it. The sign above the open metal-framed gate proclaimed it as being proudly owned by a Queensland local, unlike two of the other properties Blake spotted that were housing national franchises.

Alf was outside the cavernous iron shed, hammering at a stubborn tow hitch on a six-year-old crew-cab ute when Forbes eased to a standstill beside him.

With a thick shock of greying brown hair, he eyed them keenly, dropped the hammer to the cracked and grease-flecked concrete hardstanding, and rested his hands on his hips as they got out.

'Expected you twenty minutes ago,' he said.

'We stopped to get these.' Blake rounded the front of the four-wheel drive and held aloft a cardboard carry tray with three takeout cups shoved into the holes. 'Had to guess yours.'

Some of the attitude slipped from Alf's face, exposing a weariness that seeped through his slight frame. 'Now that'll get you some brownie points.'

'Late night last night was it?' said Forbes, not unkindly.

'Yeah.' Alf took one of the coffees and three of the sugar sachets. 'And we started on Friday. My brother's sixtieth. You'd think we'd know better by now.'

'Where's the car?' said Blake, handing one of the other coffees to Forbes. He put the tray on the front of the four-wheel drive and craned his neck to see around the ute Alf was working on. 'Round the back?'

'It is.' The man took the top off the cup and blew across

the surface, dropping the cap next to the hammer. 'So, what's a copper from Melbourne doing up this way?'

'Long story. The car?'

'Right-o. Office first. There's some paperwork you'll need to sign, otherwise Coker and your bosses will have my guts.'

He led the way past an enormous tow truck and through the open double doors into the workshop.

There was a desk and chair in the far corner, bookended by a dull red shelving unit for tools and a pair of beige metal filing cabinets. A wilted calendar stood on one of the filing cabinets, its page turned to August of the previous year. A pair of coffee mugs with dubious stains were parked next to it.

Alf bent over behind the desk and unlocked its lower drawer, then pulled out a plastic folder and handed Blake a pen. 'Chain of evidence. No one goes near the vehicle pound without signing in. Got gloves?'

'I have,' said Forbes. She reached into her utility belt and handed over a pair. 'Need me to wear some?'

'No. You won't be touching anything,' said Blake. 'I need you to film what I'm doing.'

'Okay.'

Paperwork completed and gloves on, he followed Alf through a fire door at the back of the garage, blinking as his eyes adjusted to the stark light once more.

A few metres away was a secondary fenced-off area that backed onto the neighbouring industrial unit. There were CCTV cameras above the gates, and enough warning signs to put off any kids who thought about entering for shits and giggles.

'There're cameras on the back of the garage too,' Alf explained as he tucked a key into the padlock barring entry and gave it a practised twist. 'That's the one.'

Blake eyed the lacklustre white ute that was parked over to the right of the pound, its windows smeared with grime and dust. 'When did Coker's lot take a look at this?'

'About a week after it arrived. Didn't find nothing though.' Alf leaned nonchalantly against the gate post as the two officers moved towards the vehicle, his tone bored. 'What d'you need, d'you reckon?'

Blake paused. 'A knife, to start off with. A sharp one.'

Moments later, he knelt beside the ute and drove a wicked-looking blade into the front nearside tyre, a grunt escaping his lips.

Forbes held aloft her phone, filming his progress. 'You've done this before.'

'Once or twice.' He slipped the knife further into the rubber and twisted, a soft hiss escaping.

It took a few attempts, but he was soon able to dip his hand under the broken surface and run it the length of the tyre, feeling the ridges and strata.

Nothing.

He rose to his feet. 'Next one.'

Three more tyres later, he had nothing except a layer of sweat covering his neck and cramp in his left calf muscle.

Standing, he stretched his legs and eyed the ute, then turned back to the mechanic who watched his progress with a wary intent.

'I need it up on the ramp.'

'You're kidding. You couldn't think of that before you trashed the tyres?'

'I need to get to the fuel tank.'

Alf pointed at the side of the vehicle. 'Stick your hand down the hole. Or you could use some wire.'

'Can't. I need to check the bottom of it.' He resisted the urge to rub at his neck while wearing the grease-strewn protective gloves. 'And the engine manifold, and the valve covers.'

'Fuck's sake. Hang on.'

The mechanic stomped away, muttering under his breath while he disappeared around the corner of the corrugated iron shed.

Moments later, Blake heard an engine start up and then choked out a snort as Alf reappeared, this time edging the enormous tow truck between the pound's gate posts.

He leaned out of the window as he braked. 'Figure if I use this to lift the front, that'll work – right?'

'Will it hold?'

'It better.' Alf grinned. 'I don't want the paperwork hassle if you get squashed.'

'Blake, wait.' Forbes held up her hand as the tow truck

manoeuvred into position. 'This isn't a good idea. What if that cable breaks while you're underneath the car?'

'Got a phone signal?'

She frowned. 'Yes. Why?'

'Get ready to dial triple zero if we need it. Hopefully we won't. Mind yourself, he's coming in.'

He gave her a gentle shove and stepped aside, watching while Alf backed up the truck and then jumped down and connected the cable to the ute's front axle.

'Guess we better hope it passed its last roadworthy, right?' Alf said cheerfully, and winked.

'Get it up. Let's get on with it before I change my mind.'

It took another half an hour to wrestle the tank free, and then Alf took pity on him, donned a pair of gloves and started to break it open by utilising a mixture of tools and brute force. 'Fucking rusted to shit,' he muttered under his breath as he worked. 'Bet the engine choked like a bastard with all this crap going down the line.'

Blake said nothing, motioned to him to stand aside and took over.

Moments later, it fell apart and Blake dropped to his haunches. 'Got you.' His fingers wrapped around a single piece of black plastic, a few centimetres across. Holding it up to the light, he allowed himself a faint smile. 'Got an evidence bag?'

'Here.' Forbes pulled one from her belt while she kept her phone camera trained on him and handed it over. 'What is it?'

'I've got a hunch, but let's keep looking.' He rose and faced the ute. 'I'll need to check under the engine next, Alf.'

'Thought you might say that. Wait while I put a couple of jacks underneath to be on the safe side.' The mechanic moved efficiently, double-checking his work before beckoning to Blake a few minutes later. 'Go on then.'

Taking the torch that Forbes handed to him, Blake crawled underneath the raised front of the ute, shining the beam under the worn metalwork. A faint smell of oil and fuel washed over him as he traced the two exhaust manifolds either side of the engine intake, exploring the gaps between the metalwork.

It didn't take long before his gloved fingers ran over a length of electrical tape that had been placed over a piece of hard plastic.

He pulled it away, then shuffled backwards and dropped it into the open evidence bag that Forbes held out.

Standing, he brushed himself off and eyed the vehicle once more. 'There'll be more, somewhere.'

Alf frowned. 'More of what?'

'Parts for a 3D printed gun. Specifically, a 9mm pistol that fires .22 calibre rounds,' said Blake, tugging away the gloves from his fingers. He turned to Forbes. 'The same calibre that killed Mortlock.'

THIRTY-ONE

Blake tapped his heel and stared at the computer's smeared screen while the fan whirred and rattled against its plastic housing on the floor under his temporary desk.

He could hear the kettle rumbling on its stand in the kitchen before someone – Forbes likely, because he had no idea where Ryan had wandered off to – flicked it off before it finished boiling, and then the sound of cupboards being opened carried through to where he sat.

The remains of a takeaway burger mouldered next to his computer mouse, the crusty edges of a stale bap the only evidence of a hurried lunch ordered from the small family-run café halfway between the police station and the pub. The greasy aroma wafted into the air and mixed with the smell of Forbes's choice of a beef and horseradish sandwich.

The buzzer on the front door carried through to the office

and then, beyond the closed reception hatch, he could hear Ryan talking to the courier who was now tasked with transporting the two evidence bags to Coker's laboratory.

The forensic technician had been gruff upon answering his phone an hour earlier, but soon became animated once he heard what they had discovered at Merriott's yard, as well as having the professional decency to congratulate him on his breakthrough.

Wiping his fingers on a crumpled paper napkin, Blake went to take a sip from the can of soft drink beside his keyboard, scowled when he realised it was empty, and turned his attention back to the screen.

There was only one tab open, and its contents were meagre.

Mortlock had chosen not to attend the original search of Tim Charterman's broken and busted ute, even though Blake could find no record of any other pressing matters in the man's formal diary that day. Instead, the only mention of the ute since the crash was this, Coker's report, and even that was scant on detail.

Scrolling through the scanned copy, Blake could see that a typical drugs-focused search had taken place.

It was a box-ticking exercise thanks to Mortlock's lack of input, and no more.

A drug and alcohol test had also been performed at the post mortem conducted by Michael Sigford, but given that no one was sure how long the vehicle had been at the side of the road before Terry Doxon attended the scene, it wasn't surprising that those results were inconclusive.

And no stains had been found underneath Charterman's fingernails either, so the man had been careful to bury whoever's remains without getting blood on himself – or his clothes for that matter.

Closing the report, Blake pushed back his chair and made his way through to the kitchen.

Forbes was standing at the sink while she stared out the window and watched the courier's van pull away.

He jerked his chin at the kettle. 'Enough water in that for another?'

'Yeah. Should be.'

'Figured now that Ryan's finished with sorting out those gun parts we could have a briefing, see what he's managed to find out about Charterman's associates.'

'Sounds good.' She stood to one side while he busied himself with first the generic brand of instant coffee, then the sugar. 'There's plenty of milk in the fridge – I just opened a new carton.'

'Right.' He added a splash of cold water then took a tentative slurp. 'Let's get on with it then.'

The young constable was standing by the whiteboard, pen in hand and staring at the images copied from Forbes's video depicting the gun parts. He glanced over his shoulder as they approached. 'What did Alf say when you pulled these out?'

'Reckoned it was worth getting out of bed with a hangover

for,' said Blake. 'Well, almost. Want to give us an update on how you're getting on with those background checks?'

'Sure.' Ryan cleared his throat and flipped open the manila folder in his hands. 'So, it looks like Charterman's last known whereabouts was Trinity Beach, according to his social media profile. No one in Cairns is missing him – I mean, no one seems to be worried about him. As far as I can tell, it looks like he disappears from time to time and then there was a flurry of activity like comments and stuff when he was back from wherever. Luckily, some of it wasn't posted privately.'

'What about family?' Forbes said. 'Next of kin?'

'His mum lives in Manunda. No sign of a dad. He's got a sister who lives just down the road from there, in Portsmith.'

'Are they in the system?'

'No, they're clean.' Ryan flipped a page in the folder. 'But I did find two associates of his in the system – the three of them got arrested when Charterman was twenty-two. That was his second offence. They're still mates on social media. One of them works in a DIY store – I gave them a call while you were out, and they confirmed he's one of their supervisors these days. The other bloke's got a job down at the marina, on one of the dive boats.'

'Anyone else on there worth taking a closer look at?'

'Nope,' said Ryan, closing the file. 'That's it. Everyone else checked out.'

Blake peered past him to the photographs pinned to the

board. 'Makes you wonder how he got involved with the weapons then.'

'I've never seen a 3D printed gun,' said the constable as he studied them. 'How'd you know to look for it?'

Blake shrugged. 'Gut feeling. Something didn't add up. I mean, Amos was meant to be applying for a wrecker's licence but hadn't, and Prengist saw him and Mortlock arguing three weeks ago. Makes me wonder if it was about that, or whether they knew about Charterman and what he was up to. Amos got hold of his ID somehow, after all.'

Ryan's eyebrows shot upwards. 'Do you think Ivan was involved?'

'That's ridiculous,' said Forbes. 'Why would he be?'

'Two thousand bucks and a couple of passports in his safe would be my guess,' Blake shot back. 'Maybe Amos or Charterman was bribing him to look the other way.'

She opened her mouth to retort, then clamped it shut.

'Wow,' Ryan managed, his voice strangled.

Blake took a sip of tea before peering over the mug at Forbes. 'Where's the shovel that was found in the car? Still at the lab?'

'Here, in the evidence locker for now,' she said. 'Also known as the shipping container out the back.'

'Seriously?'

'It's the best we can do. Apparently they were going to extend this place to double its size eight years ago. Never happened. Still waiting for the funding, or at least that's what Ivan said.'

'Who's got the key?'

'It's a combination lock.'

'Does it use the same code as everything else Mortlock touched?'

'Yes, unless he changed it before he died without telling us.'

Blake put down his drink. 'Show me.'

THIRTY-TWO

Blake watched while Forbes released the two sturdy locks fitted to the back door of the police station and then followed her down a short wrought-iron staircase.

'This was part of the original house,' she said over her shoulder, running her hand over the metalwork. 'Before I was born though.'

'When was it converted?'

'Sometime in the early seventies.'

An old paint tin stood on the last step, and the stench of stale nicotine caught on the light breeze as Blake walked past, two half-smoked butts on the metal tread beside it as if someone had been interrupted mid-smoke.

The staircase led to several cracked pavers that ran the width of the property before giving way to dust and stones.

Grass emerged from between the slabs with weeds jostling for space alongside.

A beat-up large steel rubbish skip was off to the left, overflowing with busted pieces of plywood. An old office chair had been upended into it, the wheels sticking up in the air beside an old computer monitor that poked out from under what remained of the seat cushion, the upper corner of it just visible over the metal rim.

Beyond that, the remnants of the original lawn took over, the vegetation longer here, tangled with vine around the furthest edges.

'Do you get many snakes out here?' he asked as the grass swished against his legs.

'Sometimes. Keep a look out. They're not too active yet. Another few weeks and you'd need to watch yourself.'

She kicked an old soft drink can as she led the way towards a twenty-foot shipping container, its pale blue corrugated corten steel dull with age.

Blake ran his gaze over it, and noticed an electrical wire running from it back to a junction box under the eaves of the police station. Then he spotted the motor for an air conditioning unit fixed to the right-hand side of the container.

Forbes glanced over her shoulder. 'The air conditioning was installed a few years ago after we had a big case involving a drug bust. Okay, so it's not the same as having an evidence room in the building, but it does the job.'

'Ever had any break-ins?'

'No. But then we don't publicise that it's out here or what it's used for. You can't see it from the car park, and those overgrown banksias shield it from the house next door.'

'Who lives there?'

'An older couple in their seventies. Been living there since they got married fifty-odd years ago.'

Blake paused, taking in a three-hundred-and-sixty view of the police station's backyard. 'Do you have any cameras?'

'One, above the back door. It gives us a panoramic view out here.'

He could see it now, enclosed within a dome-shaped black plastic casing that was fixed to the timber cladding. A wire ran from it into the wall, which he assumed connected with a power supply on the inside. 'What about the feed?'

'Online. We just log in and check it from time to time.'

A padlock with a gleaming hasp dangled from a thick steel chain that had started to tarnish, and Forbes twisted it until the combination setting faced her.

She paused and frowned. 'I suppose we should change this.'

'Might be a good idea. And maybe to something not so obvious.' Blake waited while she unlocked it, then stood aside as she swung open the right-hand door. 'No need to let Terry know the code either, given that he's retiring at the end of next week.'

'True. Okay, here we go.'

In the muted light beyond the opening, he could see two

rows of folded-out workbenches. Both were clear save for a box of nitrile gloves in the middle of one. Three metal filing cabinets and a gun cabinet had been placed along the left side of the container, each drawer sealed with a combination lock.

The air conditioning unit was near the ceiling midway along the right, and when he squinted though the gloom he could see two large chest freezers taking up the far end of the container.

Forbes reached out and picked up an inspection light from the metal floor, similar to those he had seen his local mechanic use, switching it on. 'Ivan was always talking about installing some work lamps on tripods to make it easier to get around in here…'

Blake let the comment go unanswered and followed her as she squeezed past the first two workbenches and over to the gun cabinet.

Midway through thumbing the combination lock, she glanced up at him. 'This was the only place we could keep the shovel in.'

He could hear the apologetic tone in her voice, the slight trace of embarrassment. 'Whatever works, right?'

Then she swung open the door.

There was a stunned silence before she staggered backwards, her mouth forming an "o" as her breath escaped.

'What the fuck?' she managed.

He peered around her, a sickening twist clutching his

stomach as he took in the racking system that took up the lower two thirds of the cabinet.

An old shotgun was over on the far right, the wooden stock worn with use over the years and its metal barrel dull with age.

But there was no shovel.

'Where is it?'

'I don't know. Someone's taken it.'

'Mortlock?'

'I don't know. There's nothing on the system to say anyone logged it out of evidence.'

'You mean it's been stolen?'

'Maybe.'

'Why didn't the alarm go off?'

'It-it's broken.'

'When?'

'Last year.' She turned away, crossed to the nearest workbench and leaned her hands on it as if to steady herself. 'Ivan put in a procurement request for a new one back in April after we were told the original was lost by headquarters, but we haven't heard anything. We're still waiting, same as we are with getting the radio on Ryan's car fixed. We're too far down the priority list out here, I guess.'

'What else is meant to be in here?'

'Two pistols in the top compartment.'

He flipped up the metal lid.

Sure enough, a pair of 1990s-era automatics sat on the shelf.

'Where'd these come from?'

'That drugs bust I was telling you about. One of the blokes we arrested is on a murder charge up in the Territory that's dragging through the courts so we're hanging onto them until the NT lot put in a request.'

Blake stepped back and slammed the cabinet shut, re-set the lock, and stepped away from it. 'Is there something going on around here you're not telling me?'

'Like what?'

'Was Mortlock dirty?'

She turned and glared at him. 'No. He wasn't.'

'Are you sure of that?'

'He was a good copper.'

'What about Doxon?'

'What about him?'

'Is he a good copper? I mean, he isn't – he's the laziest fucker I've ever worked with. But is he clean?'

'What is this?'

'What about Ryan? Any issues with him? You said he was ambitious.'

'I… for fuck's sake – you think one of us took the shovel?' She eased away from the workbench, her shoulders slumping. 'What's next? Are you going to accuse me?'

'Did you take it?'

'No, I didn't.'

'Would Mortlock have taken it?'

'Why?'

'I'm asking you. You were closer to him than most.'

She chewed her lip for a moment. 'No. I don't think he did.'

'Who else knows about Mortlock's habit of using the same code for everything?'

Forbes gave him a hopeless shrug and looked away. 'Anyone who knew him well, I suppose.'

'Which is half this bloody town,' he snarled. Then his mobile rang, and he swore under his breath when he glimpsed the number. 'We'll finish this conversation inside. I've got to take this first.'

THIRTY-THREE

The small kitchen gave off a slight lemon-scented odour when Angela walked in, and there was a damp mop shoved into an empty bucket next to the door.

The worktops gleamed and the tiled floor had been swept clear of crumbs and a week's worth of human activity, while the stainless steel sink was bathed in the early evening sun dappling through the window blind.

She read the note left beside the kettle from the part-time cleaner who was restricted to these outer reaches of the police station and had been and gone by the time they had returned from Merriott's yard.

They needed more disinfectant and toilet rolls.

And she was away next weekend so someone else would have to clean the toilets.

Balling up the notepaper and throwing it in the pedal bin

beside the refrigerator, Angela heard a raised voice from outside.

Beyond the window blind, she could see Harknell with his phone to his ear, pacing back and forth across the car park, deep in conversation.

'Christ,' she muttered. 'As if things couldn't get any worse around here.'

Her hands shook when she took a glass from the cupboard above the microwave and filled it from the filter tap at the sink, and when she took a sip her throat constricted, making her choke.

Beating her chest, eyes watering, she tried again, this time managing to swallow properly, although that only worsened the sickness in the pit of her stomach.

She put down the glass and slid a roll of kitchen towel towards her, peeled off a handful of sheets and dabbed at the water she had managed to slop down her shirt.

'Stupid,' she muttered.

'Who is?'

Turning, she saw Ryan leaning against the door frame, his face miserable. She exhaled as the reality of finding out that key evidence was missing settled like a dead weight across her shoulders. 'Ivan's dropped us all in it this time, hasn't he?'

'I suppose so.'

'Any idea why he might've taken the shovel out of evidence?'

'No.' He bit his lip. 'Nobody really tells me anything around here.'

'Now isn't the time for a pity party,' she said, her attention returning to Harknell. 'We've got bigger things to worry about.'

He joined her by the window. 'So what did he say about the other gun? Y'know – the 9mm that missed and hit the tree instead.'

'He reckons whoever killed Ivan took it.'

'Do you think maybe Ivan shot the tree?' The young constable's eyes widened. 'But why would he have an illegal gun?'

'I don't know. I know as much as you at the moment.' She huffed her fringe from her eyes. 'Which is next to fuck all.'

'Hmm.' He nodded towards Harknell, who had his head bowed, his jaw set while he listened. 'Is he talking to Bragg?'

'Either that, or his boss in Melbourne.' She narrowed her eyes as Harknell turned around beside Doxon's ute and paced back the other way. 'I suspect it's Bragg though.'

'There goes my chance of a bloody promotion then.'

'Seriously?' She glared at him. 'Maybe instead of moping about, you could make a start on the security footage and find out who the fuck broke in – if it wasn't Ivan doing one of his solo investigations.'

He straightened at her tone, pouting. 'No need to be like that, Ange.'

'Just go and do it, Ryan,' she sighed. She pulled out her

phone as he slouched away and hit the speed dial for the forensic team. 'Jonathan? It's Angela Forbes. We've got a situation here at the station and I need you and your team to come over. Yes, today. I know it's late. I'll explain when you get here.'

She ended the call before the forensic investigator could complain further, peered through the blinds, and saw Harknell walking back, his expression thoughtful.

He came through to the kitchen moments later, brushed past her and filled up the kettle.

Folding her arms, she leaned against the stainless steel sink and watched while he busied himself with a fresh mug out of the dishwasher and lobbed a tea bag into it.

'You know Mortlock's combination code too,' she said, keeping her voice steady. 'You've known it since last week.'

He paused midway through filling the mug with milk, set down the carton and rested his hands on the worktop. 'Meaning?'

'You could've taken the shovel.'

There, it was out.

She had said it.

Holding her breath, she resisted the urge to take a step back.

'Seriously?' he said, his voice rising.

'Why not? You've just accused me of doing the same thing. You were here on your own Saturday morning until I got here – you could've taken it then.'

'Why?'

'What?'

'Why would I take it?' His eyes bored into hers. 'Come on, you've obviously put some thought into this. Let's hear it.'

'You…'

'Hey – what did I miss, eh?'

She hadn't heard the car pull up outside, hadn't heard the front door swish open, and so Terry Doxon's appearance at the kitchen door made her start.

His face had caught the sun – as well as a few beers she reckoned – and his eyes were gleeful as he looked at her, then Harknell.

'Thought you were out fishing today,' she said.

'Just got back. Fish weren't biting much.' He scowled, then held up a small esky. 'Was going to ask Ryan if he wanted some of these tiddlers for bait. Happy families in here, is it?'

'Not the time, Terry.' She took a step backwards and busied herself with folding the freshly washed tea towels the cleaner had left on the draining board.

'We'll continue this discussion tomorrow,' said Harknell, glaring at her. 'Bragg's summoned me to Caboolture first thing so you'll have to stay here while Coker's lot are processing the container. I presume you've got hold of him?'

'He's on his way. Why does Bragg want you in Caboolture?'

He shrugged. 'I guess in the circumstances, he wants to go

through the events of this past week in person. I'm going to head back to the hotel to prep for it. I should be back late tomorrow afternoon but if Coker's done here by then and you're not around, we'll have a briefing first thing Tuesday instead, okay?'

'Right,' she said.

He turned his back and walked out the room.

A few seconds after she heard his footsteps descend the front steps, Doxon raised an eyebrow. 'What's going on with him?'

'Your guess is as good as mine. But given how long I've been in this job, I bloody well know when someone's lying to me.'

THIRTY-FOUR

There was a slight late winter nip to the air the next morning when Blake parked on a mixed development street under the lush green canopy of a jacaranda tree.

Residential low-set homes were set back from the pavement, their gardens separated from pedestrians by picket fences that ranged in colour from off-white to downright rotten, while further along there were two double-storey office units with smoked glass windows that gave nothing away.

The wide thoroughfare was quieter now that the commuter traffic had eased, and as he locked the car he could hear the rumble and honk of trains from the nearby station carrying over the rooftops.

An ibis strutted across the road ahead of him, fully intent on a discarded fast food bag that had been tossed into the gutter on the other side, its long beak then probing the contents with glee.

The breeze picked up, a polite cough from the direction of Antarctica that riffled his shirt and shook the leaves above his head. It was a timely reminder that there were still two or three weeks to go before spring brought the jacaranda trees into bloom.

He buttoned up his jacket before heading towards the café that Bragg had singled out for their meeting.

It was a few hundred metres back from a busy crossroads, and a few streets away from the hospital. The police station was on the other side of town.

Some things were better discussed away from the regional headquarters.

There was a couple in their seventies sitting at a table on the covered patio outside the café, she with her back to the street consulting the mobile phone in her hand and he with his attention taken by the menu that he flipped this way and that, hawing and sighing.

Neither looked at Blake when he walked past them and up to the counter just inside the open glass sliding doors.

There were more tables inside, each covered with the café's signature yellow-and-white chequered tablecloths and an array of condiments standing in the middle. The white wooden chairs bore cushions that matched the tablecloths, the nearest ones to the counter already taken by mothers with babies and prams or businesspeople staring at laptop screens.

One or two looked up from their work to acknowledge a newcomer, but their interest soon waned.

A young waiter in his twenties stacking cups beside a coffee grinder paused his work and smiled. 'It's table service, so sit anywhere you like and I'll be over.'

'I'm meeting someone actually…' Blake peered into the furthest reaches of the café as a man raised his hand from a table at the back on the far left, away from the sign for the toilets on the opposite wall. 'I'll have a flat white please.'

'No worries. I'll bring it over.'

'Thanks.'

Weaving his way between a cluster of tables, he noticed that Bragg had taken the chair with its back to the wall, leaving him with the one facing away from the room.

The hairs on the back of his neck protested, all his instincts telling him to move the chair so it was off to the side, but instead he left it where it was and folded his hands on the table.

Forced himself to relax.

Nobody knew him here.

'Morning, guv.'

'Sergeant.' Bragg slid his half-empty coffee cup towards him and took a sip before speaking again. 'How did Coker get on?'

'Forbes phoned me while I was on the way over here – his team finished at one this morning. They've lifted prints from the container's doors and handle, and the gun cabinet. Ryan Darke has checked the security footage – there's nothing on it.'

'What d'you mean "there's nothing on it"? It's a bloody motion detector-triggered system isn't it?'

'No, time lapse.' Blake paused at the sound of movement, and then the waiter leaned around him and set down his coffee. Two sugar sachets and a complimentary miniature cookie accompanied it. 'Thanks.'

The man's footsteps retreated while Blake emptied both sachets into the cup and stirred.

'Apparently Mortlock requested a motion-detection system but the procurement team haven't processed the purchase order yet,' he said. 'The time lapse system that was put in is the original one from eight years ago that runs on WiFi, and the signal – according to Ryan – has a habit of cutting out, depending on when the neighbourhood kids are home from school. Four in the afternoon is a bitch, he says.'

'Do you believe them?'

Blake stared at the viscous liquid and set down his spoon. 'Forbes says they've printed out the data logs that show the image capture times, and they're consistent with what Ryan says. There's a trend in the timings that backs him up.'

Bragg's gaze roamed the café while he digested the news. 'So, all four of the officers at Hangman's Gap knew about the signal lag, all four of them knew how often images were captured by the camera system, and all of them knew the code for the lock. That means any one of them could've removed the shovel from evidence.'

'Yes.'

'Who do you think took it?'

'I'm not sure. I'm focusing on why at the moment. And we need to bear in mind that if Mortlock was that lax about security, others in Hangman's Gap could've guessed the code too.'

'You mean, other than my police officers?'

'Exactly.'

'So without the footage, we're fucked – unless Coker can identify a sixth print that doesn't belong to any of you.'

'I didn't take it.'

'Good.' The senior officer's smile didn't quite reach his eyes. 'In the meantime, have you managed to find out anything else about the cash and passports that Mortlock had hidden in his office safe?'

'Not yet.' Blake ventured a sip of his coffee and grimaced. Replacing the cup in its saucer with a clatter, he pushed it away. 'None of his colleagues appear to know where the cash came from – or where he was planning on going.'

'Interesting. Quite the dark horse, wasn't he?'

'You could say that.'

Bragg's phone screen lit up, and he groaned. 'I'm due back at HQ for a meeting that's going to start in twenty minutes. You'll keep me updated?'

'Yes.'

'Keep on top of it, Blake. I don't need to tell you how important this is.'

'I know.'

'What about you? Do you think your cover story's going to hold up?'

Blake turned the coffee cup in his hand, brow furrowed while he contemplated the chequered tablecloth pattern for a moment. 'Yes, I think so. For now, anyway.'

'Good.' Bragg gathered up his mobile phone and car keys, then stood. 'It had better.'

THIRTY-FIVE

'Didn't we give you a big enough breakfast?'

Blake smiled at Simone's gentle teasing and followed her into the main bar of the pub, where the late morning sun was casting pyramids of light across the worn and uneven wooden floorboards.

'You did, so no – I'm not here for lunch, thanks.'

Dust motes spiralled in the air, and he could hear a clattering of stainless steel pans coming from the kitchen beyond the swing doors at the far end, the noise cutting through the 1980s rock track playing over the bar's speaker system.

Two wizened regulars that Blake recognised from Saturday night propped up the far end of the bar, both unshaven, both in shorts and vest tops covered in grease. Their biceps bulged while they clutched at half-finished schooners of amber liquid, and Blake was reminded once more how hard most of the people in Hangman's Gap worked to make ends meet.

Even if they did end up spending what they earned in the only pub in town.

David was behind the bar, writing an updated gig list on a blackboard under the smaller of the room's two televisions using a bright blue chalk pen. He glanced over his shoulder.

'I need a word with you both,' said Blake.

He received a nod in return before the other man went back to his work.

The smell of disinfectant filled the whole room while Molly Tanner swished a mop back and forth beside the chrome-framed stools lining the bar.

Simone sighed under her breath as she walked past the twenty-something. 'Honestly, Mols – another spill?'

'Sorry,' said the younger woman, blushing under the scrutiny of the two customers who cackled at the far end of the bar. 'It was an accident.'

'Okay, well keep an eye on things while Dave and I are in this meeting. Won't be long. Give us a shout if it gets busy.'

'Will do.'

Blake heard the clatter of the chalk pen being dropped into the pot with others beside the till register, and then Simone was ushering him through the swing doors and out along the hallway.

The sound of heavy footsteps across the landing reached

his ears before Laura launched herself down the stairs, almost barrelling into them.

She flushed, her mouth open in shock.

'Everything all right, love?' Simone said. 'Thought you were still cleaning.'

'I was.' Laura swallowed. 'Sorry – there's a bloody big huntsman in room two. I was going to find David and get him to squash it.'

'Oh, God – you and your spiders. Off you go then. He'll have to do it after we've spoken to Detective Harknell though, and make sure he doesn't splat it on the wall like last time, otherwise you'll never get the stain out.'

'Okay.'

Simone shook her head as Laura barrelled out the door to the bar, and then led Blake into a small room at the far end of the hallway.

'Ignore the state of it,' she said cheerily. 'It isn't a priority with everything else that needs doing around here.'

'No worries.' He cast his gaze around the cluttered space, which seemed to be a mixture of storage cupboard and home office.

Invoices and receipts from various suppliers were arranged into three different piles on a lop-sided oak desk that was chocked up at one end with a concrete breeze block, and an ancient laptop wheezed and whirred beside the stacks of paperwork.

Two flat-pack bookshelves took up the left-hand wall, their shelves bending under the weight of five-litre plastic bottles of cleaning products and laundry supplies for the bar, kitchen and guest rooms. A large plastic bag of plain-white generic-brand toilet rolls had been shoved into one corner out of the way, and there was a filing cabinet behind those, its middle drawer open and a pile of colourful manila folders left on top.

'Sorry, I'm in the middle of trying to sort out the book-keeping,' said David, his hands on his hips while he surveyed the room. 'I keep meaning to tidy up in here too, but…'

'Doesn't matter,' said Blake. 'At least it gives us some privacy.'

On cue, Simone gave the door a gentle push and walked over to the desk, leaning against it. 'What do you need?'

'The tourists who were here last week. There was a British bloke, and a German couple. When did they check in?'

'The Brit was only here a few nights,' said David. 'He got here on Monday, and was gone by Saturday morning. The Germans were drop-ins – they just turned up on Tuesday.'

'And checked out Saturday too.' Simone's brow puckered. 'I think they would've stayed longer, if it wasn't for…'

'Yeah, they were definitely spooked by Ivan's death once word of that got around on Friday,' said David. 'They came and asked me how long it would take to get to the Gold Coast that night. I think they'd had enough of rural Queensland by then, the way they were talking.'

'Oh?' Blake looked up from his note taking. 'In what way?'

'I overheard them telling Laura when they were checking out that they wanted to spend some more time on a beach before heading home, and that they only had another week or so left of their trip.'

'Did they say to either of you how long they'd been here?'

'No, but I got the impression they'd used up their visa,' said Simone. 'They'd certainly seen a lot – they were up north for a bit, because the woman was telling me about being in Port Douglas for a few days last month.'

'Was the Brit much of a talker? I mean, I had to have words with him on Friday night when he wouldn't leave Molly alone, but what was he like the rest of the time?'

'He wasn't much of a talker,' said David, before smiling. 'But then he did have to contend with most of us taking the piss out of him about the cricket while he was here.'

'I think he got a bit tired of it, to be honest,' Simone added. 'Poor bugger.'

Blake chuckled. 'You almost sound sorry for him.'

'Almost.'

'Have you overheard any threats between the locals?'

'No,' said David, 'which is what makes Ivan's and then Amos's murders so shocking. I mean, people have their disagreements – you know what it's like when blokes have a few beers in them – but I wouldn't have thought any of them would've done something like that. Most find a work around—'

'Or a way to avoid each other if they can,' said Simone. 'Which can be tricky sometimes given the lack of choices around here. I mean, there's only one small supermarket so if you fall out with someone there, you're stuffed. You have to go to Caboolture.'

Blake lowered his pen, a memory resurfacing. 'When we spoke to Miles Prengist last week, he reckoned he got a reconditioned carburettor off Amos. Do you know if he'd fallen out with Jeff Tanner or something? I mean, I know Prengist has a reputation for violence, but Tanner's is the only garage around here. Is he still violent?'

'Well, Miles hasn't been in the pub for two years. Not after I barred him,' said David. 'I would've accepted him back here after he'd cooled down if he bothered to come in and say sorry, but he's just avoided the place ever since.'

'What'd you bar him for?'

'He started a fight after accusing Carl Upshott of doing some work over at his place and then overcharging him. I kicked the pair of them out that night. Only Carl came back a week later, apologetic as anything.' He shrugged. 'Turns out Miles overreacted – it sounded to me like Carl's pricing was fair in the circumstances given the state of that place.'

'And you reckon he'd had a falling out with Tanner as well?'

'Maybe. He can't stand the bloke, anyway.' David gave a

tired sigh born of long hours. 'Mind you, he doesn't get on with most people.'

'Oh, that's a little unfair,' said Simone. She aimed a patient smile at Harknell. 'I think Miles is just shy really, that's why he keeps himself to himself.'

THIRTY-SIX

Angela rested her chin in her hand and stared at the computer screen, her eyes bleary.

The clock above Mortlock's office door read eleven thirty – only nine hours or so since she had left the police station after the forensics team had finished their work.

Her cheeks were flaming by the time Jonathan Coker had shot her a final glance over his shoulder and climbed into the forensic team's van before driving away.

It didn't matter what he and his colleagues found out.

She would be forever tarnished by the visit, as would the others.

The smell of fresh coffee from the kitchen carried through to where she sat, and she straightened with a start, having forgotten she had switched on the machine.

She moved trance-like through to the kitchen, her

movements automatic while she sought out a reasonably clean mug and heaped sugar into it.

Her ears still rang from the bollocking that Bragg had given her over the phone late yesterday, his words stinging. She was left with no doubt as to the prospects of her career following the disappearance of such key evidence, no matter that – in theory – she hadn't been in charge.

Wandering back through to the office, she shot a glare towards Mortlock's open door.

Whatever he had been up to, whatever he had been investigating, he had dragged her into it – even from the grave.

'Thanks a lot, Ivan,' she muttered, taking a sip of coffee before slouching in front of her screen once more.

She heard the front door then, moments before an urgent rap against the frosted reception window rang out across the office.

The fuzzy form beyond the glass shifted from foot to foot while she crossed the office, the figure familiar.

'Laura? What're you doing here?'

Her younger sister's face was flushed. 'I can't stay long – David's upstairs in the pub trying to find a spider that doesn't exist.'

'What—'

'I've got something for you.'

'How did you get here?' Angela craned her neck to see beyond her sister. 'Did Simone bring you?'

'What? No. I ran, all right? Listen. You were talking about

Blake the other night. Wondering about what he might've been doing with Ivan.' Her sister caught her breath, then held up her phone. 'I found this, sticking out of his bag in his room just now. It might help, right?'

'You...' Angela sighed, then looked at the photograph on the screen. 'What's this?'

'It's a letter, see? To him. But check out the address. It's a property in Morris Beach.'

'His aunt lived there. She passed away the other month.'

'Yeah, I know. But you said he was cagey about it. I thought this might help. I thought—'

Angela held out the phone. 'What have I told you before about snooping around the hotel guests' rooms? What if David and Simone found out?'

'They won't.' Laura crossed her arms. 'Aren't you going to check it out?'

'Why?'

'Look at the writing. It's Ivan's, isn't it? I recognise it from those reports that you had at your place the other week.'

'You've been going through my stuff too?'

'I just wondered what they were about, that's all.'

Exasperated, Angela looked closer at the photo once more, then frowned. 'Shit. It's dated the week before he died.'

'Yeah, and obviously weeks after the aunt died too, yeah? Which makes you wonder why they were using it as a correspondence address rather than email or phone, right?'

'Was it open?'

'It had been, but he'd taped it closed again. He's there at the moment, talking to David and Simone.'

'What about?'

'I don't know – Simone was heading into the office with him when I left.'

Angela looked up to see a smug look on her sister's face, then handed back the phone. 'Get back to the pub before they realise you're missing. And not a word, understood? To anyone.'

'As long as you tell me what you find out.'

'Go.'

Angela slid shut the frosted glass, then hurried to her desk, picked up the keys to the four-wheel drive, and hurried outside.

Heart racing, she paused while scrolling through her phone contacts, then hit the dial button.

It almost rang out to voicemail before a familiar voice answered.

'Angie?'

'Tess? I need your help.'

'Well, hello to you too.'

'Sorry.' She wandered over to the vehicle, leaned against the door and then thought better of it when the heat from the metalwork began to burn through her uniform trousers. 'How's everything?'

'We're fine, cuz. But you need to phone my mum soon –

she's been talking to yours, and there're all sorts of rumours going around between them. Are you okay?'

'Yes. I think so. Got a moment?'

'About two minutes before I'm due in a briefing. Why?'

'I need you to check on an officer's name for me. He's from Melbourne.'

'Why?'

'Please? Just do it for me.' Angela gripped the phone tighter. 'I'll explain everything when I can.'

Her cousin's tone turned to one of curiosity. 'Okay, well the boss has just gone to a meeting so I'll check the system. You didn't get this from me though, all right? I'm using a temp login to access this.'

'I understand, and thanks.'

'What's one of our coppers doing up your way anyway?'

Angela pulled open the door of the four-wheel drive and climbed in. 'That's what I'm trying to find out.'

THIRTY-SEVEN

Angela gripped the steering wheel as the tyres rumbled over an uneven surface of asphalt that had been chewed up and spat out over a decade ago without regular maintenance.

Beyond the windscreen, clumping bamboo shuffled for space amongst overgrown verges and tangled vines, while clutches of banksias battled for elbow room between she-oaks and acacias, all of which encroached upon the twisting narrow road.

She drove at a little more than crawling pace, twisting her neck left and right, her eyes seeking out battered mailboxes or signs nailed to tree trunks, looking for anything that would indicate where number 174 Melaleuca Drive might be.

Despite the house number, Morris Beach was a tiny place comprising a cluster of properties squashed between Coochin Creek and the sprawling outer limits of Donnybrook.

There were no shops, no cafés, and no petrol stations.

It was a dead-end road, leading nowhere in particular.

There wasn't even a beach.

She had already discovered that on her previous drive by, finding herself at a muddy spit of land that drooped into the waters between the mainland and Bribie Island.

There were no residents in sight beyond the dirt track driveway entrances she passed, and only a glimpse here and there of lichen-covered tin roofs and ramshackle clapboard hoardings. Here and there, bright splashes of early spring flowers poked out from the undergrowth on each side of a driveway and despite the run-down appearance of some of the properties, others looked well-kept.

Number one seventy-four was not one of those.

She found it half a kilometre from the beach, its wooden sign bleached grey from years of sunlight and almost split in half in its position on a rotting five-bar gate that straddled the entrance.

Pulling over to the side of the road, Angela checked her QLITE radio and phone. Both still had a strong signal despite the remote feel to the place.

She glanced out her window to the dirt track leading away from the wooden gate, its route curling away to the left. Beyond the bamboo, beyond the trees, she could see a seventies-styled tiled roof, its pale-green finish mottled with age.

Rolling her shoulders, she climbed out and glanced up the road.

There was no one else around.

Angela tapped her forefinger lightly against the QLITE's plastic casing on her belt while she chewed her lip, and then exhaled and locked the vehicle.

A metal mailbox leaned precariously beside the gate post, its rusting slit of a mouth gaping with junk mail.

She pulled it loose, then looked around the back.

A gleaming padlock barred entry to anything else that might have been inside.

Biting back frustration, she flicked through the junk mail, then shoved it back in the mailbox.

The gate gave easily under her touch, not even emitting a theatrical creak when she pushed it open. Biting back surprise at the lack of a lock on it, she hurried along the narrow driveway before she could change her mind.

There were old tread marks in the dirt, deep ruts where vehicles had passed over the years, and a few scuff marks that might or might not have been footprints.

Beyond the boundary with the neighbouring property she could hear faint music, some sort of mainstream radio station playing while someone whistled along with it. Then a power saw started up, obliterating the remaining peace.

She picked up her pace, keen to reach the house and look around before someone wondered about the police vehicle parked on the road.

It was a two-storey building, with a rusting garage door and wide window set into the lower floor and two windows above those. Broken guttering hung from one end of the eaves, leaving a dark stain that streaked down the once-white wooden cladding.

Angela pulled a pair of protective gloves from her belt and slipped them on before trying the garage door handle.

It remained firmly closed, but whether that was from being locked or because it was rusted with age, she couldn't tell.

Peering through the smeared window beside it, she could see two sofas covered in dust sheets, the bookshelves behind them bare. A further window at the far end of the room appeared to look out over a garden.

Circling the house, she found a path leading down the left-hand side of it and discovered an overgrown spread of scrubby grass that gave way to a vegetable patch that had gone to seed. Rotting herbs wilted amongst thriving weeds, and what remained of the flower borders had morphed into a tangled mess.

Angela walked the length of the house, then along the right-hand side to an outer staircase that led up to an external door.

A shallow porch sheltered the landing from the sun, but had done little against the other elements. Rotting wooden decking creaked under her feet, and she kept a firm grip on the railing in case one of the planks gave way.

She rapped on the door, and was rewarded with silence.

Turning away, her gaze swept over the driveway leading down to the road and the mailbox.

There was a woman standing beside the gate, staring at her.

'Shit.'

She thundered down the stairs, then caught herself and slowed to a walk as her boots found the dirt once more.

As Angela drew closer, she could see that the woman was probably in her early seventies, hair dyed a paler shade of blonde to hide the white or grey, skin wizened from decades of sun exposure, and a considered poise to her slender form.

'Can I help you?' She rested her arm on the gate. 'Is there a problem, officer?'

'No problem.' Angela shot her what she hoped was a reassuring smile and waited until the woman had stepped aside to let her through. 'Thanks.'

'What's going on?'

'Just a routine check of the property, that's all. Do you live nearby?'

'Over the road, number thirty-eight.' She rolled her eyes. 'And yes, I know that doesn't make sense with the numbering.'

'And you are?'

'Misty Hargreaves.' The woman squinted at her badge. 'Officer Forbes. You're not local, are you? Haven't seen you around here before.'

'I've just been transferred down from Bundy. Thought I'd get a feel for the place.'

'Oh, you're a long way from home, aren't you?'

'Have you seen anyone else checking out this property recently?'

'Maybe a week or so ago.'

'Another police officer?'

'No, some bloke in a shirt and jeans. Baseball cap. Taller than you.' Misty squinted up at her through wire-rimmed glasses that accentuated rheumy eyes. 'Didn't see his car though, so he must've parked it somewhere else and walked.'

Angela smiled. 'Sounds like you're a great neighbour to have around to keep an eye on the place.'

'As you can see, there aren't many of us around here, so we all look out for each other. Did you see the mango trees round the back? She grew veggies too. Frances loved her garden and was always sharing the spoils with us.'

'I'm sorry for your loss. She must've been a good neighbour to have around.'

'Oh, don't apologise,' said Misty, flapping her hand. 'We're all just surprised the family haven't put it on the market yet.'

'Well, I guess these things take time to go through probate,' said Angela, moving to open the four-wheel drive's door. 'It's only been six weeks or so, hasn't it?'

Misty frowned. 'No, darl. That's why we're wondering what's taking so long. It's been over a year now since Frances passed away.'

THIRTY-EIGHT

The distinct smell of burning charcoal wafted on the air as Angela climbed from the four-wheel drive outside Jeff Tanner's house.

Opposite, a group of four kids were skateboarding back and forth along the short stretch of road, using the kerb to perfect flips and jumps. The scratch and whirr of the tiny board wheels carried across to her as she locked the vehicle, the sound pausing as all four of them stopped and stared.

'How's it going?' she called.

The eldest kid's eyes widened before he looked at his companions before answering. 'All right, I s'pose.'

Angela eyed the short plank of timber that had been propped against their driveway's gate post. 'If you're going to use that, best get the bandaids ready. I've still got gravel rash scars on my elbows from practising that stunt.'

The kid grinned, then turned away, his attention taken by the youngest lining up for the next trick.

Angela pushed through a low metal gate in a wire mesh fence, the hinges squeaking as it snapped back into place. An excited *yip* preceded a bundle of fur that dashed from the side of the low-set brick house, and she smiled as the young Rottweiler tore across the scrubby lawn towards her.

'Roscoe, how're you doing boy?' she gushed, reaching out her hand as he braked to a standstill, his tongue lolling.

The front screen door swung open, and a woman in her late forties appeared, a knife in her hand and a smile on her face. 'You after Jeff, Ange?'

'Is he in?'

'Round the back, doing the barbie while Mols and I get the salad ready. You want to stay?'

'Can't, but thanks. I won't keep him long.'

'No worries. Tell him not to feed anything to the mutt – he's meant to be on a diet.'

'Will do.'

Angela looked down at the dog. 'Where's your dad, then, huh? Go find him.'

Roscoe tore off round the side of the house, and she followed at a more sedate pace, taking in the small motorboat under a worn tarpaulin on the dirt driveway to her left and the tired flower beds that had been abandoned some time ago, the remaining plants browned and wilted.

Jeff Tanner was armed with a set of tongs and a cold beer when she rounded the corner, his face quizzical.

'Thought I heard voices.'

'Sorry – I won't keep you long. Smells good.'

''S okay.' He turned each of the three steaks on the grill, then added sausages before setting down the tongs and the beer can on a teak table laid out with three sets of cutlery. 'You staying?'

'No, that's okay.' She folded her arms and managed a smile. 'Thanks anyway.'

He reached into his shorts pocket and pulled out a crumpled half-empty packet of cigarettes and a Zippo lighter, expertly flicking the wheel before taking the first drag and peering at her through the ensuing smoke.

'Want one?'

'I'm meant to be giving them up.'

'How's that going for you?'

'Oh, give it here.' She plucked one from the outstretched packet, then leaned in as he flicked the Zippo, a golden flame leaping into the air. 'Thanks.'

'So, is this a work visit or a social call? I'm presuming work if you're not planning on having dinner.'

'Yeah. Work.' She took another drag on the filched cigarette, savouring the nicotine hit as it met her lungs.

He watched her for a while, then picked up the beer and took another swig. 'Something troubling you, Ange?'

'Is it that obvious?'

'How long have I known you?' His eyes softened. 'You know, if it helps, the missus and I never believed the rumour about you and Ivan. She figured it was just Jill being jealous.'

She sighed. 'Jealous of what? Long hours, not enough manpower, all the politics he had to deal with?'

'I don't know.' He squinted through the cigarette smoke. 'She's always been like that, though. Bitter. Resentful. But that's not why you're here, right?'

'No, you're right.' Angela looked over her shoulder and saw Molly and her mother through the kitchen window, the pair of them laughing about something while they prepped the salads and whatever else the Tanners were having with their dinner.

When she turned back, Tanner was watching her with keen interest.

He raised an eyebrow. 'Well?'

'Look, I'm just following up some notes, going back over things in case we missed something.'

'Okay.'

She exhaled. There was no turning back now. 'Did you see any vehicles near the burn site prior to Ivan's body being found?'

'No, not even Ivan's. I reckon he must've rocked up after I'd left.'

'What about Harknell? Did you see him?'

He rubbed one of his huge hands across his chin, scratching at the stubble forming. 'I didn't, no, not until I saw him with you. But that doesn't mean he wasn't there, does it? He could've heard me coming and hidden or something. Why? Do you think he killed Ivan?'

She stared at the steaks sizzling on the wire rack, the meat turning black in places, and bit back bile. 'That's what I'm starting to wonder.'

THIRTY-NINE

Blake checked the speedometer, the car's tyres rumbling over an uneven surface of asphalt, potholes and occasional roadkill of dubious origin. Throat dry, he cursed under his breath as he remembered too late that he had downed the last of the water before his meeting with Bragg. The plastic one-litre bottle now rolled around in the footwell of the passenger seat, taunting him.

The radio went from an old Rolling Stones song to a constant hiss of static, and he thumbed down the volume on the steering wheel rather than scroll through to a talk radio station.

The GWN system was also turned down. He had no wish to hear about routine police work and had been tempted to switch it off, but then there was always the nagging doubt that he might miss being contacted by one of the officers from

Hangman's Gap. Especially given the way the mobile signal on his phone was fading the further he drove west.

Besides, he needed time with the thoughts that were troubling him after his conversations with Bragg.

'Shit.'

The sign to Amos Krandle's property appeared sooner than he thought, and he braked hard, remembering to check his rear-view mirror at the last minute and mouthing a silent thanks that there wasn't another vehicle behind him. Swerving onto the track leading to the poultry farm, he corrected the slight skid across the stones and dirt and then glanced across at the dam. A dive team had been sent to dredge it yesterday, but had turned up nothing to help the investigation.

He could see where their dinghy had been dragged out of the water, the skid marks carving a wide flat strip amongst the baked earth before flattening the grass where it would have been manhandled onto a trailer.

Passing the two broiler sheds, he saw that the doors were still open.

A clutch of chickens mooched about on the threshold of one, pecking and scratching at the dirt, ruffling their thin layer of feathers, and Blake wondered who was feeding them now that Amos was dead.

Maybe Sheena Lerwick, maybe not.

He slowed as he approached the house, taking in the churned-up dirt where police and forensic vehicles had cluttered the space the past forty-eight hours, and braked beside the first of the timber sheds.

After switching off the engine, he sat for a moment listening to the engine tick and cool, the interior losing its battle with the warmth from the late afternoon sun as soon as the air conditioning died.

Beyond the windscreen, a single strip of crime scene tape barricaded the shallow wooden steps leading up to the veranda. Whoever had fixed it before departing the property had tied it in a hurry, the tape twisting in the middle and obliterating the printed words across it.

He got out, straining his hearing.

A light breeze caught at a stray piece of rope that had been tied to the trellis at the far left of the veranda, tapping it against the wooden latticework. Turning, Blake took in the sight of a discarded feed bag as it tumbled nonchalantly across the yard, and then looked over his shoulder at a dull thud to see a skinny cat with one eye watching him from a pile of discarded timber beside a galvanised water tank at the side of the house.

But there were no voices.

No other vehicles around.

Reaching into his pocket, he pulled out a pair of disposable gloves and slipped them on before striding up the steps and lifting the twisted tape.

Ducking underneath, he stood on the veranda for a moment and checked the yard again.

He was alone.

The front door was closed beyond the fly screen, and someone – perhaps one of Coker's team – had fixed a brass padlock to it upon leaving yesterday.

Blake twisted it this way and that before letting it drop back into place, then sidled over to the front window and peered in, shielding his eyes with a gloved hand. The dusty black remains of fingerprinting powder covered the sill, and he kept his clothes well away.

There would be no time to get changed before returning to the police station in Hangman's Gap, and he had no wish to explain himself.

Not yet, anyway.

The living room appeared the same as it had been when he and Forbes had left on Saturday, save for the paperwork he had found – all of that had been transferred to the station for recording into evidence and filing, a laborious task he reckoned would fall to Ryan Darke.

Blake turned away, couched under the tape and made his way around the house, eyeing up each of the dirty window panes that looked out over the yard.

He froze when he reached the bathroom.

The window was open ajar, and there was movement within.

Drawing his service pistol, he cursed his spiked heart rate and took a deep breath before creeping closer.

The sill was level with his chest, and he had no wish to lose his head if the intruder was armed.

Choosing the left-hand side, leaving his dominant hand free to aim the pistol through the gap first, he shuffled closer, his jaw clenched.

Another step, and he was almost level with the opening.

Then he swung around to face it.

Opening his mouth to issue a warning, his words died on his lips, replaced with a guttural yelp as a solid ball of fur launched itself at him, clawed his chest, and dropped to the ground at his feet.

He stepped back, eyes wide, heart chasing.

The possum glared at him, then scampered away, disappearing behind a large galvanised steel water tank.

'Fuck.'

Blake leaned against the clapboard wall beside the bathroom window and closed his eyes.

When he was sure his hands had stopped shaking, he holstered his pistol and swallowed before rubbing his chest where the animal had lashed out in its haste to escape.

Exhaling, he choked out a relieved laugh, then made his way around to the timber sheds.

It seemed that Bragg had passed on the news about Blake's discovery at Merriott's yard, because Coker's team had taken apart Krandle's vehicles with a violence that resembled a high-speed car crash.

Scattered across the dirt floors of each shed were a mixture of split fuel tanks, ripped tyres and battered plastic dashboard vents. Thin layers of mud-streaked carpet from the footwells of both vehicles lay torn and discarded beside wheel rims, and there were wrenches and other tools left in disarray on top of those.

As Blake walked around them, he ran his gaze over what was left, eyeing the broken door mirrors, their shattered pieces glinting amongst the dust motes that spiralled around him. He crouched beside each vehicle, craning his neck to see underneath, only to discover that the floor pans had also been removed, exposing the guts of the machinery.

Coker had been thorough this time, that much was certain.

Turning his attention to the workbench, half tempted to return the tools to their rightful places on the rack above it, he saw that each of the drawers had been tipped out onto the floor. The contents had been sifted through, old moth-eaten envelopes torn open, and yellowing business cards tossed to one side.

He gave the pile a cursory glance, but saw nothing that provided an answer as to who had killed Amos, or why.

Walking out from the second shed and into bright sunshine, Blake shielded his eyes and surveyed the yard.

The house was out of bounds given the padlock barring entry, and he was in no mood to incur Bragg's or Coker's wrath if he used one of Krandle's tools to remove it.

Instead, he wandered over to the water tank beside the

shaded clapboard wall and ran his hand over the galvanised steel surface.

It was cool to the touch, and when he rapped his knuckles against it, a good three-quarters full. Raising his gaze, he eyed the bulging cover of a maintenance hatch half a metre above his head.

'You sly old git,' he murmured.

He ran back to the second shed, returning with an extension ladder that had been propped up in one corner. After climbing up, he could see that the opening was accessed by a simple hatch, except that six large bolts held it in place.

'Bollocks.'

Five minutes later, he returned with a wrench.

It made short work of the bolts, and then he pulled out his phone and shone the flashlight into the cavernous hole, his movements echoing within the steel container.

Dark water pooled under the light, the coolness seeping over him while the sun heated his neck. Sure enough, the level was as he suspected, and he reckoned on a bore hole somewhere on the property contributing to the majority of Krandle's supply rather than the scant rainfall collected via the gutters.

He edged his hips closer, kept a firm grip on his phone and rolled his chest over the lip of the opening.

Working anti-clockwise, he checked the water's surface and the steel walls, holding his breath.

He found it halfway, right underneath him.

A thin line of rope was secured to a hook in the ceiling of the tank, snaking down the side of the structure and disappearing under the water.

'Got you.'

He tucked his phone away and stretched his fingers out, wrapping the rope around his hand and pulling.

It moved easily, the weight on the end no more than a few kilos, and as he straightened to sit on top of the tank he belayed it up through the hatch.

At the end of the rope was a rectangular package, waterproofed under several layers of plastic that Blake made short work of with his car key.

Tearing the last of the wrapping away, he reached inside, a smaller object sliding to one side. He paused, then pinched at it with his thumb and forefinger, a faint smile crossing his lips.

'I knew it.'

The pistol was Glock-like in appearance but lighter, less refined than the one he carried. Turning it in his hand, he spotted the file marks where the serial number had once been engraved.

'You're going to kick yourself again, Coker.'

He shook his head and returned the gun to the parcel. He would put it in an evidence bag when he reached his car.

That left the rest of the package.

Reaching inside once more, his gloved fingers brushed against a pile of paper.

He pulled it out, revealing a selection of magazines and pamphlets.

'Shit.'

There were some familiar ones, the right-wing publications that were available via different websites from around the world, but it was the pamphlets that were the most disturbing.

Some had been produced on cheap home printers, the text fading where toner cartridges had started to run out or blotchy from overheating, but the premise of each was similar.

And all spouted the same hate-filled speech he was all too familiar with.

Except one.

As he turned over a simple A4 page and read the short instructions, a shiver ran across his shoulders.

Because it wasn't only hate speech and ghost guns they were dealing with now.

Whoever killed Amos Krandle was trying to make a bomb.

FORTY

Angela loosened her utility belt and swung it over the back of her chair before sinking in front of her computer.

The incident room was deserted.

Ryan was nowhere to be seen, and given that his shift wasn't due to start until two o'clock she expected no less, especially since Doxon had noted he'd seen the young copper in the pub with Molly the previous night.

The older constable was out, following up a lead on a house break-in on a nearby street according to the log, and Harknell…

She blew out her cheeks and eyed the clock.

Harknell could be anywhere.

He hadn't taken up Ryan's offer of using Mortlock's old QLITE radio, saying he preferred his mobile phone, and until now it hadn't seemed a problem.

Except there was no way to track his whereabouts.

Still, she checked over her shoulder before her fingers rested on her keyboard.

Because it seemed strange that Harknell went to meet with Bragg in Mortlock's place, even though he had only been in Hangman's Gap for less than a week.

Or had he?

Scooting her chair closer, she bit her lip.

There was no turning back once she started down this route, that was for sure.

'Fuck it.'

She opened up the phone log for Mortlock's mobile number and started scrolling.

At the crime scene last week, Harknell had told her and Bragg that he and Mortlock had spoken on Tuesday morning when he had checked in to the Hangman's Gap pub.

Pausing, she slid her notebook towards her, flicking through the pages until she found those from last Wednesday.

There.

He had said eleven o'clock.

Next, she checked the number she had for Harknell's mobile in her phone.

Then kept scrolling up and down the computer screen.

And again.

Her heart lurched.

It wasn't there.

'Shit,' she whispered. 'You lied.'

And yet, he was meant to be the last person to speak to Mortlock while he was still alive.

Hand shaking, she dialled a number from memory.

'The Royal, Simone speaking.'

'Hey, Simone. It's Angela Forbes.'

'Hi – everything all right? D'you need Laura?'

'No, that's okay. I was just wondering…' She broke off, guilt washing over her.

What if she was wrong?

'You still there, love?'

'Sorry, yes. I'm just running thorough some paperwork and things and I wondered –what time did Blake Harknell check in with you last week? Tuesday, wasn't it?'

'Hang on, I'll have a look. There should be a time stamp on our system to say when David allocated the room pass key to him… Yeah, here you go. Four o'clock that afternoon.'

'Four?'

'That's what it says here.'

'Did he eat there first before checking in, or have a drink at the bar when he arrived?'

'I don't think so. Well, if he did, he didn't ask for it to be charged to his room.'

'Okay. Thanks.'

'Everything all right?'

'Yes. Just trying to sort out some expenses receipts and stuff. Thanks again.'

'No worries.'

Ending the call, Angela kept the phone in her hand, then sent a text message that started with an apology, included an excuse, and ended by asking a favour.

'Quiet shift?'

She jumped at Doxon's voice. 'Jesus, Terry – why d'you have to sneak up on me like that?'

'Why? Feeling guilty about something?' he sneered. He dropped a battered grey backpack under the desk opposite hers, sank into the chair and leaned forward, running a hand through hair that looked as if it had missed a shower that morning. 'Christ, what a fucking mess. What time did you leave here last night?'

'Two.'

'What did Coker say?'

'Not much. You missed Bragg's call this morning.'

'Pleasant, was it?'

'No. Where've you been?'

'Doing my job. Checking out that break-in, then speaking to witnesses about Ivan. People who dealt with him on a day-to-day basis around here, that sort of thing.'

'Ryan already did that.'

'I thought he might've missed something.'

'Did he?'

'No.' He looked disappointed. 'But it was still worth double checking. What about you? What are you up to?'

'Speaking to witnesses,' she retorted.

'Is the vehicle free now, then?'

'Yes.'

'Good, because I want to have another chat with some of the witnesses we've interviewed.'

'Why?'

'Because we're getting nowhere, that's why. Because you lot think just because I'm retiring and like a drink that I can't do my job. Because Ivan died out there last week with none of us around him, and that just doesn't sit right with me.' Doxon jutted out his chin as he snatched the keys from her hand. 'Doesn't matter what he might've been up to, he was a good bloke and looked after me, so I'm going back to the beginning with this and speak to everyone again, starting with Carl. We missed something. Had to. *You* missed something.'

'Go for it. About bloody time you pulled your weight around here.'

'Screw you.'

'Did you take it?'

'What?'

'The shovel. Did you take it out of the container?'

Doxon's face reddened, his eyes bulging. 'Are you out of your mind? I've got ten days until I retire. Why the fuck would I risk my pension by doing a stupid thing like that?'

'Did you?'

'No, I bloody didn't. Did you?'

'No.'

'Are you going to blame Ryan next?'

'I—'

Her phone rang and she snatched it up, shot a glare at Doxon and then headed out the door. She kept going until she reached the car park and swiped the screen before it went to voicemail.

'Tess? Did you find anything?'

'I did. What the hell are you up to?'

'Why? What've you got?'

There was a delay at the other end while her cousin switched her phone to hands free, and then the frantic tap of fingertips on a keyboard rang out. 'How old is he?'

'Thirty-five, I think.'

'Are you sure you spelled his name right? And that he's a DS?'

'H-A-R-K-N-E-L-L. Hang on.' She paused as Doxon emerged through the front door and stalked across to the four-wheel drive. 'First name's Blake, not sure if he's got a middle name. He's out of Melbourne, but I don't know which area.'

'No, that's okay – I've pulled up the records for the whole state.'

'And? Has he got anything against his record? Any old disciplinary hearings or anything like that?'

'No, there's nothing.'

'Damn it.' Angela turned and glared at the flag at half-mast. 'So he's clean.'

'That's not what I meant, Ange.' Her cousin lowered her voice. 'He isn't on the system.'

'What? How can that be?'

'That's what I'm trying to tell you. There's no record for him. Your DS Blake Harknell doesn't exist.'

FORTY-ONE

The agricultural supply store was quiet the next morning when Blake parked his vehicle beside a wooden pallet stacked with horse feed pellets. Traffic ambled past the crossroads, and when he opened his door there was a sultriness to the air that suggested the possibility of a late afternoon rain shower.

As he got out, he nodded to a youth in his late teens who pulled a supply cart laden with coils of uPVC piping towards a ute with sunken suspension, the trolley's metal wheels jangling across the concrete hardstanding.

The owner of the ute, a man in his late forties, eyed Blake with interest before helping the younger version of himself unload the trolley, biceps bulging under a T-shirt that had the sleeves hacked off at shoulder height.

Blake turned his attention to Tanner's service station over the road at the sound of a deep rumble to see the mechanic's tow truck easing out into the street before heading in the opposite direction.

The ute drove away seconds later with a belch of exhaust fumes, leaving the supply trolley abandoned in the middle of the car park.

Loosening his collar, Blake aimed the key fob over his shoulder and heard the distinct *thunk* of the central locking as he walked towards the ag store entrance.

The twin glass doors swooshed open at his approach, a blast of cool air resting across his shoulders the moment he stepped inside. Taking a moment to let his eyes adjust to the softer interior lighting, he saw Sheena Lerwick standing behind a long beech-coloured counter to the left serving a woman with a phone in one hand and a young toddler cradled in the crook of her other arm.

He turned away while the two women laughed and finished their conversation, his attention taken by a row of shovels and other tools that stretched away to the right. The photos he had found on file of the shovel that had gone missing from the evidence locker matched a big-name brand that could have been purchased anywhere, and sure enough he found its twin halfway along the aisle.

The blade reflected the artificial lighting, casting a muffled reflection of his face that warped across its steel surface.

'Help you, detective?'

He glanced over his shoulder at Sheena's voice to see the woman walking towards him, her face quizzical.

'Do you know if Amos bought one of these in the past three months or so?'

She frowned. 'Not that I remember. You can imagine how busy it gets in here though. Why?'

'No reason.' He shrugged, then led the way back towards the till. 'What was he like to work with?'

'Easy, most of the time.' Sheena circled the counter before leaning on it and stared past him to the car park. 'He wasn't always available to cover extra shifts, but that was usually because he was busy at his place, or mucking in somewhere else.'

'Was that normal for him? I would've thought the poultry farm would take up most of his time.'

'Amos was like that. Always helping everyone out.'

'Including Jeff Tanner, right?'

'Mostly Jeff, yes. I suppose it was convenient for both of them, given Amos could see when things were busy over there.'

'What was he like around the tourists?'

'All right, I s'pose.' Sheena wrinkled her nose. 'If they were white, anyway.'

'Oh?'

She shrugged, and looked down. 'He could be rude to the… others.'

'Did you say anything to him about it?'

'If I overheard him, yes.' She sighed. 'And of course, I apologised to the customer. He would just walk off, then try to lecture me about how they were taking all the jobs. Not that there's any jobs around here anyway, but…'

'Did he seem bitter about it?'

'Yes. And once he got on that soapbox, there was no stopping him. David had to have a word with him about it in the pub when he'd had too much to drink.'

'Tell me about the shooting incident over at your place earlier this year. You said he was taking pot shots at vermin on your property line.'

'Yeah, down at the creek where the old trees are. Not that they'll be there much longer if we don't get a decent rain soon.'

'What was he using? Did you see?'

Sheena's brow creased. 'No, I didn't. I assumed it was a rifle – it didn't sound anything bigger than a .22, and I should know because I have one.'

'Registered?'

She aimed a bemused glance at him. 'Of course it is, but Ryan would've already checked that, right?'

'Go on,' he said. 'Tell me what happened.'

'I heard a couple of shots, really close to where I was standing next to one of the trees, checking for any disease. It made me bloody jump, I tell you. He was only a couple of hundred metres to my right, I reckon.' She played the simple gold chain at her neck back and forth through her fingers as her gaze found a distant spot over his shoulder. 'I called out. Told him to hold his fire unless he wanted to kill me.'

'What happened then?'

'He came stumbling through the undergrowth, patting down his shirt and his face all flushed. Apologised profusely. Said he didn't realise he'd strayed so far over my land, and that he assumed I'd be working at the ag store that day.'

'Why weren't you?'

'I had to wait for a delivery at home that morning. Once it came, I got on with some jobs. Like checking the trees.'

'Did you notice anything different, or something about Amos that seemed out of place?'

'Only that he seemed out of breath. I mean, it wasn't that hot that day. He seemed… embarrassed, more than anything else.'

'What about the rifle?'

'Pardon?'

'What was he doing with it while you were talking?'

'Huh. That's something I'd forgotten.' Sheena dropped the necklace and stared at him. 'He didn't have his rifle with him.'

FORTY-TWO

Angela paced across the uneven and cracked pavers lining the yard beyond the police station's back door, her jaw clenched.

She clutched a half-smoked low tar cigarette between the fingers of her right hand, the guilt seeping through her at the same time the first nicotine hit met her lungs.

Every now and again, she paused to glare at the corrugated sides of the storage container, then at the camera lens above the back door.

The long grass between here and there was trampled now, flattened last night by the steady stream of forensic technicians who had eyed her with undisguised suspicion bordering on disgust.

Her cheeks flushed at the memory, of having to sign Coker's paperwork to say she agreed to the search, and then having to stand back and watch while he and his team sifted through the contents of the container, looking for…

What?

Glancing at her fingernails, she scowled at the stains around her cuticles that persisted despite showering that morning.

All of them had been fingerprinted on Sunday night, except for Harknell, who had already gone before Coker's team arrived.

She snorted, then coughed and lowered the cigarette. 'You timed that well, you bastard.'

A breeze snaked itself around the rear of the building, and she turned her back to it in an attempt to stop the wind whipping tendrils of hair around her face.

Somewhere in the distance, the Rural Fire Service's local contingent was conducting another hazard reduction burn and the smell of wood smoke wafted across the town, staining the air.

Her eyes stung then, the thought that it was almost a week since she had lost someone so dear to her. A mentor. A friend. A—

'Ange? Here you go.'

She stopped pacing and saw Ryan walking down the back step towards her. She took one of the coffee mugs he held out and murmured her thanks.

He might have been young and inexperienced, but she had

been impressed in the short time they'd been assigned shifts together.

He hadn't asked any awkward questions, kept quiet while she was talking, and quickly worked out that she operated on caffeine, the occasional cigarette, and a healthy dose of snark.

He'll go far.

'What are you thinking, Ange?'

'Harknell's lying.'

'Lying to cover something up? Or lying because he doesn't know the truth and wants to cover his arse?'

'I'm not sure yet.' She reached into her pocket and then held up her lighter to his cigarette. 'Your mum would kill you if she knew you smoked these.'

'So don't tell her. Anyway, I thought you were meant to be quitting?'

'I'm working on it.'

He took the first lingering inhalation and blew smoke above her head. 'Shit, I needed this.'

They stood in companionable silence for a moment, and she let her gaze drift back to the storage container.

A headache was starting to form, niggling away at her temples while she wondered what to do with Tess's news, and what the protocol might be.

Bragg would be the obvious choice, but he and Harknell seemed close. Whether that was through rank or circumstance, she wasn't sure, but Ryan was too young, and Terry was on his way out the door.

That left her alone to make a decision, a realisation that left a dull emptiness in her stomach.

She eyed the warm glow at the cigarette tip, and took a savouring drag before ploughing on. 'Do you think maybe Harknell took the shovel?'

'I don't know what to think at the moment. What did he say when you asked him?'

'He denied it, of course.' She took another drag on the cigarette, cleared her throat. 'Are you absolutely sure there was nothing on the camera?'

'Yes.' He exhaled, narrowing his eyes through the noxious smoke. 'You can check it yourself if you don't believe me.'

'No, that's okay.'

'I don't get it,' said Ryan. 'How did Ivan get involved with weapons smuggling?'

'We don't know for sure that he was involved.' She realised the rest of her cigarette had burned down without her noticing, and took a quick drag. The things were getting too bloody expensive, and she couldn't afford to waste them. 'Let's not jump to conclusions.'

'Fair enough, but it doesn't look good, does it? I mean, apart from the four of us he was the only one who knew the code for the lock on that container, wasn't he?'

'Maybe. We know he used the same combination for everything around here, but surely he wouldn't tell anyone else would he?'

'Might've just been a lucky guess.'

She sighed, trails of nicotine escaping her lips. 'We're just making excuses now, aren't we? Even me. Trying not to face up to the fact that our boss might've actually been involved in smuggling 3D printed weapons.'

'And might've killed someone to protect himself.' Ryan raised his hands in defence. 'Well, someone died, didn't they? Otherwise, where did the blood on that shovel come from? It didn't belong to Charterman, and Mortlock was still alive back then.'

'I don't think it was a simple as that,' she said eventually.

Ryan's eyebrows shot up, but he didn't say anything, instead gesturing with his cigarette that she should continue.

'I just can't believe that Ivan had it in him to kill someone.'

He snorted. 'Are you sure? Just because you and he—'

'We didn't, okay?' she snapped. 'That's just a rumour Jill started because she was sick of him spending so much time at work. She hated him being a copper, and he didn't like being at home because of it. Half the time, he wasn't with me anyway.'

'Where was he?'

'I don't know. I suppose—'

Angela didn't move.

Couldn't.

There it was, the niggling thought that had been teasing her all day.

And she could finally grasp it.

A chill prickled her neck.

What if I'm wrong?

Her stomach twisted and lurched.

What if I'm right?

She stubbed out her cigarette and flicked it towards the sand-filled paint tin.

It missed, pinged off the rim and hit the dirt next to the front steps.

She ignored it, and sprinted for the back door, calling over her shoulder.

'Start the car, I'll meet you out the front. And tell Terry to phone me. Tell him it's urgent!'

FORTY-THREE

There was a storm forming on the distant horizon when they left Hangman's Gap. Shades of grey mingled with sickly yellows across the furthest reaches of the hinterland, the churning roll and yaw of ominous clouds tumbling over each other in their haste to beat a path southwards.

Angela swallowed, her throat dry as she watched its progress.

She couldn't see any lightning yet, but it would be there – and with it, the risk of fire.

The rural fire crews would be keeping a watchful eye on the wind direction while wondering if their back burning efforts were sufficient, or whether they could have done more with the limited resources available to them.

The ground around here was so dry that the first storms of the season would likely cause flooding, and the white roadside marker posts that flashed by the car window were a constant reminder of how deep the run-off could get if the creeks burst their banks.

She beat a steady rhythm with her fist on the door arm rest, her jaw clenched while the car's wheels rumbled over the uneven asphalt surface, wincing every time her colleague's haphazard driving style sent it hurtling into a deep pothole.

'Jesus, Ryan. No wonder your bloody radio's on the glitch. The wires have probably shaken themselves loose.' She tensed as another judder shot through the vehicle. 'You'll need new wheels at this rate. You do know you can drive around the holes?'

'Someone should bloody fix them. That's the problem though, isn't it? We get forgotten about out here,' he said. 'It's the same with us – we might as well not exist as far as HQ are concerned.'

She looked over at him. 'Is this about the car, or something else?'

'What?' He glanced at her, then quickly corrected the wheel as the vehicle veered to the left.

'Have you been turned down for another promotion?'

His shoulders heaved, and she noticed the worry lines that etched his brow, and the dark circles forming under his eyes.

'Ryan?' she said. 'Want to talk about it?'

'No.' He sighed. 'You can't do anything anyway.'

She turned her attention back to the road then, spotting Jeff Tanner's tow truck barrelling towards them.

A plain white hatchback was on the flatbed.

As the truck flashed past, Ryan raised a hand in greeting to Tanner, who was hunched over the steering wheel.

Angela twisted in her seat, automatically seeking a glimpse of the licence plate on the broken-down car before watching the truck disappear from sight. 'Victoria plates.'

'Tourist.' The young constable slapped the radio console again, to no avail. 'Reckon anyone will stay at the Royal in future, or keep driving once they hear about the murders?'

She groaned. 'God, don't mention that to anyone else or they'll be onto us asking why we haven't solved them yet. Bad for business, blah blah blah. Never mind what it's like for the families involved.'

'Who told Amos's lot about him?'

'Bragg. Turns out Amos's stepbrother is a councillor up north so I'm guessing he wanted to make sure he got in there first. Politics, y'know.'

'Huh. Reckon Bragg'll go down that route one day?'

'I wouldn't put it past him.'

Another five minutes passed in silence, broken only by one of them taking it in turns to try and get a signal from the car radio.

Angela checked her mobile phone screen. 'I'm down to one bar of signal.'

'I'll check mine when we get there.' Ryan nodded his head towards the fringes of the state forest that was now encroaching on their route, chasing away the last remains of Miles Prengist's grazing land.

She watched a rag-tag group of Brahman cattle mooching across the pasture, their pale forms stark against the brown grass while they headed towards a watering hole.

A solitary battered windmill idled above it like a forlorn lighthouse amongst a sea of baked earth, the stainless steel sails dormant in the afternoon heat.

Life was hard enough out here, and hope was all that sustained it sometimes.

'We're here.'

Ryan's voice jerked her from her thoughts, and then the wheels were lurching off the highway and onto the stony fire trail that led into the scrubby eucalypts framing the fringes of the forest.

The terrain changed the further they ventured, following a steady incline that twisted and turned amongst granite boulders discarded millennia ago when the glaciers retreated from the land.

Angela reached out for the strap above the door as the car slid to the right. 'Slow down, or you'll have us into the gulley at this rate.'

'Sorry,' he mumbled.

The speed decreased, and she let out the breath she had been holding.

On either side of the trail, the telltale signs of the previous week's back burning exercise were evident, with the remaining ironbark and eucalypts bearing the brunt of the scorch marks up their thick trunks.

There was no grass left here, no scrappy saplings or dead wood, although she knew from previous experience that upon closer inspection there would already be traces of fresh shoots poking out through the ash and charcoal remains.

Nature remained defiant, despite their best efforts to control it.

'So why are we out here again?' Ryan said, braking while at the same time unclipping his seatbelt.

She blinked, realising they were only half a kilometre now from where Mortlock's body had been found.

The dirt track was churned up here, the earth trampled by Coker's forensic technicians, herself, Harknell, Bragg, Sigford, everyone else who had borne witness to what had been left of the senior sergeant's remains.

'I need to check something. I think we all missed it.'

'What?'

She climbed out and eyed her colleague across the roof of the car. 'Can we wait until I see if I'm right?'

'Clutching at straws?'

He smiled, but she noted the sadness in his eyes, and wondered just how much he had relied on Mortlock for mentoring and fatherly guidance in his career to date.

'Maybe.' She jerked her chin towards the beaten path through the trees. 'Let's go. Wait, I don't suppose you've got a crowbar or something in the boot?'

'Might have. Hang on.'

A moment later, they were trudging between the skeletal trees.

A lone bellbird pinged somewhere ahead, a lonely call that rang out and echoed off the tree trunks.

All around her were stringy barks devoid of the detritus that gave them their name, wizened red gums that remained resolute after the onslaught of flames that had ripped through here, and – as she had guessed – the first pale green signs of new life in the form of a pair of shoots that raised themselves from the ground like a two-fingered salute to the destruction that had swept through the area.

Angela placed one foot carefully in front of the other and swept her gaze left and right, not wishing to trip over a snake.

Five minutes later, they reached the small clearing where Mortlock's body had been found.

A tangled thread of crime scene tape clung to the trunk of an ironbark, and she tore it away, absently wrapping it around her hand while she walked around the perimeter.

'How far away is Prengist's land from here, d'you reckon?' she said, squinting through the trees.

'A couple of k's, no more.' Ryan removed his cap and scratched at his hair. 'An easy walk.'

'Especially if you've got a quad bike to get away once you reach it, right?'

'I didn't notice any breaks in the cattle fence on the way in.'

'We'll check when we leave here, but he could've left it on the other side of the fence and just climbed through it. It wasn't electrified, was it?'

'Not that I noticed.' Ryan donned his cap again. 'Reckon Prengist shot Mortlock and killed Amos too?'

'Maybe. But we still need a motive…' She resumed walking, turning her attention to the undulating landscape beyond the original crime scene, peering through the trees and scorched earth.

Stepping between them, taking a wider route as she circled the clearing again, she zigzagged between a clutch of older eucalypt trees.

Her gaze swept over the terrain, spotting granite boulders here and there, piles of ash blown up against the base of those and scattered wherever she looked. Throat parched, she shivered despite the humidity as she imagined the intensity of the heat that had seized this place almost a week ago.

Then she stumbled, cursed under her breath and glared back at the uneven earth that had nearly sent her flying head over heels.

She froze.

'Ange? You all right?' Ryan called over.

She said nothing, moved back to the clearing and then looked at where she had been standing.

The ground was raised, as if—

'Someone's been digging here,' she murmured.

Her colleague's footsteps crunched over the scorched remains of branches and saplings towards her.

'That storm might be turning, Ange. Reckon on lightning strikes heading our way if we're not careful.' Ryan looked up as a distant rumble of thunder shook the sky. 'D'you want to give me your phone? I'll see if I can hot spot it off mine in case we get split up or can't get a signal on the QLITES or something.'

'Yeah, good idea.' She unlocked it and handed it over. 'You do that – I want to take a better look around here.'

'Okay. Won't take long.'

'Give me the crowbar while you're doing that.' She glanced over her shoulder at the gentle rise in the earth. 'I've got a feeling I might need it.'

FORTY-FOUR

Terry Doxon walked into the incident room five minutes after Blake.

The older constable didn't acknowledge his presence. Instead, he crossed to the whiteboard and tilted his head this way and that, reading the notes and peering at the photographs that covered its surface, apparently lost in thought.

Blake dropped his keys onto his desk and wiggled his computer mouse to wake up the screen, casting his gaze down the list of new emails that had appeared while he had been out the previous day.

'Where've you been?' said Doxon over his shoulder. 'You didn't show up yesterday.'

'Amos Krandle's place on the way back from Caboolture, then the ag store this morning.'

The constable turned, frowning. 'Why?'

'Just a hunch.' Blake reached into his backpack, then held up the evidence bag. 'What do you make of these?'

Doxon wandered over. 'Magazines?'

'Amongst other things.' He waited while the other man pulled a pair of protective gloves from a box on a shelf above the photocopier, then handed over the bag and watched while he sifted through it. 'Did you know that Amos had an interest in far-right politics?'

'No. I… I never heard him mention anything like this. I mean, he could be a racist bastard when he wanted to be, usually when he'd had a few beers, but this…'

'Yeah, Sheena Lerwick said something similar when I had a word with her just now.' Blake pointed at the leaflets and magazines. 'I found that lot in the water tank by his house.'

'Really?'

'They were in that waterproof pouch.'

'Someone else could've put them there.'

'But why? Doesn't make sense.'

'None of this makes sense.' Doxon handed back the evidence bag and its contents. 'I spoke to Carl Upshott yesterday, and Mitch and Elsa Evatt. I figured we missed something so I wanted to re-interview everyone, but so far, no one's got a clue what Ivan was doing near that burn site.'

'Okay, what about the Bressetts? You're a regular at the Royal. What'd you make of them?'

'Dave and Simone?'

'Yes.'

'They're good at what they do. Run a tight ship, know how to keep beer, and the food isn't bad.'

'That's not what I meant.'

Terry's eyes narrowed. 'Then try bloody saying what you meant.'

'Okay. Do you think they could be involved in smuggling ghost weapons?'

His question was met with a bark of laughter. 'Are you fucking kidding me?'

'No, I'm not.' Blake pushed back his chair and wandered over to the whiteboard. 'Think about it – they're hosting tourists on a regular basis who go back and forth across the country. It'd be easy for any couriers like Tim Charterman to stay at the Royal and hand over the weapons to someone else staying there without being noticed if Dave and Simone were making sure they weren't disturbed. And when I was talking to them, Simone was quick to defend Miles Prengist too, even after they had to ban him two years ago. Reckons he's shy – everyone else reckons he's got a violent streak—'

'He has. What's that got to do with the tourists?'

'Prengist could be their go-between. Or at least managing this side of the operation. You said yourselves that there was a strong suspicion he owned illegal weapons, so maybe he's been developing a sideline in the ghost ones too. Amos might have been involved as well. After all, Sheena's told us he was firing a .22 on her property line. What was he doing all the way out there, unless he was worried Mortlock was going to make another unscheduled visit?'

He paused, eyeing the other man, who didn't look convinced.

And then Doxon laughed. 'You're clutching at straws, mate. Dave and Simone aren't dirty. They've been running the Royal for near on twelve years now. You've seen how busy that place is on a Friday and Saturday night. Why would they throw that away?'

'Right, so I suppose you've got a better idea have you?'

'Not yet, but at least I'm not walking around making stupid accusations.'

'It's a theory.'

'It's deflection.'

Blake blinked. 'It's what?'

'Deflection.' Doxon took a step closer. 'Angie reckons you've been lying through your teeth since you got here, and I'm starting to think she's got a point.'

Blake sighed, an exhaustion washing over him. He held up his hands. 'You know what? We're getting nowhere, I've got Bragg breathing down my neck, my boss in Melbourne wondering if—'

'Melbourne?' Terry sneered. 'Angie checked, did you know that? She has a relly who works for Victoria Police, who told her that you aren't even a copper.'

Blake took a step back, his mouth dry. 'When did she do that?'

'She got a phone call this morning while you were out meeting Bragg.'

'Jesus.' He pinched the bridge of his nose and closed his eyes.

'So you need to explain who the fuck you really are. Did you come here to kill Mortlock?'

Blake glared at him. 'Of course I bloody didn't.'

'Yeah? So, help me out here. Like, what about that aunt of yours who died six weeks ago? You lied to us about that too, didn't you?'

'She—'

'Died a year ago.' Doxon raised his chin. 'You don't work for Victoria Police. Never have, have you? So who exactly are you, Blake Harknell? And what the fuck are you doing in Hangman's Gap?'

'I don't appear on Victoria Police's records because I'm not with them, Forbes is right about that.'

'Go on.'

Blake sighed. 'I'm *Federal* police. I'm a sergeant with the Counter Terrorism and Special Investigations Command. I was working undercover in Melbourne until last month but we were struggling – we couldn't tie in how or where, or even who was running the weapons smuggling. We knew the guns were turning up there, and we had a lead that suggested Cairns was where they were coming in, but not how they were getting them across country. Then Mortlock got in touch because he'd had a breakthrough.'

He paused as Doxon's jaw slackened.

'Are you saying Mortlock was killed because he told you?'

'Not me, my boss. Inspector Troy Finchton. He's leading the investigation into the weapons smuggling. We've got parts coming in from Malaysia and making their way down to Melbourne – there were some arrests made last month, but there's still a proliferation of handguns making it through. We always reckoned that there was a staging post somewhere along the route being used, and that they were splitting up the parts to make them hard to find but we had nothing – until Mortlock started investigating that car crash.'

Doxon narrowed his eyes. 'But we didn't find anything until you and Angela went over to the wrecker's yard yesterday.'

'Mortlock found something, and that's when he got in touch with us.'

'Not Bragg?'

'No.'

'Why not?'

'I don't know. I never got the chance to ask him.' Blake shrugged. 'And Mortlock wasn't willing to say much over the phone, or put anything in writing. He said he didn't know who he could trust here.'

'What about the passports and the money in the safe in his office?'

'I'm guessing he realised pretty quickly how dangerous

the people are who we're dealing with, and wanted to make sure he and Jill could get away fast if they needed to.'

Doxon faced the whiteboard once more while he listened. 'What did Ivan find?'

'He said he'd need to show us, and that it was enough to confirm that Hangman's Gap was the waypoint we'd been searching for. I was sent up here to liaise with him, find out what it was that he'd found, and then report back. Except when I got here last week…'

'He'd already been murdered.' Doxon turned around. 'So, who killed him?'

'I don't know, but I think Mortlock was right – I think he'd found evidence that could bring down the whole smuggling operation.'

'D'you think Amos was just inquisitive about the far-right stuff, or…?'

'I doubt it. I found this as well.' Blake extracted the A4 page he had discovered alongside the magazines, now encased within its own evidence bag.

Doxon's eyes bulged at the contents, then he wiped his hand over his mouth as he handed it back. 'You think Amos was building that?'

'Or supplying the parts, or… I don't know. I was going to check QPRIME to see when Mortlock visited Amos over the past six months. His diary, too.'

'It's on my desk.' The older constable crossed the office

while he spoke. 'A bloody shame Ivan reckoned he couldn't trust any of us.'

'He must've had his reasons,' said Blake. 'Maybe he was simply trying to protect the rest of you. I'm keeping an open mind until we have more information. Besides… What?'

Doxon was staring at his computer screen, consternation clouding his tanned features. 'Angela's buggered off somewhere.'

'What do you mean?' He crossed to where the other man held out a pink sticky note.

It was brief, her looping scrawl looking as if it had been written in a hurry.

We missed something, Terry. I'll be back by four – will explain then, but reckon I'll have some answers.

Blake's stomach lurched as he checked his watch. 'It's half four. We need to go.'

'We?'

'Yes, we – you drive. I'll get onto my lot and let them know where to meet us.'

'Why?'

'Because I think I know where she's gone, and I think she's in trouble.'

FORTY-FIVE

Angela strode back through the trees, the steel crowbar in one hand while she used the other to hold onto the eucalypts to steady herself.

Despite the adrenaline coursing through her, despite the excitement causing her heart rate to spike, she forced herself to slow down, not wishing to roll her ankle out here and have to walk back to the car in pain.

As she drew nearer to the raised profile of earth, she changed direction, approaching it from a different angle.

A flutter of fear shot through her guts as she cast her gaze over the dimensions.

From this angle, there was no doubt in her mind at all.

It resembled a grave.

Her grip tightened on the crowbar, and she moved forward, a renewed determination in her stride. Checking its weight, she dropped it to the ground beside her, knelt and started shovelling away the dirt with her hands.

It came away easily at first, evidence that no rain had passed this way since the hole was first dug. The earth was unpacked and loose to the touch, especially after the controlled burn had sucked away any remnant moisture.

She scooped it out, concentrating on the left-hand side with the knowledge that if she was right, if she did find something, then Jonathan Coker's team would excavate the rest.

Halfway down, the rocks started.

They had been thrown in haphazardly, as if someone needed to fill in the hole in a hurry, or—

She froze.

The hole was shallower than she thought, and she had found her answer only half a metre down.

There was an unmistakable iron-coloured stain across the sandstone and granite rocks that remained.

She looked over her shoulder.

Ryan was nowhere to be seen. How far had he had to walk back to the car to get enough signal to pair with her mobile phone?

Angela let out an exasperated sigh, then turned back to the shallow trench she had uncovered and extracted a pair of gloves from her pocket, imagining both Coker and Bragg's wrath if she contaminated any potential evidence with her own fingerprints.

'Okay, let's do this,' she whispered.

Starting at the furthest point, she began lifting the last of the rocks from the hole one by one, placing them in a line beside her.

Each of them carried a similar stain, each one reinforcing her belief that it was blood.

There was nothing else in the soil or the environment around her that provided an alternative.

'Jesus.'

She recoiled in shock when she uncovered the man's empty eye socket, the eyelids and eyeball long despatched by worms, beetles and other insects.

The side of his skull was caved in, a crashing blow that looked as if it had been caused by—

'A shovel.' Angela placed the rock she had been holding next to the others and eased back onto her heels. 'So that's what you were doing out here, Tim Charterman. You buried a man. But did you kill him?'

She closed her eyes for a moment, trying to imagine the scene, then frowned.

Looking back into the hole, she reached down and began removing the rest of the rocks surrounding the man's head, scooping out the smaller ones that had fallen either side.

As she worked, a satisfied smile formed – and then she saw it.

Under his left shoulder, a dull black form took shape, then another, and another.

'Holy shit,' she murmured. 'It's a weapons cache.'

She scooped out more soil that had tumbled into the space she had carved out, then more until the man's upper chest was exposed.

Grunting with the effort, she manoeuvred him towards her until she could wiggle her hand underneath and extract one of the guns.

It was the shape and size of a Glock 19, but nothing like one she had ever seen before.

It was made entirely from plastic.

'Fuck,' she breathed. 'Harknell's right.'

She pulled out her QLITE radio, thumbed the switch, and tried to order her tumbling thoughts. Checking the radio was still set to the Caboolture control room rather than the Hangman's Gap station, she took a deep breath.

'Angie? What's going on?'

She turned at the familiar voice, then frowned. 'What are you doing out here? Where's Ryan?'

FORTY-SIX

Blake watched the blackened clouds that tumbled over one another on the horizon in their haste to travel south as Doxon drove through the town.

The air was charged with anticipation born from the lightning forks that stabbed at the distant sky, the flashes already several kilometres ahead of the storm cell. The rain hadn't reached them yet – maybe never would – but lightning had a habit of striking in unexpected places.

The car rolled to a standstill at a set of traffic lights on the crossroads at the furthest reaches of town where the agricultural store, service station and an empty lot crowded the junction.

The ag store was still a hive of activity, with Sheena Lerwick and other staff hurrying to bring in sacks of pet food, dog beds and more from the display pallets before the storm cell reached the town.

The lights turned green, but instead of accelerating away, Doxon turned the car into the service station and braked behind six white rental vehicles that were parked facing the road.

'Why are we stopping?' said Blake. 'We need to get back to that place where Mortlock was killed.'

'Because I've got my own theory.' The older constable shoved open his door. 'And it's not going to be popular.'

Frowning, Blake unclipped his seatbelt and climbed out.

'I don't think David and Simone had anything to do with Ivan's murder, because of these,' said Doxon, eyeing the three hatchbacks, a six-year-old four-wheel drive with dirt speckling its white paintwork, and two wagons.

Blake peered over the roof of the car at him. 'Why?'

'When I re-interviewed Carl Upshott earlier, he said Jeff Tanner couldn't be contacted when they were doing the checks before the controlled burn. He reckoned he was out of range. I didn't think anything of it at the time, and figured he just couldn't get a signal out there. Angela went and interviewed Tanner last night. About you. She thought you might've been out there before the burn started. She's convinced you're involved.'

'Why the hell didn't you tell me this when I got back to the station?'

'I didn't get a chance – you were talking about David and Simone and then started going on about your secret bloody mission, that's why.'

'That's fu—'

'Your theory, the one about David and Simone being the go-between for the gun smugglers. What if it's Tanner, using those hire cars? Makes more sense to me.'

Blake's attention turned to the compact breeze-block office building and the larger corrugated steel-roofed service area beside it.

There was no movement from outside the service bays, no radio playing – and no tow truck either.

'How many people does he have working for him?'

'A part-time admin person, Adele, and two part-time mechanics. Reckons he can't afford full-time ones so he does most of the work himself.'

The sign on the reception door read "Open" so Blake hurried over.

A cluster of small brass bells of different sizes hanging from a frayed red-and-white rope clattered to life when he pushed it open, and a woman in her forties glanced up from a puzzle book, her surprise turning to a keen interest.

'Aren't you the new copper?' she said by way of greeting.

'I am. Where's Jeff?'

'Out on a pick-up. He said that someone from Victoria got a puncture over the weekend out near Baxter and they couldn't fix it themselves. They needed their car retrieved this arvo before the hire company invoices them for another week.'

'When's he due back?'

Adele glanced at her computer screen, then frowned. 'Should've been back about half an hour ago.'

'What's his number?'

He punched in the digits she read out, then cursed as it went straight to voicemail. 'Anyone been looking at the hire cars recently?'

'Only an English bloke who was staying at the Royal – he dropped off the hatchback on the right out there last week, and left with one of the crew-cab utes that turned up the day before. Glad to see the back of it to be honest – they're not as easy to rent out to tourists.'

'How many tourists use you?'

She shrugged. 'Not many, to be honest. Maybe one or two a month. Between you and me, I've told Jeff he ought to drop that side of the business – it doesn't make much money. But he wouldn't have it. Says it's useful.'

'Useful?'

'That's what he said.'

'Do me a favour? When he gets back, let me know?' Blake turned for the door. 'Just phone the station – the calls are diverted.'

'Will do.' Adele's gaze drifted to the window. 'Is Terry still planning on retiring?'

'I reckon, yes.'

'A shame. He was a good copper in his time, before his wife died.'

Blake paused, his hand on the aluminium push panel. 'When did that happen?'

'Three years ago. Devastated him. I don't think he's ever going to get over it.' She shot him a sad smile. 'Hence the drinking.'

Doxon was pacing the concrete forecourt when Blake emerged. He looked fraught. 'Well?'

'I think you're onto something.'

'And I think you were right about the pub,' said Doxon. 'Sort of. Some of the tourists who stay at the pub aren't tourists – they're couriers.'

'We need to go. If you're right about Tanner, then Angela's in more danger than I thought.'

'I can't get through to her or Ryan,' said Doxon. 'Her phone's not connecting, and his goes straight to voicemail.'

'Have you tried the radio?' Blake climbed in while Doxon started the engine.

'Yes, but no one's answering. It only works intermittently on Ryan's car anyway, remember?'

'Shit. Right – get us to where Mortlock's body was found. And don't hang about. No more stops.'

Doxon pulled out of the service station, the tyres bouncing over an iron drain grille before finding purchase. He pushed his foot to the floor. 'You keep trying to phone them while I'm driving. It might just be this storm buggering up the signal.'

'Is that what you think?' Blake's thumb hovered over the speed dial.

The senior constable glanced over. 'I'm trying to stay positive. We've already got three dead people on our conscience, after all.'

FORTY-SEVEN

Angela cringed as a bolt of lightning shot across the forest canopy, sending her hair on end and filling the air with the scorched scent of fresh ozone.

A split second later, the ground shook when the energy found purchase amongst the rocks and undergrowth, the sonic wave that emanated from the strike leaving her breathless.

Her shirt stuck to her skin, sweat pooling under her arms.

'Your tow truck passed us ages ago,' she said, slicking back her fringe from her forehead with the back of her hand. 'Why'd you come back?'

'I heard about the storm on the radio and thought I'd better check you were okay, just in case. I saw Ryan's car off the road.' Jeff Tanner gave a slight shrug. 'I figured something else might've gone wrong with it. He still hasn't had the radio fixed, has he?'

'No.' She removed the protective gloves, turned them inside out and balled them into her pocket. 'Not yet. How'd you know we'd be here?'

'There's nothing else going on out this way. Figured you might be having another look.' He craned his neck to see around her. 'What've you found?'

'You know I can't comment on an active investigation, Jeff.'

'Fair enough.' He stuck his hands in the back pocket of his jeans and cast his gaze around the trees. 'Looks like the burn's going to get tested this arvo.'

On cue, another rumble of thunder echoed off the hillside.

'Reckon this'll start a fire if it gets any closer?'

'Hard to tell. Land's bone dry around here. Figured I'd better keep an eye on it, just in case.'

'Makes sense.' She frowned. 'Did you see Ryan? He was walking around trying to get a better phone signal. It's cactus here.'

'I didn't, no.'

She walked over to the large granite boulder where Mortlock's body had been found, staring at the ground for a moment.

From here, the fire trail she and Ryan had followed was hidden from view, the thick gnarled ironbark trunks jostling for space despite their scorched lower limbs.

'We should probably head back to the car and your truck. I don't fancy standing under these trees if that cell hits.'

A jagged bolt of lightning shot across the purpling sky, and she blinked to offset its assault on her vision.

When she opened them, Tanner was frozen to the spot, staring into the hole she had dug.

'Jeff? You need to move away from there – it's a crime scene. I haven't had a chance to tape it off yet.'

He didn't move, and instead crouched at the lip of the shallow trench, his back turned to her. 'Such a shame.'

'What is?'

'It was working so well.'

Angela swallowed, her mouth drying as goosebumps freckled her arms.

The crowbar was next to the hole where she had dropped it, well within Tanner's reach.

Her left hand wrapped around the top of the capsicum spray canister in her utility belt a moment before she glanced around the small clearing once more.

Two men had died here, their bodies left to be picked apart by animals and insects, their killer remorseless.

She changed her mind.

Her right hand moved to her holster, and she gently released the top of it, exposing the black grip of the 9mm pistol she carried.

She had last been on a firearms training course ten months ago, her scores adequate to pass – but she had never fired her gun in defence, only at targets.

Her guts twisted.

'Jeff? I said you need to move away from there. Now, please.'

Despite her heart trying to thrash its way through her chest, her voice remained calm, her training overcoming her instinct to run.

Then Tanner slowly rose to his feet to face her, and she saw what he had been concealing while his back had been turned.

It was dull grey, matt against the glint of his belt buckle, but the shape was unmistakable.

'You?' she said, hearing the disbelief in her voice. 'You're the one who's been smuggling the weapons? Why?'

'Take your gun out – slowly – and drop it on the ground, Ange.'

'But—'

'*Now*.'

His voice filled with malevolence, Tanner took a step closer, his eyes not wavering from hers.

'Ryan will be back any minute, Jeff. Think about it.'

'Drop the gun.'

Palms sweaty, she did as she was told.

'Kick it away.'

She tapped it with her toe, the ash-laden earth slowing the gun's momentum so it only moved a tantalising metre or so away.

'Now the radio.'

Hand shaking, she pulled the QLITE from its pouch. Her

thumb brushed against the panic button, and then she tossed it towards him.

'Nice try, Angie. I reckon they'll never pick up the signal in time to help you.' He picked up the crowbar, crushing the radio with three hard swipes before turning his attention to her once more. 'Come over here.'

'No.' She raised her hands instead. 'Tell me why you killed Ivan.'

'I didn't.'

'I don't believe you.'

'I don't care what you think,' he spat. 'Amos killed him.'

'What? Why?'

'Because Mortlock found us moving the weapons before the burn was due to start. I was trying to convince him we'd discovered them while I was checking the area prior to lighting it up, but he'd heard us arguing. Amos panicked. Pulled out one of the 3D guns we'd already loaded.' Tanner exhaled, a fleeting regret crossing his face before it was gone. 'Mortlock tried to defend himself using one of them 9mm guns he managed to grab out of the cache, but he didn't stand a chance. Amos has been shooting vermin on his land for years. He doesn't miss.'

'Why didn't you stop him?' Angela demanded. 'You could have stopped him.'

'I didn't want to die.'

'But you could've said something,' she persisted. 'You could've told me. Reported him.'

Tanner choked out a bitter laugh. 'And give up this lot? Are you kidding me?'

'You covered up the death of a serving police officer, Jeff. Did you think we wouldn't find out?'

'Doesn't matter. No one knows you're here.'

'They'll see your truck parked next to Ryan's car.'

'I didn't bring the truck,' he said, a malicious smile forming. 'I brought the hire car I was towing once I'd changed the tyre on it. The truck's tucked away somewhere safe.'

'No one will believe you, Jeff. They'll know you came back here to find me.'

He shrugged. 'I'm just re-checking the area after the burn, keeping an eye on this storm, just like any good RFS volunteer would.'

'Ange?'

She jumped at the sound of Ryan's voice.

He was somewhere off to her left.

'Call him,' murmured Tanner. 'And don't try anything stupid.'

'Over here.' She wet her lips, hearing the desperation in her voice. 'Jeff, Ryan phoned Harknell and Terry before we left the station. He's told them where we are.'

Tanner's gaze moved over her shoulder as she became aware of footsteps in the dirt behind her. 'Did you?'

The young copper appeared a few metres away then turned to face her, a broken expression clouding his features. 'I'm sorry, Ange.'

'Youngsters are all the same today,' Tanner smiled. 'He's easily led, this one.'

Angela took a step back, staring at the young constable. 'What have you done?'

'I—'

'Like I said, he's easily led,' said Tanner, then swung the gun around so it was pointing at Ryan. 'I told Molly to keep away from you. She should've listened.'

FORTY-EIGHT

Beyond the windscreen, the late afternoon sunset was obliterated by churning grey clouds in the distance. They crowded the valley, funnelling the storm across the landscape and increasing its intensity as it made its way south.

'I'll try the radio again,' said Blake.

'Good luck with that – the one in Ryan's car is still playing up so you probably won't get through, I told you.' Doxon swore under his breath. 'She should've waited.'

His words were prophetic.

Blake tried again, but all that he heard was more static. He lowered his phone. He had managed to alert his Melbourne superiors as Doxon had powered their vehicle out of Tanner's yard, but backup was hours away. There was no time to wait for a tactical team to arrive from Brisbane, not if Forbes was in danger.

He shoved the radio back into its cradle then glanced down as his phone rang.

Bragg's number.

'Harknell.'

He put a finger to his right ear to hear the detective inspector better as the radio sprang to life, Doxon toggling the volume while he intercepted the message from HQ.

Bragg raised his voice over a similar cacophony at his end of the line. 'We've just received an alert from Angela's QLITE.'

'The panic button?'

'Yes. Last known location—'

'Got it,' Doxon said, flooring the accelerator. 'You're right – she's gone back to where Mortlock was killed.'

'We're sending reinforcements,' said Bragg. 'Wait until they're there.'

'Screw that.' Blake ended the call. When he looked at Doxon, he saw that the man had paled. 'How far?'

'Two minutes.'

'Fuck it.' He beat his fist against the door. 'Can you go any faster?'

'Not unless you want me to land us in the ditch, no.'

After what seemed an age, Blake peered through the windscreen. His heart stopped. 'Whose car is that?'

'I don't know, but that's the access track through the back of Miles Prengist's land.'

'Where Mortlock left his car?'

'Yep – and it's the easiest route from here to get to where Ivan's body was found.'

'Shit. Keep going. If he's around, I don't fancy him taking a pot shot at us.' He craned his neck. 'Ryan's car is behind it.'

Doxon slowed as they passed the white hatchback, his hands clenching the steering wheel. 'Can't see anyone, can you?'

'Not from here.'

The older officer braked half a kilometre down the road and turned the car around. He glanced across at Blake. 'What do you want to do?'

'You're armed, right?'

'Yeah. I don't have to hand in my service weapon until Thursday. You?'

Blake patted the shoulder holster concealed beneath his jacket, the hard surface of his 9mm pistol sending a shiver across his shoulders. 'I am. Hopefully we won't need them, but…'

Doxon said nothing, slipped the car into drive and accelerated back to where the white car blocked off access to the dirt track.

He parked across the back of it, boxing in the vehicle, and shot Blake a resigned smile. 'So much for easing into retirement.'

'Yeah.' He squinted against the low sun. 'Victoria plates.'

'Adele said Tanner was picking up an abandoned hire car from Victoria, didn't she?'

'She did.'

Blake climbed out and circled the vehicle.

Three of its wheels were splattered with weeks-old mud, with one bearing a new tyre. Dirt streaked up the bodywork and dulled the headlights, and a motley collection of dead bugs were splattered across the windscreen.

It was devoid of life. The seats were strewn with discarded energy drink cans and takeaway cartons. A phone charging lead snaked across the dashboard, but there was no mobile phone in sight, and the doors were locked.

He glanced over his shoulder as Doxon joined him, then both men walked over to Ryan's patrol vehicle.

The door was open, but there was no sign of a struggle.

'The crowbar's missing.'

Blake straightened at Doxon's voice.

He was standing at the back of the car, peering in. 'Maybe they found something.'

'Or perhaps they—'

Then he heard it, an unmistakable sound that cut through the distant crackle of thunder and turned his guts to liquid.

A single gunshot.

FORTY-NINE

Ryan cried out and slumped to the ground. He lay awkwardly with his left leg crumpled under his right, his face turned away from Angela. Blood streaked down his uniform pants.

'No!'

She only made it a few paces before Tanner swung the gun around and aimed the dark maw of its short barrel at her chest.

'Don't move.'

'I need to help him, Jeff. There's a first aid kit in the car.'

'Stay where you are.'

The young constable rolled over, clutching his calf muscle and groaning. 'You bastard.'

'Shut up.'

Hands trembling, Angela took a shaking breath. 'Are you okay, Ryan?'

'No, I've just been fucking shot.'

She watched while he eased himself up into a seated position, his fingers already covered in fresh blood. 'Did you take the shovel out of the evidence lock up?'

'No.'

'Huh.' Then it hit her. 'You tampered with the security camera footage though, didn't you? Or you switched off the camera while he took it.'

'I didn't know he was going to take the shovel. I didn't know he… he and Amos killed Ivan, honest.' He gulped. 'He said he wanted to get into the storage container 'cause there was something of Molly's in there he needed.'

'What?'

'He said Ivan had pulled her friend's car over a few weeks ago and she'd tested positive for cannabis. He said Molly was in the passenger seat, and he found the drugs in her bag. Jeff said Ivan put the evidence in the container, and that all he wanted to do after Ivan was killed was remove it.'

'What did Molly say when you told her?'

'I didn't. He said she didn't know he was trying to help her. He said that no one but Ivan knew it was in there because they were going to work something out off the books so she didn't get into trouble.'

'Ryan…' Her shoulders slumped. 'You…'

'I didn't have a choice,' he mumbled. '*He* said I didn't have a choice, not if I wanted to see Molly again. I didn't know he was lying about the drugs. I didn't know he was going to take that shovel instead. And then when I did work it out, it was too late.'

'Christ, Ryan.' She shook her head. 'Seriously? You've only been going out with her for a few months.'

'She's pregnant.' He took a shuddering breath before his eyes finally found hers. 'I'm going to marry her.'

'Not bloody likely,' Tanner said, glowering. 'Not now.' His gun swung back around to the young constable.

'No, Jeff – wait.' Angela risked another step forward. 'There's still time to fix this. Just put the gun down, and let's talk, yeah?'

'Fix it?' The man choked out a bitter laugh. 'It's a bit bloody late for that.'

'Tell me how you got involved,' she persisted, desperate to keep him talking. 'Who asked you?'

He sneered. 'I ain't telling you nothing about them, Angie.'

'Okay, then at least tell me why.'

'Are you kidding me? You've seen what's happening around here.' He waved the gun at her. 'Before this, I was losing money hand over fist back in town. No one's interested in Hangman's Gap – it's dead. Most of the tourists pass right through here these days. There're less and less people coming here each year, more people moving away…'

'So, the weapons smuggling is your pension plan, is that it?' She turned her attention to the rough grave. 'Who was he?'

'One of the regular couriers. But the boss found out he was

talking to Harknell's boss down in Melbourne. He was about to grass up the whole operation.'

'So you killed him.'

'No – they killed him up in Townsville and the other bloke – Charterman – was told to bury his body here on the way down as a warning to him not to try anything similar.' He choked out a laugh. 'Fucking bad luck he hit a bloody great 'roo afterwards though.'

Angela listened, horrified. 'Don't you care what happens to your family when they find out about all this?'

'I'm *doing* this for my family,' he snapped. 'Don't you get it? I want them out of Hangman's Gap, away from all this. There's nothing here for them, not anymore. My son will never take over my business when he's old enough – he's already told me he's not interested after he finishes uni, and the minute that one over there gets his promotion, he'd have taken Molly with him too. It's why he got her pregnant, isn't it?'

'That's not true,' Ryan pleaded. 'It was an accident. I already told you that. But I'll look after her, I promise.'

'Shut up.'

'What if the couriers get pulled over while they're transporting the guns?' said Angela.

Tanner gave a smug smile. 'Never happened yet. We've never had anyone stopped.'

'Which one of you graffitied that warning on my garage door?'

'Me. Figured you'd be smart enough to take the hint, but here we are.'

'You could help us, Jeff. Help us put them all away. Stop this, before it goes any further.'

'Shut up.' Tanner reached into his jeans pocket. 'Enough.'

When she saw the glint of the Zippo cigarette lighter in his hand, she bit back bile.

'There's not enough fuel,' she said, looking around the ash-laden earth in desperation. 'It won't work.'

'It will, trust me.' He kept the gun aimed at her, and walked over to one of the thick eucalypts behind Ryan. 'I came prepared, just in case.'

A chill crept down her spine when he reached out and lifted a metal jerry can from behind the tree and removed the cap.

The stink of gasoline and diesel carried across to where she stood, frozen, her mouth dry while he carried it back towards her, pouring a steady stream of the noxious mix across the ground.

'They won't believe you.'

'They will. Everyone knows you're been trying to quit smoking, Angie,' he said. He emptied the can, tossed it aside and then lifted the lighter aloft. 'Maybe you couldn't resist the risk once you got out here. Maybe the stress of losing Ivan got to you, right?'

'You'll never get away with it, Jeff. Put it away.'

He shot her a malicious smile, spinning the lighter wheel

with his thumb. 'Of course I'll get away with it. Your fingerprints will be all over this.'

FIFTY

Terry Doxon wiped sweat from his forehead and unholstered his service pistol before peering at Blake through the trees. 'I can't bloody see anything from here,' he hissed.

'Shhh, they'll hear us.' Blake shook his head to stop the other man from saying anything else and turned his attention back to the eucalypt and ironbark trunks that peppered the sloping landscape.

Remnant ash clung to the dirt and stones under his feet, and the stink of burning wood filled his nostrils despite it being almost a week since the controlled burn.

The two men had made steady progress towards the direction of the gunshot, but now the forest canopy encroached above their heads, each tree blending into another until, to Blake's untrained eyes, they all looked the same.

Pulling out his phone and noting the single bar of signal strength remaining, he checked the compass app.

The original crime scene where Mortlock's body had been found was north of their current position, and he was sure that was where the gunshot had originated from.

But why?

What had Forbes found that sent her racing back here?

And who had fired the gun?

He put the phone away and hurried over to Doxon. 'This way. Stay behind me a few paces just in case.'

The man's eyes widened. 'Reckon we should head back to the car and wait for that backup?'

'I don't think there's time.' Blake didn't wait for him to answer, and set off once more.

The stark terrain made for slower going than he wanted. Even though the back burning had removed the undergrowth, there were still the hazardous remains of twisted and gnarled branches and fallen trees to manoeuvre his way around.

The incline increased as he walked, his breath now laboured while different scenarios plagued his thoughts.

Was Forbes okay?

Where was Ryan?

And was Tanner the one shooting, or had one of their colleagues discharged their weapon?

Mouth dry, he ploughed onwards, his eyes sweeping the trees ahead.

And then he glimpsed a flash of pale blue on the ground, a moment before hearing an unmistakable groan.

He froze beside a ghost gum devoid of its lower limbs and held up a hand, then lowered his voice. 'Wait.'

Except when he looked over his shoulder, Doxon was nowhere to be found.

'Shit.'

Heart racing, he scanned the trees for movement, but saw none.

Doxon had gone.

'You bastard,' he muttered.

Then he heard movement, and dropped to a crouch as Tanner appeared between the trees and lifted a jerry can from behind one of them.

'Christ.'

He crawled closer, his heart racing, and kept a wary eye on the ash-flecked dirt beneath his hands and feet for snakes until he rested beside one of the thicker ironbarks at the fringes of the clearing.

He could hear Forbes now, pleading with Tanner.

He closed his eyes for a split second, wondering if he had any other options, then pushed himself to his feet and stepped around the tree, gun raised in a two-handed grip.

'Put the lighter out, Jeff.'

Tanner spun on his heel, his jaw slack for a moment.

Blake risked a glance across the clearing to where Ryan

lay and saw the young constable's hands wrapped around his bloodied leg.

When he turned back, Tanner was watching him from beneath hooded eyes.

'It wasn't meant to happen this way,' Tanner said, his voice barely above a murmur. 'If Ivan had just done what he normally did and pretended he hadn't seen anything, he'd never have wound up dead.'

'But instead, you killed him.'

'No, I told her.' His shoulders slumped as he looked at Forbes. 'Amos did. And then all he wanted to do was tell you lot. Confess. I couldn't let him do that. He would've ruined everything.'

Blake's skin puckered with goosebumps.

There was no remorse in the man's tone, no apology for what he had done. Instead, he seemed resigned.

'You can still help us,' Blake said, keeping his voice steady despite his soaring heart rate. 'Work with me to expose the rest of the smuggling operation, tell me who's in the far-right group that's been buying these, and I'll try to help you.'

'It's too late.'

'It's not. There's still time. Before anyone else has to die.'

A gentle breeze caught the flame, its orange-yellow glow mesmerising despite the harsh sunlight.

It flickered, bobbed and swayed, lapping at the oxygen that surrounded it.

'What the hell.' Tanner paused, then shrugged. 'I'm a dead

man anyway. If I go, I might as well take the whole bloody lot of you with me.'

With that, he straightened his back, held aloft the lighter with a mania in his eyes that precluded any further pleas for calm, and spun the wheel.

A three-inch flame shot from the nozzle at the tip, illuminating his tanned features and casting a glow beneath his brow.

'Wait,' Blake felt his legs trembling as he moved closer, every instinct screaming at him to put as much distance as possible between him and the inevitable inferno. 'Don't do it, Jeff. Think of Molly. Of your wife and son.'

'I'm *doing* this for them,' Tanner said, anguish etching his features.

'You bastard.'

A familiar voice, and then movement from the left caught Blake's attention too late.

Too late to stop Terry Doxon launching himself from Tanner's flank.

Too late to stop the senior constable sliding forward and tackling the man's legs, sweeping them out from under him.

Too late to stop Tanner losing his grip on the cigarette lighter, sending it spinning up into the air, the flame flickering in anger as it began to free fall back towards the fuel-soaked earth.

FIFTY-ONE

Blake watched in horror as the Zippo's flame flourished with the rush of air flow from its fall.

The overpowering stench of diesel and gasoline filled his nostrils, made his eyes water, and stung the back of his throat.

He heard a strangled cry from Doxon as the man's courage turned to anguish.

Blake's instincts screamed at him to turn around, to run, to get as far away as possible before he was engulfed, but his feet wouldn't move.

Frozen, fear crawling through his veins and unable to react, he wondered how much pain he would have to endure from the ensuing flames before death claimed him.

'No!'

A blur appeared from his right, and then Forbes was surging past him, her hands outstretched.

She dived to the ground, sending small stones and dust flying in her wake, her face etched in agony as the gravel dashed her uniform trousers and pierced her exposed arms.

But her eyes never left the cigarette lighter.

It tumbled from the air, gathering speed.

Blake held his breath, unable to look away.

And then she caught it. Both hands, cupping them together and simultaneously rolling away from Tanner, away from the trail of fuel that pooled at his feet.

The pain hit her a split second later, fire burning into her flesh, and she cried out in agony.

But she didn't falter.

Instead, she hauled herself up and away, away from the clearing, not stopping until she reached a stretch of burned-out dirt and ash from last week's controlled burn.

The cigarette lighter fell from her grip, and at that moment she threw back her head and bellowed a string of expletives.

'Don't let him run,' Blake hollered at Doxon, then tore across the clearing to where Forbes had dropped to her knees, cradling her hands in her lap while tears streaked down her face.

'Let me see.'

She trembled under his soft touch, a whimper escaping when he turned her hands in his.

Her skin was raw, pinkish red and angry, the blistering welts already weeping.

Blake exhaled. 'Let's get you back to the cars. I'll patch

you up as best I can, and then I'll drive you to the hospital in Caboolture. Can you walk?'

She nodded, leaning against him as he helped her to her feet.

'Are you okay?' said Doxon.

Blake looked over his shoulder to see him leading a handcuffed Tanner towards them, the older sergeant's face etched with worry. 'She needs medical treatment, and fast. Can you stay here with him while I phone for backup and arrange an air ambulance for Ryan as soon as I get a signal?'

'No worries.'

'Get onto Carl Upshott on your way back to the station. Tell him an RFS crew will need to come out here and clean up that fuel pronto.'

'Will do.' Doxon gave Tanner a shove and led him towards a bare patch of earth. He lowered his voice as he returned to Blake. 'Hell of a catch. You ought to consider auditioning for the local cricket team, Angie.'

She grimaced. 'I might have to, if Bragg decides to fire the lot of us for not waiting for backup.'

FIFTY-TWO

'There'll be an internal affairs investigation of course, starting now. You'll be suspended from duty until that's complete. You too, I'd imagine Harknell.'

Cameron Bragg shoved his hands in his pockets and eyed the myriad of photographs and notes strewn across the whiteboard at the end of the compact office, shirt sleeves rolled up and his tie askew.

The air conditioning unit above Ryan's empty desk rattled against an ever-increasing ambient temperature while the ceiling fan did little more than waft a tepid draught across the room, ruffling paperwork and lifting the various flyers pinned to the health and safety notice board beside Doxon's chair.

Blake watched while the detective inspector paced the bare floorboards, each step producing a lazy creak from the uneven surface.

Doxon sat with a thunderous expression aimed at the Caboolture detective's back, drumming his fingers on the pockmarked surface of his desk and ignoring Forbes's murmured pleas to remain quiet.

Finally, Bragg turned to face them. 'Should you be here, Angela?'

'I'd rather stay, sir.' Forbes straightened her shoulders, her palms covered in protective bandages that wound around her fingers in places. She waggled them at Bragg. 'The doc said I was lucky – the lighter didn't stick to my skin, and these are mostly superficial.' She frowned, and lowered her hands. 'Still bloody painful though.'

'Got some painkillers?'

'She's been swallowing them like they're going out of fashion,' Doxon said, aiming a disapproving glance over his shoulder at her. 'He's right, Ange. Give your mum a call, and see if she can come and get you.'

'No.' She jerked her chin at Bragg. 'Not until we're finished here. If that's all right. Sir.'

Blake buried a smile under a yawn and looked away, admiring the woman's defiance despite her injuries. His gaze found the empty desk in the corner, a sobering twist to his gut pinching him at the sickening realisation that the station's youngest recruit was facing a bleak future.

'Any news about Ryan's surgery?' he asked Bragg.

'He's in post-op recuperation at the moment,' came the answer. 'According to officers who've been placed on guard outside his room, he's expected to make a full recovery – although that could take six months. Myself and a senior constable from head office will start interviewing him tomorrow as soon as his doctor gives us access.'

Blake nodded in response.

No doubt most of that six-month period would be taken up by extensive physiotherapy – and legal wrangling.

He wondered what Tanner's daughter, Molly, was doing right now and whether her loyalty to the young father of her unborn child would remain. How the twenty-something and her mother would fare in the small township now that her father was also under arrest for murder was something he dare not contemplate.

'What's the latest from Jonathan Coker?'

Bragg's question tore Blake from his thoughts, and he turned his attention back to the senior officer still pacing the floor. 'He's advised that another team from Brisbane arrived twenty minutes ago, so he's split his personnel into three main areas. One to process the grave site and weapons cache that Angela discovered, one to concentrate on today's events, and the other is auditing the site based on what we know now about Mortlock's murder.'

The detective inspector rubbed his chin while he listened, his face pensive, then looked up at a knock on the door before it opened and a uniformed officer entered the room.

The newcomer eyed each of them with suspicion before turning to Bragg. 'Ready when you are, sir. We'll have to use Mortlock's office though, given the lack of space in here.'

'Right.' Bragg turned back to them. 'I'll need statements from you, Blake, and Terry before you leave tonight – Angela provided hers at the hospital. Officer Whitley will take those, and they'll form part of the internal investigation into what the hell's been going on around here, and why the hell you chose not to seek my input before putting yourselves in danger.'

Blake stiffened. 'I thought I would be debriefed by my superior officer, sir.'

'That may well be the case, but you'll be interviewed here first.' Bragg raised an eyebrow. 'I trust that won't be a problem?'

'I guess not.'

'Good, then you can go first. Do you need a representative?'

'It could take another hour or more for someone to get here,' said Blake, heaving himself from his chair with a sigh. 'So, let's just get on with it.'

FIFTY-THREE

Alec Whitley turned out to be a proficient interviewer.

He and Blake had entered Mortlock's office each sizing up the other, the ceiling fan above the previous occupant's desk beating a steady rhythm that echoed Blake's heart rate as he took one of the chairs facing Whitley and placed his hands in his lap.

He forced himself to relax his jaw while the senior sergeant set up the recording equipment and read out the formal caution, then recited his rank and number, all the usual details that would leave no doubt about his purpose for being in Hangman's Gap and his role within the investigation.

'To confirm before we start with the questions, are you happy to proceed without union or legal representation?' said Whitley.

Blake shrugged. 'It'll save time. Yes, I'm happy to proceed.'

'Good. How did you come to be in Hangman's Gap?'

The questions went back and forth for another twenty minutes, establishing facts and the history of the investigation into Mortlock's death.

Within minutes, Blake sensed that the man was his equal, and that Bragg had chosen wisely.

'Who do you believe shot Ivan Mortlock?' Whitley said, pouring two glasses of water from a condensation-heavy jug and sliding one across to him.

'Thanks.' He took a gulp. 'Jeff Tanner informed us earlier today that Amos Krandle had killed Mortlock with one of the 3D printed weapons from the cache.'

'Do you believe him?'

'Without being present at any subsequent interview, or without having sight of what the forensic investigation finds, I'm unable to comment on that.'

'How did Mortlock discover the grave site?'

'There's nothing on record to show that. We do have a witness, Miles Prengist, who stated that he saw Mortlock arguing with Amos but we don't know what that was about.'

'If you were to hazard an educated guess?'

'It may be that Mortlock spotted something while out on the road doing his routine checks that piqued his interest and decided to take a look. He and the others here cover a lot of distance every week following up on different cases and welfare checks, and of course there was still the fact that no one had identified the car crash victim at that time.'

Whitley looked down and consulted his notes. 'That would be Tim Charterman.'

'Yes.'

'Do you think Mortlock was involved in the weapons smuggling?'

Blake blinked. 'I don't think so. He came to us, after all.'

'He came to *you*, not us.' Whitley steepled his hands under his chin, his gaze steady. 'It appears that he may already have had his suspicions about his co-workers here.'

'Which were justified, because Ryan was involved.'

'Just him?'

'I've found no evidence to suggest anyone else is.'

'What about your aunt's house?'

'We planned to use it as a dead letter drop – my bosses in Melbourne didn't want to risk anything getting intercepted here or at Mortlock's place until we figured out who might be involved.' Blake shrugged. 'The house was convenient, that's all.'

Whitley glanced at his notes once more. 'Constable Forbes found cash and two passports in the safe in here, which we assume were placed there by Mortlock. Why would he do that?'

'We've been working on the premise that after he found

out about the smuggling and chose to notify us, he felt his life was threatened, and he'd covered his back.'

'Why wouldn't your lot offer to protect him and his wife?'

Your lot.

Blake let the comment go, and instead kept his gaze steady. 'We might've done, given the chance. I was due to meet with him last Wednesday morning to see exactly what he'd found out. I never got the chance.'

'Because they got to him first.'

'Indeed.'

'Would you see that as a failure by you and your superior officers to protect a vital witness to your investigation?'

'You'd have to ask them. I was just following orders.'

Blake sipped at a fresh mug of coffee and rubbed at exhausted eyes.

His interview with Whitley had finished an hour ago, and now Doxon was being questioned.

'Any more of that stuff, and you won't sleep.'

He glanced over his shoulder as Forbes walked into the kitchen, and pointed his mug at the coffee pot. 'Do you want one? I don't think any of us are going to get much sleep tonight.'

'I'm good, thanks.' She managed a wan smile. 'I think I'm sky-high on the painkillers as it is.'

'How're you holding up? Can I get you anything?'

She shook her head in reply.

'What about a cigarette? I mean, I know you're trying to quit and everything, but…'

A shudder passed through her body, her gaze falling to her bandaged hands. 'I… no. I don't.'

'Okay.' Blake looked down as his phone vibrated, answering the call when he saw the displayed name. 'Boss?'

'Just wanted to let you have an update. We've got a team out of Brissy that are currently tearing apart Jeff Tanner's home and business. They've already found details about the people behind the weapons smuggling and the far-right group that's been buying them. Arrests are imminent in both Cairns and Melbourne. Has Bragg interviewed you formally yet?'

'About an hour ago. There's a bloke by the name of Whitley doing the interviews. Bragg reckons he's going to interview Tanner—'

'He won't be. We have jurisdiction over that given our interests in the smuggling operation. Keep your head down – it probably won't go down well. We've still yet to establish who's the head of this outfit from the arrests we're making tonight, and I don't want Bragg's lot alerting a potential suspect until we're ready.'

'He won't like that.'

'Don't worry about it – he's going to have enough on his hands trying to explain why one of his officers was involved without his knowledge.'

There was a commotion at the other end of the call then, and Blake strained to hear what was being said. 'Sorry, boss – what was that?'

'Never mind. I've got to go. I'll be in touch as soon as I've got more news.'

The call ended and the sound of an engine carried through the flyscreen beyond the drawn blinds over the sink, headlight beams reaching through the gaps.

Then footsteps and voices calling out to each other.

Blake lowered the phone and lifted one of the slats, blinking against bright lights as a large outside broadcast truck swung into the car park behind a smaller van.

Spotlights were being set up, and a woman in a crisp business suit stalked back and forth with a microphone.

'Christ,' he said. 'The media circus has begun. That's one of the nationals that's just turned up as well.'

Forbes snorted. 'Great, just what we need.'

The front door slammed and Cameron Bragg's form passed the window, closely followed by Alec Whitley, the senior detective buttoning up his suit jacket while he hurried towards one of the camera crews.

'Someone's happy about it anyway.' He let the blinds snap shut, then turned to see Doxon in the doorway. 'How'd it go?'

The older constable shrugged. 'Like you'd expect. Reckon I'll have to postpone the retirement party until next month.'

'Sorry to hear that.'

'It is what it is.' Doxon shot him a sly smile. 'Reckon I'll get some fishing in if I'm suspended too.'

Blake grinned. 'There's always an upside, right?'

FIFTY-FOUR

Four weeks later

The pub was heaving by the time Blake pushed his way through the front door.

A cacophony of noise greeted him as a four-piece band crashed their way through an energetic rendition of an old Go-Betweens song, the chorus echoed by a growing crowd that surged towards the stage, leaving a trail of spilled beer in their wake.

Simone Bressett spotted him first, waving him over to where she stood beside a man and a woman he hadn't met before, her introduction lost amongst the other shouted conversations around him.

He smiled politely, then indicated he was going to attempt

to make his way to the bar, and stepped aside as Laura Forbes walked past with a teetering stack of pint glasses cradled between her arms.

Blue balloons in different shades had been tied to the rafters and supporting beams throughout the pub, a sign in gold lettering dangling between them wishing Terry Doxon a happy retirement.

The man himself was propped up against the bar, a relaxed smile on his face. Tanned, freshly shaven and sporting a short-sleeved polo shirt, he looked ten years younger than when Blake had last seen him.

Doxon held out his hand as he approached, his grin widening as he shouted above the noise. 'You made it.'

'Flew up this morning. Wouldn't miss it for the world.'

'Bullshit. You were here for the arraignment hearing.'

Blake nodded in response, aware that a lot of the regulars were staring, then pointed at Doxon's near-empty glass. 'What're you on?'

'The usual, thanks.'

The song ended, and the singer announced a ten-minute respite as Blake reached the bar.

Jostled from every angle, he raised the two fresh pints above his head and followed Doxon over to a far corner, away from the burgeoning queue.

'Happy retirement. Got to say, it looks like it suits you.'

'Cheers.'

Simone came over, a laden platter of fried food in her

hands. 'Come on, you two. Eat some of this – especially you, Terry. You need something to soak up the beer otherwise you'll never last the night. And your girlfriend says she needs you to pose for some photos while you still can.'

'Girlfriend?' Blake raised an eyebrow at Doxon.

'Yeah.' A faint blush crossed the other man's cheeks. 'She's an old schoolfriend. Got in touch three weeks ago out of the blue…'

'Things are going well by the look of it.'

'They are, thanks. I'll be over in a sec, Simone – promise.' Doxon waited until she had moved on to a pair of regulars with the food, then turned to Blake.

'Ivan would've loved this. At least we found the bastards responsible.' Doxon threw an arm around Blake's shoulders, alcohol-heavy breath in his face. 'Couldn't have done it without you, mate.'

'I reckon you would've,' said Blake, extracting himself from the other man. 'Team effort, right?'

Blake angled his body so his back was to the wall and surveyed the crowd. 'No sign of Molly Tanner – what's the latest?'

Doxon took a slurp of beer and lowered his voice a little. 'She and her mother left town the day after you. The servo site is up for sale – someone saw a surveyor there on Thursday so I guess they'll be instructing an agent to deal with getting rid of it ASAP. Rumour has it they're staying with a relly on the

Gold Coast. Far enough away, but close enough to keep your lot and Bragg happy. Talk of the devil.'

Blake glanced round to his right as the front door opened and Cameron Bragg walked in, wearing the same suit he had been wearing in court that morning.

He shook Doxon's hand. 'Congratulations, Terry. Can't stay long – Sarah's on her own with the kids tonight and they're both down with some sort of lurgy from school.'

'No worries, guv. Thanks for coming. First drink's on me – just let David know what you're having.' Doxon shot him a malicious grin. 'If you can get to the bar, that is.'

'Right. Back in a minute.'

Blake watched him go. 'Reckon he'll make it?'

'If he does, he'll be lucky to make it back here without spilling a drop.' Doxon's gaze shifted. 'Christ, Carl's trying his luck at chatting up Angie again. You'd have thought he'd have learnt his lesson.'

Blake looked over, and almost dropped his pint.

Forbes had switched out her uniform for a figure-hugging navy satin dress that clung in all the right places, a swirling tattoo covering her left bicep. Her hair was left loose and tumbled haphazardly over her shoulders as she jabbed a finger at Carl Upshott.

Blake smiled, bemused, as her voice grew louder and then Upshott's face flushed red. 'Guess he has now.'

She came stomping across to them, shaking her head. 'Seriously, what's the matter with him?'

'Hero worship,' said Doxon, then executed a quick sideways step as she aimed a none-too playful punch at him. He laughed. 'Back in a minute – I've got to take a piss before I do my speech.'

'Speech?' Blake raised his eyebrows. 'More than two sentences? You?'

'Fuck off.'

Grinning, the retired constable walked away, his gait unsteady as he was stopped by other people on his way to the exit.

'Well, it'll be an interesting speech at that rate,' said Forbes. She took a delicate sip from a glass of white wine. 'Hope someone's recording it, because I doubt he's going to remember any of tonight.'

'As long as he's happy.' Blake looked down. 'The bandages are gone.'

'Yeah.' She held up one hand, then the other, both with simple dressings now covering the soft skin. 'The docs are really pleased with progress. No nerve damage, and the skin's healing well. Another couple of weeks and these can come off too.'

'And you? How's the investigation going?'

She eyed him carefully. 'You know how it's going.'

'The Federal one, yes. What's happening here?'

'Bragg's reinstated me – things got a bit out of hand with no one manning the local side of things for a while there, and he's allocated three officers on a rota basis to help out.' She wrinkled her nose. 'I guess he's still looking for someone to replace Ivan and Ryan, although that could take time.'

Laura pushed her way through the crowd, making a beeline for her sister. 'Can I borrow the car keys?'

'What for?' Forbes narrowed her eyes.

'I need to take Mum over to Christie's place. She's forgotten the present.'

'You're kidding me. I'll drive. You've only just passed your test.' She turned to Blake. 'I'll be back in five. Don't let Terry start his speech until I get here.'

'I won't.'

After she and Laura disappeared through the back door with an older woman in tow, Blake leaned against the wall and watched the ebb and flow of people around him.

There was a different atmosphere in the town now, a resigned acceptance that – despite the camera crews and rubberneckers losing interest in favour of the next news story – their lives had been changed forever by three of their own, one of whom had been a promising young police officer.

From what he could tell from the different licence plates out in the car park and the motor homes cluttering the camp site down the road, the tourism trade was holding steady. Whether that was because of what had happened here and whether it could be sustained as attention waned remained to be seen.

'Didn't think we'd see you back here.'

He turned to see Miles Prengist stalking towards him, the

man's broad shoulders making easy work of getting through the throng. 'I thought—'

'David lifted the ban.' The man sipped from a stubby beer, condensation running down the glass. 'About bloody time, too.'

'I take it you apologised at last.'

Prengist managed a sheepish grin. 'Something like that. You staying long?'

'Just tonight. Simone's stuck me in one of their spare rooms. Seems the place is keeping busy.'

'Yeah. We'll see.' Prengist looked around. 'Anyway… be seeing you.'

'Sure.'

Blake went to take another sip of beer, then, realising his glass was empty, reached across and put it on a low table beside him, aiming an apologetic smile at the group of four sitting around it.

Awkward, aware that he didn't belong to this town or its people and was probably only being tolerated for the sake of Terry Doxon, his attention wandered back to the band as they traipsed towards the stage to begin their second set.

The guest of honour was nowhere to be seen, so no doubt his plans for a speech would have to wait for now.

'For someone at a party, you look bloody miserable.' Bragg shoved a fresh pint under his nose as the guitarist started to retune and the drummer tapped at a snare drum. 'Get that down your throat.'

Blake complied, the first mouthful slipping down with ease as the atmosphere turned convivial around him, his shoulders relaxing.

Then he saw the way the detective inspector was looking at him, and lowered his glass. 'Is there a problem?'

'I need a new officer in charge here. And soon.'

'You do.' Blake nodded. 'I've been thinking about that, and the sooner you get someone in to put their own stamp on the place, the better. It'll go a long way to help the community cope with what's been happening here.'

'It's yours.'

'What?'

Bragg chuckled. 'Come on, don't play bashful, Harknell. There's only so much you can take at the Federal level before you burn out. You said yourself you had to get out of Melbourne for a while. Why not go the whole way and turn your skills to something regional for a change? You'd be ideal for here. People trust you.'

Biting back the urge to groan – or bolt for the door – Blake jerked his chin towards the bar as Forbes reappeared, her mother and sister at her side. 'What about her?'

'Too junior,' said Bragg. 'And although she's got potential, she made some critical mistakes that could've got her – and her colleagues – killed. Having said that, there are people in Brisbane who think a promotion's in order. Just not yet.'

'She's a promising copper. Well respected locally, too.'

'I had a word with your boss. He's aware I'm making this

offer.'

'Seriously?' Blake spluttered on his beer and blinked. 'You already asked him?'

'He feels that your life may be in danger if you return to Melbourne. You're too well known amongst the local gangs to go back undercover, let's face it.'

Blake sighed, and contemplated his half-empty glass. 'True.'

'You'll consider it then?'

'I'll think about it. Thanks for the drink.'

He was saved from saying anything further by the band launching into a belting version of a Paul Kelly song that had the floor vibrating as everyone jumped to their feet.

Bragg drifted away after that, and Blake concentrated on the music, tapping his foot and murmuring the words as the set list progressed through a steady stream of pub rock anthems, not trusting his voice to raise it any higher like some of the others around him.

He caught sight of Terry Doxon at the far end of the room, the man swaying to the music with an arm draped around his girlfriend, the pair of them smiling as well-wishers congratulated him on his retirement.

And then the constable was stumbling towards the stage, a microphone was thrust under his nose and he pleaded for quiet as he delivered his promised speech, his words growing stronger as he spoke of his pride at being such an integral part of the community, and his sadness at recent events.

He finished to thunderous applause, and as Blake turned back to his pint he saw Forbes walking towards him, her face flushed.

'You look happy,' he said. 'And… different, out of uniform.'

'Who'd have thought it, right?'

'That's not what I meant.'

She grinned and took a sip of wine. 'Bragg says you're going to be joining us.'

'Did he?' Blake looked over her head to see the detective inspector raising a fresh drink at him. 'I told him I'd think about it.'

'Ivan would've approved. He would've liked you. You should take it.'

He looked around at the gathered crowd and the familiar faces, feeling the warmth that emanated from the conversations and laughter enveloping him.

Then thought of the bitter memories he had left behind, of the dangers and uncertainty he had faced over the years, and the bleak prospects if he returned.

'Okay, I guess I could do with a change of scenery,' he said. He smiled, then clinked his glass against hers. 'Let's go and tell Bragg he can make it official.'

THE END

ABOUT THE AUTHOR

Rachel Amphlett is a USA Today bestselling author of crime fiction and spy thrillers, many of which have been translated worldwide.

Her novels are available in eBook, print, and audiobook formats from libraries and retailers as well as her website shop.

A keen traveller and accidental private investigator, Rachel has both Australian and British citizenship.

Find out more about Rachel's books at: www.rachelamphlett.com.

Printed in the USA
CPSIA information can be obtained
at www.ICGtesting.com
LVHW030735280624
784156LV00014B/174

9 781915 231864